Ice Angel

By the same author

The Paradise Will

Chapter One

Spring 1815

O N a damp evening, a mud-splattered post-chaise laden with portmanteaux came to a halt outside a fashionable town house in Curzon Street, Mayfair. Its sole occupant, a slim young woman dressed in a high poke bonnet and dark-blue pelisse, alighted a few moments later and, after thanking the postillion who had jumped down to assist her, she hurried through the drizzle to the front door.

It was opened by a smartly dressed servant. 'Welcome back to London, Lady Vane,' he said. 'Everything has been arranged just as you requested.'

'Thank you, Silwood,' she replied, in a lilting voice, stepping into the elegant, marble-floored entrance hall. 'The journey seemed to take an age although it is not so far in distance. I am anxious to see Dominic. Is he still awake or has Harriet already sent him to bed?'

Before Silwood could reply, there was a cry from the top of the staircase. 'Mama! Mama! You are here at last – I have been waiting this past hour and still you didn't come.' A fair-haired boy ran down the sweeping stairs and threw himself at his mother, putting his thin arms around her waist and burying his face in her skirts.

'Hello, my dearest.' Her expression softened as she returned his bearlike hug. 'I am late, but the coach was delayed for almost an hour and not much can be done to hurry sheep when they are blocking a country lane.'

'Sheep?' he said, looking up keenly into her face, having latched on to the only word in her explanation that interested him. 'Were there any lambs among them? If so, I hope you brought me one to keep, for I should like a lamb of my own very much.'

'No, Dominic,' she replied with a smile. 'It is not possible to travel in a post-chaise with a lamb. The poor thing would be quite distressed, you know, and miss its mother. Besides, you have enough animals here already.'

'Oh, well, I suppose if it would miss its mother, I could not keep it – I would not want anyone to take my mama away.'

'Of course you would not, love. Where is Aunt Harriet?' As she spoke, Lady Vane removed her gloves, pelisse and finally her bonnet to reveal glorious golden hair, pulled into a simple knot at the back of her head.

'Lying down in her room. She has a headache because Joshua scratched at her embroidery until it was ruined.' Dominic looked up in concern as he continued, 'Please don't be angry, Mama – I know Joshua shouldn't have done it, but he is playful and always finding mischief.'

'That kitten of yours will have to learn better manners if he is to live in London,' replied Lady Vane, amusement in her voice. 'Was Aunt Harriet angry?'

'Oh, no! She never is. She just sighed, like this,' – Dominic imitated a faint sigh of resignation – 'and said "that is the trouble in sharing a house in the city with so many creatures".'

'Poor Harriet! I'll speak to her, and perhaps her headache will improve when I give her my news.'

'Is it good news then?' he asked eagerly.

'Yes, it is, Dominic,' she replied. 'Go and find Mary and when you are ready for bed, I'll come and share my secret.'

He whooped with excitement and ran back up the stairs, holding on to the handrail and taking the steps as fast as his legs would allow. She smiled as she watched him, relieved to see her son in such high spirits.

'Will you be requiring dinner in the dining-room this evening,

Lady Vane?' queried her butler, who was still awaiting further instructions.

'I'm not certain, Silwood – has Mrs Forster already eaten?'

He gave a small, deprecating cough. 'Er, no, Lady Vane – that is, she was upset following the incident Master Dominic has described and said she did not desire food.'

'I understand,' said Isabella, with a knowing look at the fleeting expression that crossed Silwood's features. 'Perhaps I can coax her out of her megrims. See that my luggage is dealt with and arrange for dinner to be served in half an hour; Mrs Forster and I shall dine together if I can persuade her to come downstairs.'

'Very good, ma'am.'

Silwood went away, and Lady Vane made her way upstairs to her aunt's chamber to knock on the door. A feeble voice bade her enter and she went in to find Harriet sitting up in bed and sipping a cup of tea, a fetching lace cap set slightly askew on her soft brown hair.

At the sight of her niece, Harriet replaced her cup on the china saucer too quickly, spilling some of its contents on the pristine white sheet, but she did not appear to regard it as important and held out her hand in greeting. 'Isabella! Thank goodness you are back. My head aches and it is the fault of that silly kitten – my embroidery is quite ruined.' She sniffed in a prosaic fashion. 'Of course, I did not chastize Dominic because Joshua always manages to escape from wherever one puts him. However, that is not the whole of it: you will not believe what that parrot has learnt to say while you have been in Sussex, and what it has done to the curtains in Dominic's room—!'

'Oh, Harriet,' interjected Isabella, laughing as she squeezed her aunt's slim fingers and bestowed a kiss on one delicately perfumed cheek. 'I see you have endured a trying time while I have been at Haystacks, but let me give you my news for I shall burst if I do not tell someone soon.'

Harriet sat forward and opened velvet brown eyes wider in anticipation. 'You have met Mr Longville then?' she asked urgently. 'How are things situated – is the house fit to live in, or is it in bad repair?'

'Everything is settled,' replied Isabella, sitting on the edge of the bed. 'The property has three acres of ground which will be perfect for Dominic to explore and it is near to the coast, so that, too, will be excellent for the summer. The only problem is the state of the house; Great Uncle James did not keep it in good repair, and although the exterior is reasonably sound, the rooms will need attention before we can occupy it. I stayed there while I have been away, but it was not comfortable, even though Mr and Mrs Johnson, Uncle James's old servants, did their best.'

'But what shall we do for funds?' queried Harriet, a note of despair in her voice. 'You know that we have none.'

'That is my good news. It seems that Great Uncle James lived a parsimonious existence, and consequently he had a respectable fortune to his name. Mr Longville informed me that Uncle James bequeathed his money to me, as well as Haystacks.' Isabella's luminous blue gaze rested on her aunt, a glow of pleasure briefly replacing the wary look that lurked there. 'Now we are independent, Harriet. We have enough money to be comfortable, and to provide for Dominic's future. All the arrangements are in place and Mr Longville has agreed to oversee the repairs.'

With a cry of delight, Harriet embraced her niece. 'My dear, such wonderful news! When shall we be able to leave London?'

'Not for several weeks. The work will take time and we must manage here until then. It is not an ideal arrangement when we have Dominic's animals for company, but we must endure it as best we can. In any event, the rent here is paid until September so we may as well take advantage of that.'

'With these animals running wild, I shudder to think what state this house will be in by then,' said Harriet, before adding bluntly, 'or my nerves.'

A smile lit Isabella's delicate features. 'It is not for long, and I could not have asked Dominic to give up his pets; it would have been too much with the other distress he has had to deal with.'

'How good it is to see you smile again,' observed Harriet. 'I declare it is an age since I have seen you as relaxed as you are at this moment – perhaps you are beginning to forget the past.'

'I shall never forget, Harriet, since remembering makes me wary. Besides, it does not signify if I am more at ease: you know that I have no intention of entertaining or even going into society.'

'But you cannot live like a hermit while we are in London,' she replied, shocked. 'It is unnatural, and there will be talk if you do.'

Isabella gave an elegant shrug. 'I don't care. While we endure this short stay in Town, I have no wish to provide fodder for the tattlemongers, and certainly no desire to attract gentlemen – the reason why most young women come to London for the season.'

'I fear we will be considered eccentric if we do not attend a few functions,' said Harriet. 'Why, my old acquaintance Lady Pargeter called in your absence and was obliging enough to leave an invitation to her evening party. Shall we not attend, then?'

Looking at her aunt's forlorn expression, Isabella realized that although she preferred to keep society at bay, her aunt had a different opinion.

Harriet was the much younger sibling of William, Isabella's father. With her gregarious nature and attractive looks, she had made a creditable marriage and enjoyed an unassuming lifestyle in London. When her husband had died, leaving her a widow and childless at thirty-two, Harriet had responded with surprising fortitude and, notwithstanding her straitened financial circumstances, had contrived to live modestly with the assistance of friends.

Then, four years ago, Harriet had received Isabella's urgent plea. Knowing something of her niece's situation, Harriet had agreed to move to Yorkshire and in so doing, had effectively cut all her links with society. During that time, Isabella, who would always be grateful for the way Harriet had left her life in

London behind without question or rancour, had come to regard her as a beloved older sister rather than an aunt.

From Harriet's tone of voice as she had asked this question, Isabella recognized that her aunt was yearning for company now it was once more available to her. Perhaps it was unfair to deny Harriet this pleasure when she had helped Isabella during her most desperate times.

With these considerations in mind, Isabella therefore replied, 'Well, you may go and enjoy yourself, Harriet, but I will not be tempted. Now, as your headache seems much better, come down to dinner.'

Harriet smiled and a short time afterwards went with her niece to the dining-room; she was already anticipating her reappearance in society at Lady Pargeter's evening party and secretly determined that Isabella would accompany her.

Some time later, Isabella crept into her son's bedroom, but the scene that greeted her was not a slumberous one. Standing unobserved by the door, Isabella watched as Mary, her long-serving maid, remonstrated with an argumentative Dominic who was disinclined towards his bed.

'It's already past your bedtime and your mama is very tired, Master Dominic. Besides, I'm sure your mama's answer would be the same as mine: you cannot have that creature in bed with you,' said Mary, pointing her finger towards a large ornate cage which housed a squawking parrot. 'It's bad enough having Jemima in the room.'

'But Mary, I cannot go to bed yet – Mama promised to talk to me before I went to sleep.' He lowered his voice and adopted a conspiratorial tone. 'She has a secret to tell me.'

Isabella could not suppress a chuckle and Mary turned around, a smile spreading across her features when she saw her mistress. 'Miss Isabella, I am very glad you are back. I was telling Master Dominic that bedrooms are not the place for parrots, but he thinks Jemima will want to sleep in his bed rather than on a perch.'

'Dominic,' began Isabella, a note of censure in her voice as she came further into the room, 'Mary is right – Jemima is happier in her cage.'

Dominic furrowed his brow with the effort of explaining. 'Well, I only suggested it 'cause Mary told me before that my pillow is full of feathers and as Jemima has feathers, I thought she would feel more at home there.'

Isabella laughed. 'I can see why you might think so, love, but I assure you she wouldn't like it at all and would rip open the pillows with her sharp beak. I see the curtains have already suffered her attentions.' She raised her fine brows at the large tear in the fabric drawn across the window and then frowned when the parrot uttered 'bacon-brained' and 'gudgeon' in a loud clear voice. Hiding a smile, she added severely, 'And I also see what Aunt Harriet means about Jemima's new words.'

Colour rose to Dominic's cheeks. 'Sorry, Mama,' he said, with a guilty look. 'I only said those words twice and didn't mean for Jemina to hear them.'

'I see. Then we must hope that Jemima does not repeat them at an inconvenient moment,' replied his mother.

'Never fear about the curtain, miss,' said Mary, 'it will be fixed in a trice tomorrow. Now, Master Dominic, if you want your mama to tell you secrets, it's time for you and Jemima to go to bed.'

Dominic argued no further and watched as Mary threw a blanket over the parrot's cage. Then, he meekly climbed between the covers, folded his arms and lay still, his blue eyes wide with excitement. Isabella exchanged a wry glance with Mary as she left the room, then sat by the bed and grasped her son's hand.

'What is your secret, Mama,' he asked. 'Is it something I shall be pleased to hear?'

'I believe so, love. Do you remember I told you Great Uncle James had died and left us a house in the country?'

'Yes, but you thought it couldn't be anything very special because Uncle James hadn't seen you since you were a girl.'

'I was mistaken; Uncle James has left us a delightful house and while you have been settling here in London, I have been looking at our new home which is called Haystacks.'

He sat up and said eagerly, 'Is there room for a pony, if I only ask for a small one?'

'Yes,' replied Isabella, her mouth curving into a smile.

'And a puppy?'

'Of course!'

'Then can we go tomorrow?'

'We must wait a little while, but I promise it will not be long.'

'Will Papa be there?' he asked, after a pause.

Her heart went out to him. 'Your father died, Dominic – he is not with us any longer.'

'Oh,' muttered Dominic, looking down and twisting the bed sheet between his fingers. 'Well, I don't mind because I can't remember much about him, except that he was cross and made you cry.'

'Your papa made himself sick and then he became cross,' said Isabella gently.

'I know – I heard Mary whispering to Aunt Harriet one day that Papa was in his cups and that's what made him sick.'

Isabella raised her brows at his matter-of-fact tone – it seemed her son had overheard discussions the meaning of which he did not fully understand. 'Yes, he did, but he can't hurt himself, or us, any more,' she murmured.

Dominic nodded, gave a huge yawn and lay back against the pillows. 'I'm happy that you're back, Mama.' After a few moments, his eyelids began to drift downwards and Isabella watched in silence until slumber claimed him.

She kissed his flushed cheek and reached up to dash away the tears on her lashes; it did no good to dwell on the past. Her nightmares would stop eventually and time would heal her spirit, but, even though over a year had passed since Edward's death, her anguish was still raw. She thanked God that Dominic had been too young to remember everything. Unsurprisingly, he showed little affection for his father's memory and no interest in enquiring further about what he had witnessed. All Dominic voiced was a desire for his current circumstances to continue and the occasional fear that his father would return. He dealt with both issues in a brisk, childlike fashion, and seemed able to dismiss unpleasant memories soon after they arose. Isabella wished that she could do the same.

She was desperate to retire to Sussex and provide as best she could for her son. At least now she had Uncle James to thank for making that task appear a little less daunting.

Chapter Two

OVER the next two weeks, word spread quickly about Lady Vane. Isabella's wish to remain disengaged from society only caused more speculation about her past, her future, and if she were poor or wealthy. Her smiting celestial beauty was sufficient to arouse interest and that, coupled with a curious air of self-containment and sadness, gave her a tangible glow of mystery.

While she was regularly seen driving in the park with her son and widowed aunt, she chose never to do so at the most popular times. She refused to be drawn on polite queries into her background, but it was impossible to take offence since she managed somehow to parry every enquiry in a firm but courteous way, leaving the questioner little wiser but utterly charmed. It was therefore unsurprising that gossip regarding the reasons for her reticence soon reached a feverish pitch and everyone in London seemed to know that she had been given the epithet of the 'Ice Angel' by some wag because of her beauty and reserve.

Isabella, who remained unaware of this speculation, spent her first weeks in London organizing her household. The house in Curzon Street had been offered to her by her good friend Dr Dalton; he had urged Isabella to use his sister Lady Bingham's property as she was in Bath and would not require it again until the following spring. Although worried at the prospect of living among crowds, Isabella had become resigned to the fact that she had little option but to accept, even though she suspected the minimal sum requested in rent was nowhere near the usual rate for such an exclusive property.

Her dead husband's estate had not been entailed and while the attorney had informed Isabella that the sale of the manor and its contents would cover the considerable debts outstanding, only a few hundred pounds a year would be left to support her and her family.

Isabella had expected little, but to hear she was to receive nothing more than this small sum had come as a terrible blow and she had fretted about their future. Then, at her most desperate time when the sale was almost complete, Great Uncle James's bequest had arrived like manna from Heaven. It had been followed quickly by the offer to lease Lady Bingham's London house, along with her servants and carriages. Isabella's spirits had risen at this improvement in her fortunes and she had set off for Sussex determined to make the best of whatever state she found Haystacks in.

To find Haystacks was a more substantial estate than she had envisaged was a surprise, but to discover that her great uncle had also left her a respectable amount of money was a pleasant shock. Isabella had not realized that Uncle James possessed any wealth, nor could she understand why he had chosen to will it to her. However, she was very grateful that her relative had provided the means for longed-for independence and an opportunity to put the past behind her. The responsibility of Dominic and her aunt weighed heavily on her slim shoulders, but she carried it without complaint – it was infinitely preferable to the situation she had endured since her marriage. Sometimes Isabella found it hard to believe she was still only twenty-four. When she looked in the mirror, her features remained those of the girl who had married Sir Edward Vane, but her character was greatly altered.

Isabella had never given her beauty much consideration and now she paid no regard to it at all. She did not see the cloud of silken gold hair framing classical features, the pair of speaking blue eyes fringed with long dark lashes, the short straight nose and the luscious full mouth reflected in her mirror. During her marriage, there had been no occasion to embellish her looks for social functions and she had ceased trying to please her husband. She would have therefore been incredulous had she been told she was beautiful enough to make gentlemen stand and stare when she passed by. When she was seventeen, her dying father had considered it his duty to see her married before leaving her alone in the world apart from her widowed aunt and a distant elderly uncle. That her father had considered their neighbour Sir Edward Vane a suitable bridegroom had surprised their acquaintances, and at the time Isabella had not understood the reasons for their murmured dissent. Edward's reputation was a little wild, but she had agreed to the match after being dazzled by the dashing young man she had met on a handful of occasions. She had also wanted to comfort her desperately ill father who was anxious to see the ceremony take place before he died.

With the benefit of hindsight, however, she understood that she had no more business to marry Edward Vane than she had any of the other young men she had met in her brief time out in society. Isabella was only passably fond of him and knew nothing of his character. Still, with the age-old optimism and innocence of youth, she had believed she and Edward would deal well enough together. She would not enjoy the London season her father had always promised, but Isabella had consoled herself with the thought that her new husband would show her the city's delights when they were married.

How wrong she had been. Isabella had not realized the truth about Edward until after their marriage and then it was too late. Appalled by her wretched error of judgement, Isabella had blamed no one else for the situation she found herself in. The marriage had not been forced on her and she knew that her father had acted with the best of intentions. Besides, he could have had no notion of Edward's true character either, as Edward had kept it well hidden. Isabella was relieved that her father had died shortly after the ceremony – at least he had not witnessed what happened afterwards.

Her husband's behaviour had manifested itself after the
wedding and Isabella's nightmare had begun. Any optimism and
hope had been effectively crushed in the years that followed and
they became social outcasts. Isabella was not sorry for this,
since she was too embarrassed and saddened by her situation to
wish it to be observed by anyone else.

Now, because of her marriage, she had changed: the trusting,
naïve girl had gone forever, to be replaced by a wary young
woman. Isabella had no wish to expose herself to the questioning, albeit so far polite, of the *ton*, since she could barely
analyse her past with equanimity, let alone discuss it with
strangers. She was therefore in no mood to accompany Harriet
to Lady Pargeter's evening party, despite the pleadings of her
aunt during that same afternoon.

'You must come, Isabella; I cannot go alone. Everyone will ask
why you are not there, and so many other questions, that I shall
become muddled and say the wrong thing,' said Harriet, who
had resorted to uttering her pleas from behind a handkerchief,
which was touched occasionally to the corner of her eye.

'Of course you can go alone – you do not need me to act as a
chaperon,' observed her niece. 'I will not ask you to forgo any
pleasure, but I have no desire to seek out company, Harriet. As
for being indiscreet, confine your conversation to the weather
and the entertainment on offer and you will be quite safe.'

'I will try, but it will be difficult when everyone is asking
about you and Dominic. May I not tell them a little about our
circumstances to satisfy their curiosity?'

'No,' replied Isabella firmly. 'If details about my marriage
should somehow emerge, there would be gossip and I could not
bear it. Not that I care a rush for my own feelings, but I wish to
avoid any whispers reaching Dominic's ears.'

'I do not want that either, but people will be talking and
surely it can do no harm to give out the minimum of facts about
our situation?' said Harriet.

Isabella fell silent, considering this. After a few moments, she
replied, 'I suppose that may be preferable to allowing all

manner of ridiculous theories to emerge.' Eying her aunt's speculative look with amusement, she added, 'But you must only disclose the bare essentials, Harriet.'

'Of course – just that you are a widow and that Edward died over a year ago. It would not, I agree, be proper to give out the circumstances that led to his death.' Her voice brimmed with disapproval and the bitterness her normally placid soul still held towards Isabella's dead husband was apparent in every syllable.

'I could not endure any details on that subject being divulged,' admitted Isabella. 'My greatest concern is that Dominic will hear rumours before I have explained to him what occurred, and I do not want hearsay to influence him.'

'Edward's sins have nothing to do with Dominic,' declared Harriet, putting aside her embroidery to regard Isabella directly. 'He will not follow in his father's footsteps, I am sure of it, for his character is very different. And you cannot be held responsible for Edward's actions, Isabella. No one could have done more, despite causing yourself further distress in the process. I'll never understand why your father thought your interests would be best served by marrying Edward. We would have managed if you had come to live with me in London, but I suppose we must allow that William did not know Edward's character and perhaps his judgement was impaired by illness. Edward's behaviour was shocking and I cannot forgive or forget it.'

'Do not remind me,' said Isabella, in a voice that wavered.

Immediately contrite, Harriet put a comforting arm around her niece's shoulders. 'Forgive my foolish tongue,' she said gently. 'Indeed, I had no wish to distress you.'

'I know, Harriet,' she murmured, 'and I should not still find it upsetting, but it will take time to forget his abominable conduct. He never cared for me – he wanted my money which he soon wasted anyway – and I grew to loathe him. Perhaps I could have coped with straightforward neglect, but for him to have contemplated....' Isabella's voice trailed away and she paused, a shocked expression on her face. 'I should not speak ill of the dead, but I mean it – every word.'

'Nonsense, Isabella! You speak the truth and I shall not chide you for it; sometimes I think you have been too restrained about the matter,' said Harriet. 'But now it is time you began to live in the world again, if only for Dominic's sake, so I beg you will reconsider accompanying me this evening. It may save gossip about your behaviour reaching Dominic.'

'Is that possible?' asked Isabella, turning her troubled gaze towards her aunt.

'I don't know, but people will talk so if you do not accept some invitations. Society might christen you an odd creature if you refuse every invitation, rather than merely consider you a reserved young woman who is civil enough to attend a few select functions, but not such a will-o'-the-wisp to flit to every entertainment London has to offer now you have put off your mourning clothes.'

Isabella bit her lip thoughtfully. 'I do not rejoice at the prospect, but perhaps I could attend a few small events.'

'It will be for the best, and you will outshine all the beauties in London without putting yourself to any effort.'

Glancing at Harriet from under her lashes, Isabella said, 'I am agreeing because I do not wish to cause unnecessary gossip – I have no intention of attracting any gentleman's attention.'

'I did not doubt that for an instant, my dear,' replied her aunt primly.

That same morning, in the library of his town house in Berkeley Square, Harry Cavanagh, third Earl of Bramwell, was arguing in a good-natured fashion with his friend, Mr Frederick Isherwood, about their plans for the evening ahead.

Lord Bramwell, who sat behind the large oak desk which dominated the book-lined room, declared, 'Freddy, I've no inclination to attend a party where everyone makes tedious small talk. There is no relief to be had even at the card tables – they are inhabited by vicious old tabbies.'

'Now that's too strong, Hal,' remonstrated Mr Isherwood, using the diminutive form of his friend's name favoured by his family and close acquaintances. 'No need to refer to my aunt as a vicious old tabby. She's no such thing; in fact, she's a good sort.'

'My apologies, Freddy – I was not, of course, including Lady Pargeter in my sweeping dismissal of London dowagers,' replied his lordship with a smile. 'But you must agree that such an affair is dull work and I have an early start for Brighton tomorrow if the weather holds fine.'

Freddy, lounging in the leather chair opposite, started forward in surprise at this. 'Good God, so you've accepted Kendray's bet after all! Have you run mad? There's no way it can be done.'

'On the contrary, I have not only accepted the bet, but I shall beat his time by at least fifteen minutes. The odds on my success are currently ten to one and even you should risk a wager at such an attractive price.'

'Fifteen minutes!' said his friend. He shook his head in disbelief, 'Can't be done. Not without you ending up in a ditch with a broken neck.'

A laugh escaped Lord Bramwell. 'Show a little faith in my abilities, Freddy! London to Brighton in four and a half hours is feasible and there will be no need to break my neck to achieve it.'

Mr Isherwood was unconvinced. 'Baintree made a similar boast last year and failed. Couldn't show his face in town for three weeks out of embarrassment, as I recall.'

'But I never boast,' protested Hal. 'Having made allowances for my excellent team and new curricle, the matter is not in doubt. It will also provide sport to enliven a dreary day – London is thin of company and I crave a little entertainment. With my mother and Julia still down at Chenning Court, Theodore becoming uncommonly interested in his books after the lark he kicked up at Oxford, and Lukas and Hugo safely at school, even my animated family seem to be remarkably well behaved at present and requiring no attention from me.'

'Is Julia coming to London soon?' asked Mr Isherwood, with feigned nonchalance.

Freddy's attempts to appear indifferent to the arrival of Hal's sister made his companion's eyes gleam with amusement. 'She and my mother will be here next week. As you are aware, it is Julia's first season and that has meant the removal of holland covers from the rest of this place for the first time in years.' Hal raised an eyebrow and looked about the room. 'Lord knows, I had forgotten it was so vast, but my mother is fond of it and I suppose we must have somewhere to accommodate all the young men anxious to beat a path to Julia's door.'

Shrugging his broad shoulders, his companion muttered a little defensively, 'I only ask so that I may call and pay my respects. My mother would also be displeased if I did not pass on her regards to Lady Bramwell, who is her oldest and dearest friend.'

'But of course that is the reason, Freddy,' replied Lord Bramwell with perfect gravity. 'I'm sure my mother and sister will be pleased to see you. However, I should warn you that Julia's beauty has increased considerably since last year – you will have to work hard to obtain even a country dance.'

'How can you talk about Julia in that manner, Hal?' said Mr Isherwood, colouring. 'You treat everything as a joke.'

'My dear fellow, life has taught me to do just that.' Hal stood up and moved to the window. After observing the scene below for a moment or two, he added in a more serious voice, 'Don't worry, Freddy, your admiration for my sister will remain secret. Indeed, if that's the way of things, I wish you well – you'll have my blessing – but Julia will take some convincing. She's fond of you, but London can go to a young girl's head and the attention she'll receive will do likewise. You will recall I speak from experience in these matters, although Julia's nature cannot be compared to that of the lady I am referring to.'

'Since you mention it, I have heard that Lady Portland and her husband have returned – they have come over from the Continent, so I understand, and taken a house in Half Moon Street.' Freddy looked uncomfortable as he imparted this piece of information which had come his way just that morning.

Hal turned abruptly to scan his friend's features with a keen gaze. 'What the deuce has Felicity come back to London for?'

Freddy gave another shrug. 'I have no idea but I suppose she is entitled to if she wishes: the scandal died down years ago. They have lived mainly in Italy because of Portland's health. No doubt their return is due in part to that monster Napoleon escaping from Elba. Matters are becoming a mite uncomfortable across the water so perhaps they were minded to return to the relative safety of London.'

'I see,' mused Lord Bramwell, in a non-committal voice.

After a pause, Mr Isherwood ventured, 'Do you mind that she has returned?'

'No,' said Hal. 'Eight years as Lady Portland will not have stemmed Felicity's malicious tongue, but that is no concern of mine, thank God. I hope Portland still thinks he had a good bargain with his marriage. I know now I had a lucky escape, although I will allow that I did not think so at the time and thought my life had been blighted for ever.'

'I hear she is still considered very beautiful,' said Freddy, with an interested glance at his companion's expression. However, there was no sign of disquiet there at the return of the woman who had caused a major scandal years earlier by breaking off her engagement to Hal and eloping with the older, but exceptionally wealthy Lord Portland.

Freddy had witnessed his friend's despair following this rejection: Hal had turned briefly to drink and to gambling until his steady nature and sense of humour had reasserted themselves, and he had continued with his life. In the years that followed, Hal had proved himself to be a steadfast friend, a source of good advice for his widowed mother and younger siblings, and a forward-thinking custodian of his estates.

However, Freddy recognized the marks that the events of eight years ago had left upon his friend. Despite being one of the most eligible bachelors in society and, as a result, laid siege to by mothers of hopeful daughters and ladies of marriageable age alike, there had been no room in Hal's life for serious love affairs. Very little of what engaged the *ton*'s interest seemed to hold, or indeed even arouse, Hal's attention. The escapades he indulged in from time to time arose from boredom and the resolution, made in the depths of his despair, not to take life too seriously again. But Hal was never reckless or inconsiderate, in spite of appearing so to those who did not know him well. His devil-may-care reputation was belied by the more sober man beneath, but that man was known only to his family and close friends. Society knew nothing of Hal's wider interests and he wanted it to remain that way.

'Indeed?' replied Hal, his grim voice interrupting Freddy's musings. 'Such information cuts no ice with me. However, I am sure Felicity is inordinately pleased: beauty was her only asset and when that departs, she, too, will become a vicious old tabby.'

Freddy gave a wry smile. 'Which brings us back in a somewhat convoluted manner to this evening. Will you oblige me by attending? My aunt has implored me to go and to bring you along – she is terrified of having too many ladies and not enough gentlemen. We need stay just for an hour or two and then depart.'

'Oh, very well,' replied Hal with an exasperated sigh, 'but only to oblige you and your aunt.'

His friend, eager to offer some encouragement, winked and said with a smile, 'There may be a pretty face or two among the old tabbies.'

'If there are, I will not lose my head over any of them.'

Chapter Three

SEVERAL hours later, Isabella was regretting her decision to attend Lady Partgeter's soirée. She was unable to view the evening ahead with any enthusiasm and when Dominic had awoken from a nightmare and insisted on seeing his mother, she had suggested to Harriet that she should go alone. Harriet, however, had refused to countenance this. Her entreaties did lead eventually to Isabella climbing into the carriage, but her demeanour was that of someone stepping into a tumbrel rather than embarking on an evening of pleasure.

Despite Harriet's protestations that her niece would enjoy herself once she was there, Isabella was unconvinced and determined to return to Curzon Street as soon as possible. Her character was not naturally dour, but a joyless marriage had suppressed her lively, enquiring nature. She was aware of this and knew also that as a consequence she might be considered remote, but that did not concern her. Indeed, it suited Isabella to cultivate an aloof air because it helped to avoid questions about her past.

However, she was agreeably surprised at their reception in Green Street. There were a few murmurings when they arrived, but soon it was obvious they were no longer the main topic of conversation. At least eighty people were crowded into the elegant reception rooms and it seemed that many of the fashionable London elite were present. The card tables set up in the side rooms were well attended and while there was no dancing, a group of musicians played at the end of the drawing-room. Most people, while politely interested, seemed disinclined to enquire beyond the details that Harriet imparted, so Isabella relaxed and even began to enjoy herself, a circumstance which her aunt noted.

'I said there was no need for concern,' Harriet whispered, as they entered the saloon where the refreshments were laid out. 'Everyone is most obliging, and not odiously curious. And in spite of your reluctance to come this evening, I have received a great many compliments about you, Isabella.' She gave a little smile of satisfaction, adding, 'Naturally, I expected that to happen once you could be enticed into society again.'

'I am glad to please you, but I have no desire to impress the *ton*,' replied Isabella.

'Your modesty does you credit, but you are very lovely, my dear – it is almost criminal to keep such beauty hidden away.'

Isabella smiled at Harriet's obvious bias but by now her attention had been claimed by the gentleman talking to Lady Pargeter. He was dressed in the most extraordinarily flamboyant style, the like of which Isabella had never seen before. She tried not to stare and observed him from under her lashes, but just at that moment, he raised his quizzing glass in her direction and whispered a comment to his hostess. Isabella hid her amusement and turned her attention back to Harriet.

In fact, Harriet's sentiments regarding Isabella's beauty were shared by many present, particularly the gentlemen, for whom Lady Vane's ethereal features, slim figure and graceful carriage had cast every other young woman present into the shade. Among these was Sir Seymour Dinniscombe, the extraordinary figure already noted by Isabella. Sir Seymour, commonly known as 'Dinny' among London society, was a good-natured, valetudinarian bachelor whose obsession with his health and with visits to his tailor was well known.

Although his immense wealth of £60,000 a year had made him an attractive proposition for many ladies, an offer of marriage had always failed to materialize from Sir Seymour. He had concluded that none of the young women who had excited his attentions could be relied upon to pay due regard to his constitution. Consequently, he had remained unmarried, for which situation he felt not one pang of regret since it allowed him to spend more time upon his wardrobe and visit whichever physician was enjoying his patronage.

His mode of dress, which he himself thought of as the height of fashion, was generally regarded by the *ton* as dandyish; most young men arriving in London considered Lord Bramwell and Mr Isherwood, with their more reserved but elegant sartorial style, the mode to copy. However, Sir Seymour was oblivious to other people's opinions on this matter and was rich enough to indulge whatever tastes he and his tailor thought appropriate. These were many and varied as that wily purveyor was always ready to suggest a new way to relieve Sir Seymour of his money. This evening Sir Seymour was attired in the normal evening dress of long tailed coat and satin knee-breeches, but he had added his trademark extravagant accessories. He was resplendent in a yellow and white spotted waistcoat, black shoes with silver buckles and sported a huge nosegay in his coat. Fobs and seals adorned his waist and highly starched collar points meant that he could only turn his head with difficulty. His hair had been carefully brushed à la Brutus, while his cravat was astonishing in its intricacy: it had taken an hour and several discarded neckcloths for Sir Seymour and his valet to achieve the desired Waterfall arrangement, embellished with a sparkling diamond pin. This picture of magnificence now stood discussing the merits of hot milk possets with his hostess.

'... Indeed, Lady Pargeter, the excellent Doctor Hammond said that the benefits for a delicate constitution of taking a posset before retiring outweigh port or Madeira. It is apparently more beneficial to the digestion and, having endured a disturbed night following a glass of port at White's yesterday evening, I can vouch for the truth of this. Hammond also advised me that adding a drop of laudanum to the posset will ensure a restful sleep, and do no harm—' Sir Seymour halted mid-sentence, staring while he groped absently for his quizzing glass. 'Pray tell me, who is that exquisite young woman?' he asked faintly.

Lady Pargeter followed the direction of his gaze. 'Ah, that is Lady Vane; her aunt, Mrs Harriet Forster, is to her left. Isabella Vane is a beautiful creature, is she not, Sir Seymour? All of London is curious about her, but she seems disinclined to reveal any personal details. Indeed, society has already given Lady Vane the title of the Ice Angel because of her marked reserve.'

'Is she married?' queried Sir Seymour bluntly, still studying Isabella through his glass.

'Why, no. I understand that she has been a widow for over a year now and recently arrived in London with her aunt, who is also a widow. Apart from this, no one knows anything about her.'

Sir Seymour gave an audible sigh. 'For a moment I thought I had fallen asleep here, in this very room, and awakened in the presence of Aphrodite or Helen of Troy. Never before have I seen such a ravishing lady!' he admitted in an awed whisper. 'Lady Pargeter, will you please introduce me at once.'

His hostess, surprised by his sudden distraction with Lady Vane, did as she was bid. Once the formal introductions had been completed, Lady Pargeter moved away to greet some late arrivals and Sir Seymour sat down with care next to Isabella, straightening his waistcoat afterwards in case it had become creased during this manoeuvre.

Isabella was then subjected to blatant but admiring scrutiny from Sir Seymour while Harriet raised her brows at her niece in amusement. Sir Seymour, meanwhile, chatted easily, confining his conversation to general topics; he had no intention of being intrusive in his questioning from the outset and thereby upsetting the young woman before him.

'Do you intend to stay long in town, Lady Vane?' he asked eventually.

'Our plans are not yet fixed; we shall remain here for some weeks at least,' she replied.

'It will be a little uncomfortable, however – the house is full of Dominic's pets and they are always under one's feet,' admitted Harriet.

'Dominic?' queried Sir Seymour, puzzled. 'Is that your brother, Mrs Forster?'

Harriet laughed. 'No, Sir Seymour – Dominic is Isabella's son. He is only six years old and a delightful child.'

The change in Sir Seymour's expression was so sudden as to be comical; his mouth twisted in a parody of a smile as he tried to disguise his chagrin. 'I did not know you have a son, Lady Vane. How – how charming, to be sure! I am afraid that children are quite outside my experience.' He cleared his throat nervously, anxious not to give offence. 'That is to say, I like them well enough at a distance, but I consider them unpredictable which is particularly worrying when one is wearing a new coat or pair of boots.'

'Dominic is harmless although I agree that he has a propensity, like most small boys, to become remarkably grubby in a short time,' said Isabella, smiling.

'Exactly so!' he agreed, with feeling. 'A nephew of mine once almost ruined a pair of my Hessians. It took my valet a fortnight to remove the mud and polish them back to perfection. Most upsetting thing to happen! It was all over in a trice too – the little fellow ran straight over my feet when he came in from the garden. Complained bitterly to my brother at the time, but he just laughed and said "Dinny, stop talking nonsense over a pair of boots". Nonsense, indeed,' said Sir Seymour with a wounded expression, 'I am particularly attached to my Hessians.'

Isabella, who had struggled to keep her countenance during this speech, bit her lip to prevent her amusement from bubbling over. Observing this, Harriet came to her rescue and it was she who smoothed Sir Seymour's ruffled feelings back to serenity.

'Your discomfort was understandable – a shocking thing for a gentleman to endure,' agreed Harriet. 'My husband was most careful about his boots and always insisted that champagne be added to the blacking in order to achieve the desired effect.'

'My valet does the same,' he acknowledged, feeling on safer

ground now the conversation had moved away from children. 'It is a pity that the fellow cannot make the same excellent job of pressing my linen, but he tries his best.'

'But your style is very individual,' observed Isabella. 'Your valet must therefore find great satisfaction in his work.'

'Why, thank you Lady Vane! I shall take your comment as a compliment.' Sir Seymour, glowing with pleasure, turned his head as much as his starched collar would allow to smile warmly at her.

'Are you well acquainted with London society?' asked Harriet as she looked about the room.

'I can claim expertise in that area,' said Sir Seymour, puffing out his chest. 'Most of my time is spent in London among the *haut ton.*'

'Then pray tell me, who is that gentleman watching us so earnestly? I do not know him at all and yet he has been staring for some time. Is he perhaps an acquaintance of yours?'

In response to Harriet's query, Sir Seymour raised his quizzing glass.

Isabella, whose eyes had followed the direction of Sir Seymour's gaze, saw a tall, broad-shouldered man who was indeed staring at them, but most particularly at her. He, too, was dressed in the normal evening attire of longtailed coat, waistcoat and satin knee breeches. However, he wore them with a nonchalant grace completely at odds with Sir Seymour's extravagant style. Dark hair fell across his brow, giving him a rakish appearance and his eyes scanned Isabella's features intently. Under his scrutiny, Isabella felt strangely breathless and colour began to warm her cheeks. The more he stared, the more her anger rose; if he were rude enough to study her like a specimen under a magnifying glass, he would only succeed in earning her contempt. However, she evinced no outward signs of annoyance, having become skilled at concealing her feelings during her marriage.

'That is the Earl of Bramwell, who is at this moment being joined by Mr Frederick Isherwood,' explained Sir Seymour, observing the second gentleman who had come to stand next to Lord Bramwell. 'It is unusual to see either at an event like this, but Mr Isherwood is Lady Pargeter's nephew so that must be the reason for their attendance this evening.'

'Lord Bramwell cuts a very handsome figure,' said Harriet in a low voice.

'He is considered a Corinthian, a man who excels in every sporting pursuit, but I think him a little reckless,' remarked Sir Seymour. 'He has a devil-may-care approach to life which seems attractive to ladies. However, it would be injurious to my health to indulge in the ill-advised escapades which appeal to Lord Bramwell.'

'Ill-advised escapades?' echoed Harriet, intrigued.

'Oh, nothing too serious, you understand – he is a leader of the *ton*, after all – but Lord Bramwell is usually to be found at the centre of some harebrained scheme or sporting bet,' explained Sir Seymour. 'I hear he intends to drive down to Brighton tomorrow in his curricle in less than four and a half hours, simply to answer a wager. Madness! I should be confined to bed for a week if I attempted such a feat.'

'Any reasonable person would not attempt it,' agreed Isabella vehemently. She was aware of Harriet's look of surprise – this was severe criticism for an activity which most young men of the day took part in and was generally considered harmless – but as far as Isabella was concerned, Lord Bramwell had already earned her scorn. She had endured enough reckless and inconsiderate behaviour to last a lifetime and had no desire to become acquainted with anyone who followed that path.

However, this stern resolution was destined to be quickly broken: Isabella, alone for a few moments some time later, found Lord Bramwell's tall figure had suddenly appeared at her side.

'I have appealed to Lady Pargeter for the last hour to introduce me, but either you are engaged, or her attention is diverted before she can do so, and I can wait no longer,' he said. 'May I introduce myself and hope that you will excuse my abominable lack of manners? It is only because I am impatient to meet you.'

He bowed and smiled engagingly. 'Lord Bramwell, at your service, Lady Vane.'

Forced to acknowledge him, Isabella turned to look up into his face. Lord Bramwell was undeniably handsome; his features were well defined and attractive, there was no dandyish affectation in his courteous manner and his physique was clearly that of a sportsman. A smile lurked in the grey eyes which gazed down into hers and he was close enough for Isabella to have momentarily felt his warm breath on her cheek as he spoke. The smooth rich timbre of his voice washed over her and, unbidden, the thought flashed into her mind that Lord Bramwell was the embodiment of her ideal. She pushed it away ruthlessly; having already been introduced to Sir Seymour and the amiable Mr Isherwood, who was quite as handsome as Lord Bramwell, with no similar effects, Isabella felt annoyed at her reaction.

Reluctantly, she gave him her hand, aware of the latent strength in his grasp. A quiver ran through her as he unexpectedly bent his head to brush his lips over her knuckles. 'Good evening, Lord Bramwell,' she replied in a voice of cool disdain and snatched her hand away.

He raised his brows at her icy tone but merely said, 'Are you enjoying Lady Pargeter's hospitality?'

'She has been most kind; Lady Pargeter is an old acquaintance of my aunt's.'

'I see. I understand that you are newly arrived in London and have taken a house in Curzon Street?'

'Yes.' Isabella felt her animosity rise: had he been making enquiries about her? She knew she was being unjust – his comments were innocuous to say the least – but she only felt secure if the relative anonymity she had built around herself and her family remained intact, and Lord Bramwell's keen gaze seemed to reach into her innermost thoughts.

'Lady Pargeter informed me earlier when I asked to be introduced; I was not aware that you were staying in Town,' he explained. 'Do you intend to stay for the season?'

'I cannot say. The length of our stay will depend on other

circumstances,' replied Isabella, feeling a little contrite; whatever else Lord Bramwell was, it appeared he was not a tattle-monger.

'Your presence will grace London society however long you are here.'

Isabella blushed. 'There is no need to offer me approbation,' she replied sharply.

'But it is not empty praise: I merely speak the truth,' murmured Hal, who was unable to remove his gaze from the most enchanting face he had ever beheld. His expression suddenly became quizzical and he added, 'Have I offended you in some way, Lady Vane? I suspect that you do not look upon me kindly, although I cannot think why as we have only just met. That is unfortunate because I feel an overwhelming desire at this moment to kiss you thoroughly and restore your good humour. And in case you think me mad, I assure you such disregard for the proprieties is entirely out of character.'

Isabella stared at him, at a loss how to reply to this direct and wholly unexpected speech. She quickly decided he was making fun of her – it must be an agreeable form of verbal dalliance in London to suggest kissing a lady one had just met. Her annoyance towards Lord Bramwell grew, as did her indignation at his ill-judged humour. 'Are you enjoying a joke at my expense, Lord Bramwell?' she asked curtly. 'If so, I find it most distasteful.'

A tinge of colour crept into his lean cheeks. 'No, indeed. Forgive me – that was a foolish thing to say, and I certainly did not mean to embarrass you. What a graceless fellow you must think me now!'

Isabella observed, not entirely truthfully, 'But how could I reach any opinion of you in such a short time, Lord Bramwell?'

'I hardly know – I have already begged your pardon and tried to excuse any possible incivility in the manner of my introduction,' he said, with the ghost of a smile. 'Perhaps my supposed reputation has gone before me; Sir Seymour, although harmless, is always ready with his opinions.'

Isabella coloured deliciously as this accurate observation hit home. She tried to appease her conscience by saying, 'Whatever opinions Sir Seymour may have, I would try not to let them influence mine.'

'I simply ask that you form an opinion based on what you see, and not on my reputation.' He hesitated and then continued, 'Please excuse my forthright manner, but I should like permission to call upon you in Curzon Street in the near future.'

She turned her clear gaze fully upon him and, in an unguarded moment, evinced surprise and confusion.

'W – Why ever would you want to—?' stammered Isabella. 'That is, I suppose, you may call if you wish, but I – I might be engaged and unable to receive you.'

'I quite understand,' he said, smiling, 'and I should not wish to intrude upon your time too greatly, but my sister, Lady Julia Cavanagh, arrives in London next week for her first season and I cannot help but think that she would be as pleased to make your acquaintance as I have been. Would you be prepared to meet her? I am persuaded she would think it delightful if you could.'

Shocked by this request, Isabella regarded him in silence. Not an hour before, she had determined never to have any conversation with Lord Bramwell, a devil-may-care Corinthian whose way of life was abhorrent to her. Now, he had introduced himself, declared his desire to kiss her soundly and wanted her to meet his sister!

Compelled to answer as he stood waiting for her response, she cast about in her mind for an excuse but could see no way of extricating herself without being abominably rude. Isabella consoled herself with the thought that perhaps he did not intend to carry out his threat of calling in Curzon Street.

'Very well,' she replied, 'if you insist upon it, we shall be happy to receive you and your sister, but I fear you will both find it tedious.'

He smiled and said cryptically, 'I thought this evening would be tedious and I have been proved quite wrong. Please excuse me, Lady Vane; Mr Isherwood is searching for me and it appears he is ready to leave. I look forward to calling on you in the near future.' He bowed once more and moved away to join his friend.

Isabella's heart sank as she stared at his retreating figure. Her attendance here had resulted in exactly the situation she was most afraid of and now she must endure visits from Sir Seymour and Lord Bramwell. The first did not concern her unduly and she would look forward to with some amusement; the second was an entirely different matter and filled her with trepidation. It seemed Lord Bramwell had the ability to jeopardize her carefully schooled emotions and it was imperative she did not allow that to happen.

Chapter Four

FOUR days after meeting Lady Vane, Lord Bramwell strolled into the subscription room at White's. His appearance was greeted by cheers from everyone present and within moments, he was surrounded by a large group of the club's members, young and old, all clamouring for details of how he had achieved his triumph. They included Sir Walter Kendray himself, who congratulated Hal on beating his London to Brighton time.

'Never thought you would do it, Bramwell,' cried Sir Walter. 'Four hours and twenty-five minutes exactly, eh? A fine achievement and a compliment to your driving skills and your horses. Your bays are the best matched team I have seen – allow me first refusal if you decide to sell.'

'Thank you, Sir Walter, but I have no intention of parting with my horses just yet.'

'Can't say I blame you – would do the same myself.' Drawing out his pocket book, Sir Walter said, 'Shall I settle our wager now?'

Hal shook his head. 'I am dining here this evening so we can settle our account then.' He then added with a grin, 'And if we meet at the gaming tables, you may have the opportunity to regain your losses.'

'What, with your damnable luck and skill at cards?' asked Sir Walter, with an incredulous laugh. 'I sincerely doubt it, although I shall be happy to try provided the stakes are not too high – I have no stomach for losing my fortune on the turn of a card.'

'Nor have I,' acknowledged Hal. 'In spite of my reputation, I never take unnecessary risks.'

Freddy Isherwood joined them then and, after congratulating Hal once more, Sir Walter returned to the game of cards he was involved in.

'Well, Freddy?' asked Hal, 'Did you have the good sense to place a small wager on my success?'

'Matter of fact, I did.'

'At least you put your faith in my ability eventually,' said Hal, amused. 'Now, to more serious matters – did you carry out my request?'

'Yes, though I can't say it will do you much good,' said Freddy. 'Delivered the flowers to Lady Vane, just as you asked, along with your compliments. However, I didn't see her in person. Her aunt came down and was very pretty in her thanks on Lady Vane's behalf, but said she was out of the house running an errand. I don't know if that was the truth or not, but Lady Vane had already received a great number of flower posies and invitations.'

'Perhaps I should have delivered the flowers myself when I returned to London, but I was impatient to send her my compliments and to atone for a clumsy comment I made during our conversation,' said Hal.

'I see,' mused Freddy. 'Well, Mrs Forster reeled off the list of people who had called in Curzon Street. Seems Lady Vane is extremely popular although that's hardly surprising – most beautiful girl I've ever seen! Apart from,' he added, with a grin, 'your sister, of course.'

'I expected nothing less, Freddy. She is a bewitchingly lovely creature and all of London will fall at her feet. But I am intrigued by more than her beauty: she seemed offended by me.'

'Lord, Hal, why should anyone take offence at you, least of all Lady Vane? She has only just arrived in town.'

Lord Bramwell shrugged. 'I acknowledge my imperfections; perhaps I should have been more formal in my introduction and, as I said, I made an unfortunate maladroit remark. However, I do not believe she was piqued solely by that. No, there is something else and I mean to discover what it is.'

'I wish you luck but you'll have to fight your way to her through Dinny – he's already called in Curzon Street twice and Mrs Forster told me that Lady Vane had received him on one occasion,' said Freddy.

Hal raised his brows at this but said no more – he had no desire to share even with Freddy all his reflections on Lady Vane. He had been mesmerized from the moment he had laid eyes on her, feeling almost as if he had received a physical blow. Stirred by this strange madness, he had subsequently struggled to stay his planned three days in Brighton because he had wanted to hurry back in the hope of seeing her again. He had encountered many beautiful women before, and admired them, but not one had refused to leave his thoughts like Isabella Vane had.

Since Felicity Richmond had broken their engagement and eloped with Lord Portland, Hal had not sought out any women who expected more affection than he was willing to give. The optimism he had given to that youthful love affair had been dashed on the vicious rocks of reality and when, eventually, he had realized that it was his pride that had been damaged and not his heart, he had determined to stay away from any serious attachments with women in the future – they seemed to offer only pain and embarrassment.

This he had done, and the care of his family and the responsibilities associated with his estates had taken precedence. His reputation had arisen from escapades that he undertook simply for the challenge they represented. Hal did not care that most of London admired him for his sporting and gaming prowess and knew nothing of his other interests and philanthropic work.

But Hal had discovered that he did care what Lady Vane thought of him. Her curious elusive air, a mixture of sadness, reserve and striking beauty, struck an unexpected chord deep within him. He had glimpsed vulnerability behind her cold glances which, to his astonishment, appealed to his protective instincts. Yet she obviously disliked him from the outset and in the intervening hours since their meeting, Hal had struggled to think of any serious indiscretion he might have committed.

Bitterly, he cursed himself for having said that he would like to kiss away her ill-humour. He did not know what had possessed him to utter such a tactless remark, even though he admitted ruefully that it had been the truth and he had simply spoken his thoughts aloud. However, Lady Vane had not then trilled her delight and begun a determined flirtation – she seemed unaware of her allure and he had not detected an ounce of vanity – nor did he think she reacted with disdain for prudish reasons. Her dislike had been present even before his comment and it irked him that he could not account for it.

Sir Seymour might have discussed him with Lady Vane, but Hal knew that Dinny was no liar and his amiable nature possessed no malice; again, nothing Sir Seymour could have said would have induced her contempt.

There must be another reason, one that Hal felt compelled to uncover.

Harriet glanced at her niece in frustration as Isabella instructed Silwood to inform Lord Marston, who was waiting downstairs, that they were not at home to callers.

'I do not understand you,' observed Harriet, after Silwood had left the room. 'You refuse to see any of the pleasant young men who have called here since we attended Lady Pargeter's party. They are merely being polite and for you to spurn their admiration is unkind. You may be considered a cold-hearted creature if you do not show a little more interest.'

Isabella raised her brows and gave a quizzical smile. 'Do you think me cold, Aunt?'

'No, indeed! You are the kindest, most considerate young woman,' said Harriet earnestly. 'I simply believe that you could receive more of your admirers than you seem inclined to at present.'

'But for what reason, Harriet? I have no desire to encourage any gentleman.' Isabella sighed, sadness shadowing her eyes. 'Now we are in society again, I realize how much I wish to avoid people.' Noting her aunt's shocked expression, she continued, 'Oh, do not fear that I will become a recluse – I should never do so, and certainly do not want Dominic to become afraid of society. But I cannot trust anyone yet and I will not allow my— that is to say, our current peace of mind to be ruined, particularly by men who only wish to beguile the season away with an agreeable flirtation.'

'They may not all be so frivolous,' protested Harriet, indignant. 'Why, Lord Marston has called every morning this past three days, as have many others – they might genuinely wish to know you better.'

'Perhaps, but I take care for all our sakes, not merely my own. Do not think too harshly of me, Harriet. Perhaps there will be someone one day to whom I can entrust my feelings, and those of my family.'

'But how shall you meet such a person if you will not even receive morning callers?' she grumbled.

Isabella laughed outright at this, her smile lighting up her features. 'Then I make you a promise not to turn every well-meaning young man away from our door.'

'Sir Seymour is taken with your charms,' said Harriet, glancing at her niece from under her lashes, 'You seemed content to endure his visit, my love.'

'Because he does not threaten my equanimity,' replied Isabella. 'Oh, it is difficult to explain precisely how I feel. I am conscious of Sir Seymour's admiration, but I do not feel intimidated by it. Besides, he is such an absurdly eccentric creature, and I found his visit entertaining.'

'Yes, he always has interesting information to impart.'

This reply, apparently delivered with all seriousness by Harriet, drew a look of amusement and surprise from Isabella but she offered no comment.

'But why then did you refuse to see Mr Isherwood?' continued her companion. 'The poor man was quite desperate to pass on the posy of flowers and compliments from Lord Bramwell, and yet you would not see him.'

'I cannot condemn Mr Isherwood, but Lord Bramwell is a different matter – and he did not even trouble to deliver his flowers in person.'

Harriet tutted. 'Uncharitable, Isabella! You know very well that Lord Bramwell was in Brighton; Mr Isherwood said his lordship would have delivered the posy himself if he had been in town.'

'I suppose even a *nonpareil* like Lord Bramwell cannot be in two places at once,' she acknowledged, 'but I am tempted to dislike him from what I have heard.' Isabella had not told her aunt of Lord Bramwell's remark about kissing her – it would not be wise when Harriet often entertained the most ridiculous romantic notions about Isabella's future.

'Well, you will have the opportunity of discovering more on Friday. We received a card this morning advising that he intends to visit then with his sister.'

'B – But I did not expect him to call,' said Isabella, a look of disquiet skimming her features. 'I thought he was merely indulging in polite conversation.'

'Well, it appears he was not,' replied Harriet with an enigmatic smile.

In Berkeley Square the following morning, Lord Bramwell's sister shared Isabella's vexation.

Lady Julia Cavanagh had arrived in London the previous afternoon, accompanied by her mother. Lady Julia was a petite, raven-haired beauty whose slumbrous dark eyes, full lips and golden skin threatened, according to her mama, to take London by storm. But Lady Julia was as candid as she was lovely and she was singularly unimpressed to discover that her elder brother had arranged this social call.

'But who is she, Hal?' she queried, a sliver of annoyance in her voice. 'I have never heard of Lady Vane and I venture neither has Mama.'

'She has just recently arrived in London,' explained her brother, leaning his broad shoulders against the fireplace and watching his sister's animated features. 'Any facts about her existence up to that point are unknown – and she seems determined it should remain a mystery. All that is known is that she is a widow of four-and-twenty and she is accompanied by her aunt, who is also a widow, and her six-year-old son.'

'Well, I am sorry she finds herself a widow at such a young age, but what has this to do with me?' protested Julia. 'I have no time to oblige a woman who is only anxious to further her social standing.'

'That is too severe of you, Julia. On the contrary, Lady Vane is unwilling to venture into society much – she has even declined to receive several very eligible gentlemen eager to further their acquaintance. I'm surprised she agreed to receive us, although I admit that I left her little choice.'

Her brown eyes regarded him steadily, amusement now twinkling in their handsome depths. 'Ah, I begin to understand. Is Lady Vane beautiful?'

'Exquisitely.'

Julia laughed. 'Now I see! You wish to further your cause with this paragon and have had the audacity to use me as an excuse.' She tilted her head and gave him a quizzical look. 'But this is not your usual style – you have not required assistance in the past with your occasional amours.'

'And what do you know of my amours, miss?' asked Hal with an amused look.

'Only that none of them has been serious,' she replied frankly. 'Is Lady Vane so different then?'

'She is, but I cannot explain why. Our meeting was brief, but she already disapproves of me and yet, in spite of that disapproval, I feel compelled to discover more about her—'

'Naturally, if she is exquisitely beautiful,' interjected Julia, in a dry voice.

He shook his head. 'It is not just her beauty, although that is extraordinary; she has an air of diffidence, sadness even, which

45

is elusive and difficult to describe. Lady Vane is not much older than you in years, but her manner is very different – perhaps you will understand when you meet her yourself.'

His sister regarded him thoughtfully. 'Your description of the lovely Isabella is intriguing, Hal. Very well; I agree to your abominable coercion and will accompany you. At least then you shall not suffer the ignominy of being turned away!'

Hal grinned. 'As always, your presence will lend me respectable countenance. You are more than passable bedecked in all your London finery, Julia.' He studied her sprigged muslin dress in an exaggerated manner, eyes brimful of laughter. 'I suppose I must address the bills for what you and Mama have spent at various modistes and milliners?'

At that moment, Marguerite, The Dowager Countess of Bramwell, entered. She was a tall, graceful woman possessed of thick dark hair like her children, but her own was sprinkled with grey. However, she was one of those fortunate women for whom the passing of years only added to their elegance. She placed an affectionate kiss on her son's cheek in greeting, smiled and said, 'Good morning. I am afraid I did not perfectly understand your comment just now, Hal – what particular crime are Julia and I accused of?'

'Spending too much of Hal's fortune on the nonsensical fripperies of fashion, Mama,' said Julia gaily.

'Pray tell me when fashion became nonsensical?' asked Lady Bramwell, a gleam of amusement in her eyes. 'It is one of the most important matters for a young woman who is about to enjoy her first season, and you cannot begrudge Julia one penny, for it has all been well spent. Wait until you see her blue ball gown!'

'Spare me the details of the blue ball gown,' he said, smiling. 'You have no need to justify the expense; every penny will have been wisely spent as you both have ineffable taste. In my opinion, Julia needs little embellishment to improve upon nature and I am sure Freddy will agree.'

Lady Julia coloured at this mention of Mr Isherwood. 'It will be pleasant to see Freddy again, but I hope he does not expect to monopolize my attentions – I am determined to enjoy my season to the full.'

Her brother gave a nonchalant shrug. 'Freddy has expressed no such pretensions to your time.' When Julia looked downcast, Lady Bramwell and her son exchanged brief but knowing glances. 'He will be calling in the next few days to pay his respects to you, ma'am,' said Hal innocently.

'Of course,' said Lady Bramwell, 'Freddy will wish to deliver all the news from his mother. You do not need to be present if you have another engagement, Julia.'

The flush in Julia's cheeks deepened. 'Oh! Well, I – I cannot say where I shall be with all the invitations we have received and now Hal has arranged another morning call,' She gave her brother an arch look as she added, 'In recompense of which, Hal, I demand that you accompany us to Almack's on Wednesday.'

He groaned in mock disgust. 'Very well, but do not fail me in my request.'

'I shall be happy to oblige, dear Brother,' said Julia. After reminding her mother she wished to travel to Bond Street to collect her new evening slippers, she left the drawing-room.

When Julia had gone, Lady Bramwell subjected her eldest son to a careful scrutiny. 'You look well, Hal. London appears to suit you although no doubt by the end of the season, I shall be anxious to return to Chenning. Have you heard from Theodore? I received a letter from him last week, but it made no mention of his recent troubles.'

'Because he does not wish to worry you,' explained Hal. 'The matter is resolved – I wrote to his tutor at Oxford, who assured me it was no more than a prank which got out of hand. Theo has been reprimanded and will be encouraged to rusticate until the fuss dies down. I expect him to arrive in London during the next few weeks, as he will surely not miss the opportunity to descend on us while we are here.'

"I suppose driving a herd of cows on to the college green was childish rather than dangerous, but I shudder to think what wild scheme Theodore will think of next,' said Lady Marguerite, shaking her head. 'At least you can guide him; London can be a perilous place for a young man with money and time to enjoy himself.'

'Do not concern yourself unduly about Theo, ma'am – it is just youthful high spirits.'

'You are right, of course.' Lady Bramwell hesitated for a moment, then continued with a quizzical look, 'And what of you, Hal? What engagement have you thought it necessary to add to Julia's list?'

'I have asked her to accompany me on a morning call,' said Hal. 'The lady in question is a young widow, Isabella, Lady Vane, who has recently arrived in Town. Do you know her?'

'I do not believe so. However, if you are keen to visit and introduce your sister, you must consider Lady Vane worth the effort,' she ventured.

'Yes,' he replied, with a grin.

'Then I shall not enquire further until you are ready to tell me,' declared the countess. 'A mother who delves into her adult son's affairs is someone to be pitied, don't you agree?'

He was obliged to laugh at this, but merely said, 'Matters are not what you may think: we have met only once and she already regards me with disdain.'

Lady Bramwell looked at him in astonishment, 'Whatever for?'

'I don't know exactly, but I intend to find out.'

'Well, that is certainly not the reaction you would hope for,' exclaimed Lady Bramwell. 'How curious; I look forward to meeting Lady Vane myself.'

Chapter Five

As she waited for Lord Bramwell and his sister to arrive, Isabella grew more nervous even though she chastized herself for being faint-hearted. What harm could a morning visit do? It would be over within an hour, and yet still she could not relax. The beautiful posy of yellow roses she had received an hour ago, along with Lord Bramwell's card and compliments, had already brought the colour rushing to her cheeks. Instinct told her that Lord Bramwell threatened her current calm and ordered existence, something she had longed for during the turbulent years of her marriage, and indeed, he had haunted her thoughts in recent days with tormenting regularity.

As an antidote, she reminded herself of his reckless character, but in this she enjoyed limited success; Isabella was honest enough to admit that it was unreasonable to allow Sir Seymour's comments to dictate her view. Harriet had heard nothing exceptionable about Lord Bramwell – he was, she confided to Isabella, considered a Corinthian and a nonesuch, but his sporting wagers were generally thought to be great fun and stylish rather than the reckless madcap schemes epitomized by the likes of the Earl of March. Despite the fact that sport and gambling was woven into everyday life and that most men, both young and old, devised wagers and tests of stamina to occupy their time, Isabella remained wary. Gambling held painful memories for her and she determined to keep Lord Bramwell firmly at arm's length and treat his visit in the same way as she had Sir Seymour's. But when Silwood informed her of his arrival, her treacherous heart defied this resolution and began to beat faster. Clasping her hands together and taking a deep breath, Isabella fervently hoped that this ordeal would be brief.

The butler announced her visitors and Lord Bramwell strode into the first-floor saloon. 'Good Morning, Lady Vane,' he said. 'May I introduce my sister, Lady Julia Cavanagh?'

He moved aside to allow his sister to come forward, and Isabella found herself looking into a pair of brown eyes which twinkled with friendly amusement. 'Delighted to meet you,' declared Julia, 'and I see that descriptions of your beauty have not been exaggerated.'

Isabella blushed and replied quietly, 'It is kind of you to say so, but since my beauty or otherwise is of no importance to my family, it is of no consequence to me. I admire your gown, Lady Julia – it is by Mrs Trentham of Bruton Street, is it not?'

'Why, yes,' said Julia in surprise. 'How clever of you to notice.'

Isabella smiled. 'Not really – my aunt ordered a gown from Mrs Trentham recently and I recognized her particular style.'

'Are Mrs Forster and your son well?' enquired Lord Bramwell.

Isabella, aware that he had not removed his gaze from her face, endured his scrutiny with all the self-control she could muster. After thanking him for the roses, she murmured, 'Yes, they are both in good health. Harriet is helping Dominic learn his letters; we share the task and spend an hour with him each morning. He is progressing so well that he will need a tutor when we to move to Haystacks— that is to say, our new home in the country.' Isabella bit her lip in annoyance; she had not meant to reveal even this small detail and hoped that her visitors had not noticed.

'When my brothers were young, they found it extremely annoying to be confined to London,' said Julia. 'They were never happier than when in the countryside, climbing trees, riding their ponies, or fishing.'

'We were the grubbiest urchins in the neighbourhood and

roamed the Chenning estate from dawn until dusk,' said Hal, with a smile. 'And although you would not think it from her elegant appearance today, Julia was never far behind, begging to be allowed to join in.'

Julia laughed. 'It's true – I was a hoyden who didn't enjoy the more sedate activities that girls are supposed to adhere to.'

'Then you have four older brothers, Lady Julia?' queried Isabella, a trace of envy in her voice. As a child, with no mother and only an elderly father for company, she had spent many lonely hours longing for siblings and the halcyon view of childhood described by Lord Bramwell struck a chord – it was exactly what she would wish for Dominic.

'Oh no – Hal and Theodore are older, but Lukas and Hugo, who are twins, are sixteen and still at school.' Julia gave Isabella a mischievous smile and added, 'However, it is only Hal who tries to be high-handed with me—'

'—and fails miserably,' observed her brother in a dry voice. 'Julia is more than a match for her brothers, Lady Vane, both in spirit and obduracy.'

Isabella joined in with the laughter that followed this remark and began to relax. Julia's manner was warm and refreshingly open and it was clear that Lord Bramwell was very fond of his sister.

Half an hour later, Isabella had also realized that he was knowledgeable, with intelligent opinions on a number of subjects. He was well versed on the situation in Europe, including Wellington's imminent replacement at the Congress of Vienna, but he interspersed this with gently satirical observations on some of the ridiculous figures in London society and gave sensible advice on which attractions to visit and which to avoid. She found herself enjoying his company more than she had anticipated, but the instant this thought registered, she became alarmed at her weakness and her reserve returned. Isabella knew she would be happy to cultivate a friendship with Lady Julia, but her nerves soon felt strained to breaking point by Lord Bramwell's presence. She managed to remain outwardly self-possessed, willing the visit to end, and yet, when her visitors rose to leave, disappointment mingled with her relief.

'I am certain, Isabella—' Julia hesitated as she collected her reticule. 'You do not mind if I call you Isabella? I feel as if we have been acquainted for far longer than an hour.'

'Not at all – indeed, I wish you would,' replied Isabella.

'Then I am certain, Isabella, that we shall be firm friends. I shall introduce you to my mother as soon as can be arranged and, as well as sending you an invitation to my come-out ball, Mama and I will ensure you receive Almack's vouchers.'

Isabella paled and stammered, 'Th-thank you, but it is out of the question – we cannot attend.'

'Why ever not?' said Julia, looking at her in surprise. 'I understood you have put off your black gloves?'

'No! I mean, yes, I am not in mourning any longer, but ...' began Isabella.

Julia raised her brows and remarked brightly, 'Then I shall allow no objections – to keep your beauty hidden would be scandalous and besides, you deserve a little enjoyment and we shall have the pleasure of providing some of it. Don't you agree, Hal?'

'It would be a pity to deny the *ton* your company, Lady Vane,' he said, smiling.

Isabella had no choice but to accede, even though the notion of going into society filled her with dread. However, since she could not articulate her reasons for this, she remained silent. Her cheeks grew warm under Lord Bramwell's shrewd grey gaze and she felt relieved that his visit was about to end.

But just as she was preparing to show her visitors out, the door was flung open by a tearful Dominic, who rushed into the room and threw his arms around his mother.

'Mama! You must come!' he cried. 'I let Jemima out of her cage, and then Joshua came in the room and tried to catch her. Now she won't come down and ... and ... Joshua is stuck on top of the fireplace! Aunt Harriet has tried to help, but she couldn't catch him, and Mary and Silwood both look very cross. They said

I shouldn't disturb you, but I knew that was fudge and you wouldn't mind.' Dominic hiccupped on a sob. 'Please come and help me – no one else knows what to do.'

'Pray don't get upset, love,' said Isabella, putting a comforting hand on his shoulder. 'When our visitors have left, I shall come upstairs and—'

'Please do not let us detain you, Lady Vane,' interjected Lord Bramwell gently. 'Can we assist in any way?'

Dominic regarded Lord Bramwell through tear-drenched lashes. He sniffed and said, 'Can you catch parrots, sir? I should be grateful if you can; Jemima is very quick and even Mama finds it difficult getting her back to her cage.'

'Dominic!' muttered Isabella, horrified. 'This is Lord Bramwell and his sister – you must not ask for their help with something so trivial.'

'On the contrary, I have no further engagements until this afternoon and am happy to place myself at your son's disposal.' Hal turned to his sister, his lips curved in amusement. 'Are you willing to help this young gentleman retrieve his errant parrot, Julia?'

'But of course,' she cried.

'Then we are at your service, Master Dominic,' said Lord Bramwell, bowing. 'Lead us to the scene of this domestic crisis.'

Smiling broadly at this offer of help from an unexpected but impressive-looking source, Dominic showed no restraint; he took Lord Bramwell firmly by the hand and led the way. Following on behind with Julia, Isabella found herself incredulous at this sudden turn of events. Lord Bramwell had been on the point of leaving, and now Dominic was taking him to catch a parrot and retrieve a stranded kitten. She could scarcely believe a leader of the *ton* had agreed – he must surely be wishing himself elsewhere – and yet, to his credit, he had not questioned the situation and seemed prepared to indulge a small child he had only just met.

The scene that greeted them in the room at the back of the house that served for a sitting-room would have been highly amusing to Isabella had she been alone. However, in the presence of Lord Bramwell and his sister, she struggled with acute embarrassment – her first impression was that the whole household had gathered to create an unedifying spectacle for her visitors.

Two junior footmen and a chambermaid were trying energetically to entice the frightened kitten down from the mantelpiece, from where several china ornaments had been dislodged and now lay in fragments on the rug in front of the fireplace. The ornate clock in the centre of the shelf hovered precariously on the edge, in danger of following the china to the floor, while the feline perpetrator of this destruction spat angrily at anyone who approached his position behind a large silver candelabrum.

A disgruntled Jemima sat on top of the brocade curtains regarding the animated tableau below with bored disgust, alternately squawking or reciting 'bacon-brained gudgeon' to her audience; Mary was trying to comfort Harriet, who sat on the sofa, while Silwood observed in a disapproving tone that Lady Bingham's town residence was completely unsuitable for such wild creatures, and he feared for the expensive Chinese vase beneath the teetering clock.

At the appearance of Isabella and her guests, however, a silence fell over the assembled company.

Harriet, perceiving their visitors had been somehow dragged into this unfortunate scene, rose to her feet, saying hurriedly, 'Oh! Lord Bramwell, there was not the least need to trouble yourself.'

'On the contrary, Mrs Forster, my sister and I offered our services willingly,' he replied.

'Oh, a-and Lady Julia,' said Harriet, becoming more agitated by the minute, 'a pleasure to make your acquaintance. I beg you – do not think we always go along in this manner. Indeed, Dominic's pets are normally quite well behaved – it is only because of unfortunate circumstances that Jemima took fright and you perceive the results of the chase that followed. Oh dear!' Harriet stopped and sank back on to the sofa.

'There is no need to explain, Mrs Forster,' said Julia gaily. 'Now, how shall we go on, Hal?'

Lord Bramwell gave instructions to Julia, who listened closely and then spoke to Silwood. That gentleman, more than happy to be dispatched to the kitchen where order still reigned, left the room, followed by the footmen and chambermaid, who had been advised by Lord Bramwell that their assistance was not required and they could return later to retrieve the broken china.

Dominic, who was impressed with these visitors' willingness to help, moved to stand beside his lordship. Pulling at Lord Bramwell's sleeve, he said in an urgent whisper, 'Please, let me help too, sir. This is my fault and I hate to upset Mama.'

Hal smiled down at the small boy beside him. 'Now that is honest of you, Dominic, and I have great respect for an honest gentleman. I shall certainly need your assistance when your butler returns.'

Isabella, watching and listening, was torn between fascination at Dominic's instant acceptance of Lord Bramwell and annoyance at herself. Lord Bramwell had already stripped off his coat, and his broad shoulders and well-muscled torso were now visible through his fine linen shirt. He had also rolled up his sleeves to reveal strong forearms dusted with soft dark hair.

Irritated for even having noticed his excellent physique, she said sharply, 'Lord Bramwell, Dominic has inconvenienced you both by involving you in this imbroglio. I could have managed perfectly well.' Annoyance and resentment quivered in Isabella's voice – she was capable of dealing with her family's affairs.

'But my motives were mainly selfish, Lady Vane: I have not enjoyed myself this much for a very long time,' replied Hal, with an enigmatic grin.

Isabella was astonished at the way her heart reacted to his smile and, unsure how to respond, she blushed and moved away. She returned to the sofa where Julia was busy soothing Harriet's agitation, just as Silwood came back bearing two small dishes.

One contained a portion of the poached turbot that cook had been preparing for lunch and which had only been relinquished after a reassurance that it was at the request of the Earl of Bramwell himself. The other held a selection of chopped fruit.

Lord Bramwell, after selecting the latter, offered it to Dominic and said, 'Stand near the cage with this tempting morsel.'

Dominic did as he was bid while Lord Bramwell went to the fireplace and held up the dish of turbot, allowing its aroma to reach the kitten. Unable to resist, Joshua surrendered meekly, allowing his lordship to lift him down and place him on the floor where he began to eat the fish.

Jemima, sensing the danger had now passed, wasted no time in flying down from her refuge and, after a final defiant chorus of 'bacon-brained gudgeon', she re-entered her cage to peck at the fruit Dominic had now placed there.

'Oh, thank you!' cried Dominic, surveying this outcome with smiling relief. 'It was clever of you to know how to deal with Jemima and Joshua – usually only Mama can do that.'

Hal, who had restored the clock to a safer position and was now replacing his coat with the aid of Silwood, glanced down at him. 'Happy to be of assistance, Master Vane, but I do not think Lady Bingham would be pleased to see her parlour put to such er – unusual use.' His conspiratorial wink and grin robbed the words of any offence.

'Well, I shan't do so again, for I never wish to cause Mama any worry,' said Dominic.

'An admirable sentiment,' murmured his lordship, gazing intently at Isabella.

On overhearing this comment, confusion, irritation and a welter of other feelings welled up in Isabella's breast. Never before had she been subjected to such a tumult of emotions as she had during one morning in this man's company. She felt exhausted and could offer no other explanation for the sudden tears that sprang into her eyes.

She blinked them away, angry with herself and, quite

irrationally, at Lord Bramwell. 'Hurry now, Dominic and take Joshua away. Don't let him cause any more damage today.'

'Shall I see you again soon, Lord Bramwell?' asked Dominic, anxious to extract a promise from his new hero, 'and your sister, of course.'

Hal chuckled. 'Have you more creatures in need of rescue then?'

'Oh, no, I won't trouble you again in that way,' said Dominic, 'but I would like to show you my other pets: I have a few ducks and chickens, although they are kept outside.'

'If your mother will permit it, Dominic, we should be happy to make their acquaintance some other time.'

Dominic raised pleading eyes to his mother. 'Will you, Mama? Please say yes! Lord Bramwell and his sister are just the sort of people I like – they aren't too stuffy to speak to me, and they like Jemima and Joshua. Not like Sir Seymour – he says they make him sneeze and—'

'Enough, Dominic!' interjected Isabella hastily. 'Of course I have no objections, but you must remember that they are very busy and cannot guarantee to see you often.'

'We shall do our best, Dominic,' said Julia, 'and I must say that yours is the prettiest compliment I have received since arriving in London.'

Obliged to be satisfied, he nodded, grinned and left the room, taking his kitten with him.

'What a delightful child,' observed Julia. 'Engaging manners, and quite unaffected – you must be very proud of him, Isabella.'

'Thank you – I am. Dominic has endured—' Isabella hesitated, then continued, 'That is, he is remarkably level-headed and good tempered.'

'Such an undemanding little fellow on the whole,' agreed Harriet with an indulgent sigh.

'Yes, but please do not allow him to pester you, Lord Bramwell,' urged Isabella. 'He can be very persistent when he chooses.'

'I daresay I shall withstand it, having been used to the

attentions of four younger siblings, and I will enjoy getting to know Dominic – and you, Lady Vane – a little better,' he replied, his grey eyes fixing once more on Isabella's face.

She blushed in response, and when her visitors departed shortly afterwards, she was left to mull over an unexpectedly eventful morning. Dominic had accepted Lord Bramwell without reservation and had obviously enjoyed his company, but Isabella reflected that his lordship had again succeeded in unsettling her; her carefully schooled emotions had been in turmoil since meeting him at Lady Pargeter's house, and she was alarmed by stirrings of physical response he evoked in her.

Chapter Six

'IT is not what I wanted, Portland: I asked particularly for a diamond brooch. You forget that I have been used to the finest jewellery and I refuse to manage, as you so charmingly phrase it, even for a short while with this – this trinket.'

Lady Portland addressed this frank statement to her bemused spouse, but it was overheard by several other customers in the genteel, hushed surroundings of Rundell, Bridge & Rundell, jewellers to the *ton*. She was unimpressed with the amethyst brooch that her husband had sought to purchase for her and passed the item back to the astonished manager with a contemptuous flourish.

Lord Portland sighed. 'Very well, my love – of course, you shall have exactly what you wish but you will have to wait, since Sheridan here tells me that he will need to order to your specific requirements.' Lord Portland gave Mr Sheridan a glance of pained resignation, a consequence of having suffered his young wife's displeasure for the third time that morning.

'Hurry up, then, and give the man the details so we may go to the milliner's – I am already late for my appointment. I'll wait for you in the carriage,' Felicity replied.

Lord Portland gave another sigh and gratefully removed himself from his wife's environs into Mr Sheridan's office. Lady Portland swept outside, and was helped into a luxurious carriage. As she waited for her husband, she idly and rather dismissively observed those members of London society who passed by in their curricles and phaetons, acknowledging those she knew and delighted by the number of admiring glances she received from the gentlemen. Suddenly, at the approach of a smart curricle with two occupants, her attention became acute and she studied with a great deal of interest the tall, dark-haired man handling the ribbons of the matched bays. Lord Bramwell did not notice her immediately – his attention was focused on driving his high-spirited thoroughbreds through the busy street and he was also deep in conversation with the petite, dark-haired young woman at his side.

'Julia has grown into quite a beauty,' murmured Lady Portland, pleased that his lordship was, today at least, only in the company of his sister. As Lord Bramwell's carriage drew nearer, Felicity smiled and slowly inclined her head towards its occupants; she had every intention of being recognized and appreciated by its driver.

When Julia, who had persuaded Hal to take her to Rundell, Bridge & Rundell to collect her new ear-rings after leaving Isabella, observed the striking redhead in the carriage outside number 32 Ludgate Hill, she cried, 'Goodness! Do you see that woman, Hal? I swear it is Felicity Portland.'

'It is,' he said grimly. 'Freddy told me that she was back in London. Forgive me, Julia, but I'm going to drive on – I prefer to avoid Lady Portland today.'

They drove past and Julia, glancing at her brother's stern profile, raised her brows in surprise. 'But why has she returned? I thought she was living on the Continent for the sake of Portland's health.'

'She must have her reasons and they are probably selfish ones: Felicity always put her wishes above those of anyone else. Now she is back among the *ton*, I'll be civil if our paths cross, but no more. I feel nothing for her and know now that I never did.'

'Well, she is still very lovely, but shockingly *de trop* – that muslin was entirely unsuitable for a carriage dress,' observed Julia tartly.

'She always encouraged attention.' Lord Bramwell frowned, flicked his whip at his wheelers and muttered under his breath, 'Damn her to hell!' Lady Portland had proved herself in the past to be a spoilt, vindictive woman and Hal was not sanguine that Lord Portland would have subdued her manipulative nature. An easy-going man by reputation, Portland would be no match for his wife when she was determined to get her way. Hal sincerely hoped that he could avoid Lady Portland during her stay in London.

His frown was replaced by a smile as his thoughts returned to Isabella. He found that he loved simply watching her: her innate grace, the movement of her lips as she spoke, the curve of her cheek, her profile, the sound of her voice. To his relief, her manner had not been as frosty as at their first meeting and Hal had even been conscious of her tension ebbing away until something had caused it to return. Julia, it seemed, had not noticed this, but Hal had sensed her retreat instinctively.

He wanted to know what was in Isabella's heart, to earn her trust and to somehow ease the burden of her unhappiness. Was she still mourning her late husband? Perhaps she had loved him dearly, or perhaps her marriage had been an unhappy one which held painful memories. Having watched Isabella, Hal thought it more likely to be the latter; her sadness did not seem to be the desolation felt from loss of a loved one, but rather the brittle, bleak anguish of torment.

Meanwhile, Lady Portland, who was observing with impatience her husband's attempts to climb into the carriage without causing further discomfort to his gout-ridden foot, felt a shiver of anticipation. Seeing Lord Bramwell again had hardened her resolve. She had already determined that it was high time she embarked on a serious affair. Her marriage had palled long ago, and she yearned for more excitement than her husband could provide. Lady Portland had enjoyed flirtations while living in Europe, but always with men anxious to enjoy her delights. There was no thrill of the chase. Now, Felicity had glimpsed a tempting challenge: Hal had grown into a handsome, virile man who presented her not only with a target, but stirred feelings of desire which she thought had vanished from her heart long ago. How delightful it would be to make Lord Bramwell beg for her favours and then enjoy an illicit affair to enliven her dull existence.

Portland could offer nothing any more. She despised him for being so easily cuckolded and for being eager to pander to her whims; she deplored his spreading girth; his increasing ill-health irked her beyond reason, and even the power of his wealth had lost the edge of its attraction. She did not regret her marriage – after all, she enjoyed the comforts and deferential treatment that extreme wealth brought – but after glimpsing Lord Bramwell's handsome profile and impressive physique, she had felt a sharp stab of disappointment when she recalled that once he could have been hers. However, there may still be some recompense. She had the protection of being a married woman and, as long as the participants were discreet, affairs were not merely countenanced but encouraged; and she had heard Bramwell was still unmarried, so there would be no need to deceive a wife as well as a husband.

Lady Portland smiled as she listened to her husband's attempts to restore her good humour as they returned to their house in Mayfair: her thoughts were pleasant ones and concerned Lord Bramwell.

In the days that followed, Lord Bramwell called frequently in Curzon Street and Julia often accompanied him. Isabella found his patience towards Dominic surprising; she had thought his enthusiasm for indulging a small boy would soon wane. However, a mutual appreciation seemed to have developed – Dominic saw Lord Bramwell as a source of fun and a fount of knowledge, while in return his lordship seemed to enjoy his companion's enquiring mind and artless chatter. They had visited the Royal Menagerie, seen the animals at the Royal Exchange, and even explored Madame Tussauds famous waxworks.

Isabella was unsure how to deal with her son's new friendship. She was pleased that Dominic enjoyed Lord Bramwell's company, but she could not feel happy that he was forming a strong attachment to a man whose presence in their lives would be fleeting. She had seen enough to know that as well as possessing a sense of humour, Lord Bramwell was intelligent and articulate, and that his affection for Dominic was sincere. However, the glow of sensual awareness that she felt whenever he was near had intensified and, sharply disarmed and discomfited by this, Isabella's demeanour remained distant. His extraordinary ability to affect her meant that she dreaded being alone with him ... and God knows what would happen if he touched her – she must avoid that at all costs.

Despite this, she could not help being intrigued by him. He spoke only of inconsequential matters in conversation, offered her no false flattery and had not threatened to kiss her again. He had made a few gentle enquiries about her past which she had politely rebuffed. He had invited her to drive with him in Hyde Park which she refused, even though her traitorous heart had wanted to accept, but, having raised his brows in surprise at her stammered refusal, he made no further comment. Indeed, his lordship made no obvious attempts to ingratiate himself and yet, if he did not appear in Curzon Street because of other engagements, Isabella found herself longing to hear his voice.

Sir Seymour also visited regularly, but while she found Sir Seymour amusing and was flattered by his attention, Isabella felt disappointment when his arrival was announced rather than Lord Bramwell's. In contrast, Harriet entered with relish into discussions on Sir Seymour's various ailments and his tailor's recommendations, and when Sir Seymour suggested a trip to the theatre, Harriet had accepted before Isabella could think about refusing. Edmund Kean in *Macbeth* was not to be missed, observed Sir Seymour, and he promised to book a box.

However, Sir Seymour found conversing with Dominic beyond his scope. He merely tickled Dominic's chin or ruffled his hair, and referred to him as a 'charming little fellow'. This treatment was greeted afterwards with disgust by Dominic, who complained that Sir Seymour was the most bacon-brained gudgeon that ever was and he talked fustian. Isabella, biting her lip to cover her amusement, chastized her son, to which Dominic replied that Sir Seymour was very kind but not as great a man as Lord Bramwell.

On hearing her son voice this solemn encomium, Isabella became even more concerned; it proved how attached Dominic was becoming to Lord Bramwell. This circumstance had not gone unnoticed elsewhere and had been discussed in Berkeley Square between Lady Julia and her mother.

'For you know, Mama,' remarked Julia one morning when her brother had gone to Curzon Street, and she was browsing through the latest issue of *La Belle Assemblée*, 'Hal has grown fond of Dominic and takes him everywhere he asks to go. My brother has had no time to visit Chenning Court, see his man of business, or indulge in any sporting wagers as he is too busy at the Royal Exchange or some such place.' She smiled and added, 'Dominic is a delightful child though; when Isabella and I took him to Gunthers so that he might try the ices, he soon became the centre of attention. Everyone there was enchanted by him and even Scrope Davies said he should love to introduce him to Prinny one day as he was sure the child would make him laugh.'

'I look forward to meeting Dominic,' replied Marguerite, looking up from the list she was perusing. 'It seems Lady Vane's son is as charming as his mother if he is able to arouse admiration in as jaded a palate as that of Mr Davies.'

'What did you think of Isabella when you met her and Mrs Forster in the park?' asked Julia.

'Delightful in many ways, not least her lovely face. I only had time to exchange a few words with Lady Vane before Sally Jersey claimed my attention, but I see what Hal means by her reserve – her eyes hold wariness towards the world.'

'Well, she will not attend Almack's with me yet, but I have managed to coax her into society a little; we enjoyed our visit to the Pantheon Bazaar and Hal hid his boredom at shopping very well. Although he is fond of Dominic, I believe Isabella is the real reason Hal haunts Curzon Street.' Julia chuckled. 'He seems extremely taken with her ... perhaps they need some help—'

'No, Julia,' intervened Lady Bramwell firmly. 'Hal has been hurt in the past and perhaps Lady Vane has, too. It will require a great deal of patience on Hal's part to earn her trust and you will do better to let matters take their course.'

'You are right, Mama,' replied Julia, sighing as she idly scanned the items in the monthly miscellany section. 'Most of London has fallen in love with Isabella's beauty but she lets no one near. However, I am certain that Isabella harbours a spark of deeper feeling for Hal; she is growing fond of him, I know it. Isabella is the dearest girl and I would love her to be Hal's choice.'

'So would I, but it will not do for us to interfere without good reason,' said her mother, adding drily, 'and I do not think your brother would thank us either.'

Glancing up from the periodical, Julia arched a scornful eyebrow. 'Lady Portland has been showing interest in Hal again, and I cannot bear her.'

'Lady Portland! Is she back in London?'

'She and Portland have returned because of Bonaparte's escape from Elba – they have taken a house in Half Moon Street.'

Marguerite Bramwell murmured, 'I presume that Hal is aware of this?'

'Yes, and he hoped to avoid her. However, I could almost believe she – Lady Portland – has been following him. She seems to be at every event and we have encountered her twice in the park.' Putting aside *La Belle Assemblée*, Julia frowned. 'She is so forward, Mama! She approached us yesterday and started talking as if we were old friends. She even touched Hal's arm in front of her husband and was as flirtatious and sugges-tive as ever she was before her marriage, looking at Hal from under her lashes and wearing the most alarmingly low-cut gown.'

'And what was Hal's reaction to this flirtation?'

'His expression was thunderous,' replied Julia. 'He obviously found her behaviour irritating, but had no intention of causing a scene. After enquiring after Portland's health, he excused us as soon as he could from their company. Lord Portland must be very gullible – he seemed to notice nothing amiss and smiled indulgently at his wife.' She shook her head. 'Felicity Portland is … well, I believe she intends to pursue Hal.'

'Indeed?' said her mother. 'Then she will be disappointed, Julia. Hal knows he was well rid of her and I was never more pleased than when she eloped with Portland.'

'But she could cause problems: she always was a spoilt, spiteful creature, and has a temper if she does not get her way.'

'Then Portland would do well to bring her to heel before she embarrasses him further.'

'Mr Isherwood, that is, Freddy,' said Julia, a charming blush tingeing her cheeks, 'says she is the most designing harpy and he has warned Hal to be wary of her.'

Lady Bramwell smiled. 'Freddy has good sense and charming manners, but he seems always to be ringing our bell on the flimsiest pretence and I cannot conceive why – there must be a hundred and one other things for him to do in London.'

Julia blushed even deeper pink, and stammered indignantly, 'I – I am always glad to see Freddy – we have danced together at Almack's and I persuaded him to let me take the reins of his curricle in the park – but other young men call here, and I should not favour Freddy above them so I have driven out several times with Lord Dryburgh, and danced with the Duke of Hearn.'

'Such treatment only seems to make Freddy call upon you more often,' observed her mother with a smile and, as if on cue, the butler opened the door to announce the arrival of Mr Isherwood.

Lady Julia was anxious for her blushes to subside before he came into the room and fanned herself with the circulating library novel she had discarded earlier. Lady Marguerite, observing her daughter's behaviour with amusement, made no further comment, but welcomed Mr Isherwood warmly when he entered.

'Freddy! What a pleasure to see you this morning but I'm afraid you miss Hal – he has taken young Master Vane to view another of London's attractions and will not return until later.'

Mr Isherwood, who seemed to be finding it difficult to remove his gaze from Lady Julia's flushed countenance, replied abstractedly, 'Oh! Good morning, Lady Bramwell. Er – where did you say Hal was?'

'With young Master Vane,' she prompted.

'Oh yes!' said Freddy. 'Well, no matter – no doubt I shall meet him at White's later.'

'I daresay you will – you gentlemen seem to find as much pleasure in your club as we ladies do in shopping. Now, will you excuse me, Freddy? I see from my list there is a pressing matter I need to discuss with cook regarding Julia's ball. So many details still to be organized! You will be attending, I hope?'

'Of course,' replied Mr Isherwood, 'I would not miss it for the world.' He gave Julia another warm glance and grinned.

'Excellent. Please stay and take some coffee with Julia.' Lady Bramwell rose to her feet and, after taking her leave of Mr Isherwood, swept out of the room.

There was a silence for a few moments before Julia murmured, 'How nice it is to see you, Freddy.'

'I am pleased to find you at home, Julia. I have looked for you this last week.'

'Oh, I am always busy now,' she said lightly, 'We have so many invitations that I hardly know which way to turn and with all the arrangements for the ball, I don't have a moment to myself.'

Mr Isherwood frowned and replied, 'I am anxious to arrange a date for the trip to Richmond we discussed. I called yesterday, and the day before, but you were otherwise engaged.'

Julia bit her lip and looked away. 'I – I was out when you called.'

'I see. I had begun to wonder if you were avoiding me,' said Freddy with feeling, studying her long lashes, dark eyes and luxuriant ebony curls.

'I have other people to see apart from you.'

'Yes, damn it! Lately I've had to fight my way through Dryburgh, Mr Aynsworth or the Duke of Hearn,' he said, through gritted teeth.

'And how can I help that?' retorted Julia, colour rushing back to her cheeks. 'I am merely enjoying my London season, and it is no business of yours who I see and when.' Julia was piqued. There was a grain of truth in Freddy's assertion of her avoidance – she was ashamed now that she had enjoyed making him a little jealous, although her pride would not let her admit to it.

'I have no right, but I thought you might show a little partiality for my company,' muttered Mr Isherwood.

'You are a friend of the family, Freddy, but I must not offend others by refusing them in deference to you.' Julia thought she knew why Freddy was upset, but she wanted to hear him admit to his jealousy and, more importantly, the sentiment of love behind it.

Mr Isherwood, frustrated by his seething emotions, could not see this; he therefore chose to do precisely the opposite and conceal it. 'A friend of the family,' he cried. 'If that is all you think of me, perhaps I will do better not to call upon you so often.'

'If you insist on shouting, perhaps it would be better if you did not!' said Julia, a catch in her voice – the direction of this conversation was not at all what she had anticipated.

Freddy, eyes burning with emotion, opened his mouth as if to reply, but then, collecting himself, he fell silent and walked away. After a long pause, he turned back to face her. 'My apologies, Lady Julia,' he said in a clipped tone. 'As you so rightly point out, I can make no demands upon your time; you must enjoy your season in any way you choose.'

'F-Freddy,' said Julia, giving the oddest little sob, 'you know I am exceedingly fond of you and—'

'There is no need to explain further,' he interjected, his expression grim. 'I see now that I should not have come today – no doubt you find my company an unwelcome distraction. Pray give my excuses to Lady Bramwell: I find I have an engagement elsewhere in Town. Good day to you.' With that, he bowed and strode purposefully out of the room.

Julia watched him leave in dismay and tears sprang to her eyes. Sinking on to the chaise, she drew in a ragged breath, then buried her head in the silk cushions and cried.

Chapter Seven

'WELL, you troublesome cub,' began Hal with a rueful laugh, 'this is how I am rewarded for taking you to Kensington Gardens this morning – a muddy coat and paw prints over my right boot, both of which will reduce my valet to tears.'

Dominic grinned broadly in response. 'We had fun so a little dirt does not matter. Tell your valet that it was necessary or Aesop would have been taken away and punished.' He sat in Hal's curricle as they travelled back to Curzon Street and squeezed between them, flicking an adoring gaze between his two rescuers, sat a pitiful looking black and white dog, a dubious cross between a collie and a terrier.

'Aesop?' queried Hal, puzzled.

Dominic patted their canine companion. 'The dog, of course! I thought I would call him Aesop because he must know lots of tales from the scrapes he's been in. You know, I think he likes you almost as much as he likes me.'

'Hmm,' said Hal, looking askance at Aesop, 'so I observe, although our friendship was sealed because I purchased the ham he had stolen from the butcher and allowed him to finish it.'

'That butcher had a very red face; he was annoyed until you offered to pay and then he became polite – he even offered to send a sirloin of beef around to your house – but I didn't like him for beating Aesop.'

'The dog didn't approve of him either,' observed Hal in a dry voice. 'He snarled and barked at Mr Butcher in the most appallingly ill-mannered way that I was forced to reprimand him.'

'But Aesop stopped barking as soon as you commanded him to, so he must be a well-behaved dog if he is not provoked,' said Dominic. 'Poor thing! He looks like he has been starved.'

'A shabby specimen indeed, but some good meals and a bath will soon address that.'

Aesop barked as if to agree and Dominic observed appreciatively, 'You see, he is clever – I'm sure he understands every word we are saying.'

'In that case, I hope he will understand that I cannot take him to Berkeley Square. I have a houseful of family and servants, and a ball planned for the near future. To place a dog, even one as charming as Aesop, into such a cauldron of activity could be disastrous.'

'But I don't want you to take him there,' said Dominic. 'I want to take him home; Mama already said I could have a puppy, so she won't mind if I arrive with a dog.'

Hal raised an eyebrow. 'Won't there be objections in view of your existing menagerie?'

'My what?' asked Dominic, mystified.

'Your collection of pets,' explained Hal with a smile.

'Oh, that!' Dominic's brow cleared and he said confidently, 'Well, Mama never breaks a promise. Aunt Harriet is the only person who complains about my menag, menager … my animals, and she never means it. Of course, if Mama really does not wish it then I would not keep him.'

'You are a credit to your mother, Dominic.'

'I don't like upsetting her,' he replied gravely. 'Mama used to be unhappy all the time because my father was cross with everyone, especially Mama, but now she smiles and hardly ever cries – I didn't like it when she cried.'

Hal digested this in silence. Dominic's artless words seemed to confirm that Isabella's marriage had been unhappy and he wondered again what bitter memories she held. He knew that he needed to be patient and that Isabella needed time – time to know him better and to trust him. At least she had grown more accepting of his visits now, and befriended Julia, but Hal dared to hope he had detected a more profound change recently. The deep glow of affection – no, more than affection: desire – lurked in Isabella's eyes when she looked at him, but she always turned away quickly and the moment was lost. It was as if she was afraid that he would see what was written there.

Giving his attention back to Dominic, he replied, 'Very well, let us see if your mama is prepared to house Aesop temporarily. I suppose I will step into the breach if necessary, although having Aesop as a companion would ruin my reputation,' Hal observed with a grin. 'Several of my acquaintances stared in astonishment as they passed us by this morning.'

They reached Curzon Street and were followed into the entrance by Aesop, who pressed his thin body against Dominic's legs under Silwood's disapproving glare.

Lord Bramwell, passing his driving gloves and hat towards the bemused butler, said, 'Where is Lady Vane?'

'In the yellow saloon, my lord, but—'

'Then we will announce ourselves,' interjected Hal. Looking down at the dog beside him, he remarked severely, 'Try to behave, Aesop. It will not do to show your rag manners here.' Aesop wagged his tail in response and trotted after Dominic, who was already bounding up the stairs.

'Mama!' cried Dominic, bursting into the saloon, 'Look what we have found! He is the dearest thing, and you must let me keep him because you said that I might have a puppy, except I don't wish for a puppy anymore, just Aesop. An angry butcher hit him with a broom for stealing his ham, and then a crowd gathered around to see what the fuss was for, but Lord Bramwell saved him, and bought the ham, and gave the butcher some money for his trouble! Everyone was most obliging when they discovered Hal was a lord—'

'Stop, Dominic!' said Isabella, laughing at this tumbled, breathless speech. 'Who is Aesop?'

The forlorn-looking canine padded over to Isabella, Harriet and their companion, Sir Seymour.

'What is that dog doing here?' exclaimed Isabella in astonishment.

Harriet observed Aesop's arrival with dismay, 'Dominic! You cannot bring that flea-ridden creature into the saloon.'

Sir Seymour, whose expression was one of stunned confusion, had been enjoying a conversation with Lady Vane and Mrs Forster on the merits of wheat flour boiled in ale for a poultice, but a cacophony of noise had begun on Dominic's return and he eyed Aesop uneasily through his quizzing glass. 'I cannot allow that animal too near, Lady Vane,' he remarked in an enervated voice. 'He might bite.'

'Fustian!' said Dominic bluntly. 'He won't bite you – Lord Bramwell says Aesop's manners can be improved, but he has a good character.'

'I'm afraid I must take most of the blame for the dog being here,' admitted Hal as he came into the room. 'After rescuing him from an irate shopkeeper, I did not have the heart to leave him to further punishment.'

'You saved this scraggy animal?' queried Sir Seymour, incredulous, 'but why?'

'What a silly question! Because he needed saving, that's why,' said Dominic.

'Enough, you unruly imp,' murmured Hal, his lips twitching. 'I can fight my own battles.'

'Dominic, apologize to Sir Seymour for your rudeness!' said his mother.

Chastened, an embarrassed flush crept across Dominic's face and he shuffled his feet. 'I – I'm very sorry, sir, but we had fun and Aesop is grateful.'

'Is Aesop the dog's name?' asked Isabella, understanding dawning in her expressive eyes.

Hal nodded and grinned. 'Your son decided it would be an appropriate epithet.'

Isabella felt her heart quicken at his devastatingly attractive smile and, transfixed by what she saw in his eyes, she was unable to look away. Hal's expression held a quizzical half-smile as he watched her and the rest of the world seemed to retreat as warmth raced through her veins. Colour stung her cheeks and she struggled to draw in a breath as she stared at him, shocked and confused at the intensity of her reaction. Eventually, after what seemed like an age, her aunt's voice broke the spell and Isabella was able to tear her gaze away.

'But how did you become entangled in Aesop's affairs?' asked Harriet.

'When we went to Kensington Gardens, Aesop decided to run our way with the ham he had stolen,' said Dominic. 'A red-faced butcher was chasing him with a broom, but Aesop hid under Hal's carriage, growling and barking at the man, until Hal told him to be quiet and offered to pay. A crowd of people were watching us by then and—'

'I am so sorry, Lord Bramwell,' interjected Isabella, horrified that he should have been drawn into another fracas. 'You have been extremely inconvenienced.'

He laughed. 'Not unless you count as an inconvenience the cost of a ham joint, a muddy coat and paw marks on my best Hoby boots – which I certainly do not.'

'Good gracious!' muttered Sir Seymour, studying Lord Bramwell through his quizzing glass in alarm. 'You must have those items cleaned at once, Bramwell; a dose of champagne blacking will work wonders on your boots.'

'But I always get muddy and Mama says it does not matter at all,' said Dominic, puzzled at Sir Seymour's anxiety; Aesop, tongue lolling from his mouth, wagged his tail in agreement.

'Can Aesop stay here, Mama?' said Dominic. 'He can live downstairs until we move to the country.'

'I would offer to house the animal myself if I did not have house guests and a ball approaching, Lady Vane. If you can keep him in Curzon Street for a short while, I promise to send him to Chenning Court at the earliest opportunity,' said Hal.

'Mayfair is no place for a dog, and they bring on my chesty cough,' protested Sir Seymour with a shake of his head.

'Surely we do not have the room?' said Harriet, picturing paw prints over her needlework, 'although I must say, he looks a dear thing and would keep us company.'

'Aesop needs more space that we can give him, Dominic, and we shall not be leaving London for a few weeks yet—' began Isabella.

'Please, Mama!' begged Dominic, with an imploring glance. 'He is so thin and hungry.'

Hal watched as indecision shadowed her features. 'My hunting dogs are at Chenning, Lady Vane,' he said gently. 'I give you my word he would be well cared for there until you chose to house him again yourself.'

'Very well,' agreed Isabella, sighing. In truth, she was glad of Lord Bramwell's assistance in managing this unexpected situation, even though she knew it was weak of her.

'Then I suppose we must move more of Lady Bingham's china,' murmured Harriet.

Dominic, giving a cry of delight, ran to hug both his mother and Hal. 'Thank you, Mama! And thank you, Lord Bramwell!'

Hal laughed at his enthusiasm. 'Thank *you*, child, for an entertaining morning.'

Unfortunately, Aesop decided to join in this display of mutual appreciation and, placing his paws on Sir Seymour's pristine biscuit-coloured pantaloons, reached up to lick his face.

'Off!' shrieked Sir Seymour, his quizzing glass falling from his limp fingers as he looked down in horror. 'Mud, and on my favourite pantaloons too!' He leapt to his feet and began rubbing vigorously at the marks with a silk handkerchief which only spread them further. Groaning in disbelief, he raised his eyes and appealed for help from a reliable source. 'Mrs Forster, it will not do – you see they are quite ruined.'

A smile touched the corners of Hal's mouth: Dinny was rich enough to buy new pantaloons every day of the week if he chose to, but he seemed determined to make a great fuss of this pair. 'Now see what you have done, Aesop,' said Hal, addressing the dog in a severe tone. 'Rag manners indeed!'

'Can they be cleaned?' said Isabella, struggling to maintain her composure as she caught sight of Lord Bramwell's countenance.

'The very thing,' replied Sir Seymour eagerly, 'but it must be done as soon as possible.'

Harriet, who had sympathy for Sir Seymour's plight, exclaimed, 'Fuller's earth! Fuller's earth, laid over the mark and then pressed with a hot iron, is very successful. I shall write out directions for your valet while you collect your hat and gloves, Sir Seymour.'

'You are too good, dear lady,' he said, much moved. Anxious to be away before anyone else saw him in this less than perfect state of dress, Sir Seymour reminded Isabella that he had reserved a box at Drury Lane for Friday evening before hurrying out in Harriet's wake and giving Aesop, now sprawled nonchalantly on the rug, a deprecating glance.

When he had gone, Dominic giggled. 'What a fuss Sir Seymour makes over a little mud, Mama! I'm sure Aesop only meant to be friendly.'

'I'm sure he did, Dominic, but Sir Seymour's clothes are very important to him,' said his mother, a tremor in her voice.

'It might have been worse, so let us be thankful,' observed Hal solemnly.

'How?' said Dominic.

'It could have been his waistcoat,' replied Hal with a slow grin and a wink.

Unable to contain her amusement any longer, Isabella laughed outright at this and Dominic chuckled too, until she said, 'Go and wash your hands now, and take Aesop with you. Ask Mary to find a place for him downstairs where he cannot offend cook or anyone else. Oh, and ask one of the footmen to give him a bath – I daresay he needs one.'

Dominic nodded and after thanking his mother and Lord Bramwell once more, he left with the dog trotting behind.

Isabella, suddenly realizing that she and Lord Bramwell were alone, gave him a nervous glance. She was not afraid of him – she was afraid of herself. This was the moment she had been dreading and, just as she suspected, her traitorous body did not disappoint. A tingling awareness began to rush through her once more, her breathing came fast and shallow and her heartbeat hastened. Every sense seemed to dilate and heighten when he was near and Isabella looked away to cover her confusion. Her eyes fell to his Hessian boots, noting the muddy paw marks as he walked towards her. If only he were physically unattractive, or unkind, or conceited – perhaps then she might have been able to curb her response. As it was, the battle was lost. She did not know how or why, but this man was dragging her feelings and emotions inexorably back to life. 'Th-thank you for your kindness to Dominic, Lord Bramwell,' she stammered, finding her voice at last. 'He enjoys your company, and you are generous to give him so much of your time.'

'There is no need to thank me – Dominic is a delightful child. I hope you do not mind the dog being foisted upon you, Lady Vane; he can go to Chenning as soon arrangements have been made.'

'We will manage somehow. Dominic had already been promised a puppy, although I did not think to add a dog to our household while we are in London.' Isabella paused, then added quietly, 'And I did not doubt your word.'

He gave Isabella a grateful look. 'I am glad to hear it. Your opinion of me matters a great deal.'

'I worry that Dominic is becoming too attached to you,' she admitted. 'We must leave London soon, and he will be devastated to lose your friendship.'

Raising his brows, he regarded her quizzically for a long moment. 'I would never disappoint Dominic in that way. Can I ask that you trust me in this matter also? Severance of our friendship will come only from you, or from Dominic – not from me.'

'Oh, please do not misunderstand – I do not think you would be deliberately unkind,' she said, struggling to find the right words, 'but you may tire of amusing him.'

'I would do everything in my power to protect you and

Dominic from distress,' he murmured, his gaze never leaving her face. 'You have become extremely important to me, Lady Vane.'

'Oh! Pray do not say so, Lord Bramwell!' she replied, agitated. 'Indeed, you know nothing about me and I cannot—' He was at her side in quick strides, placing a finger against her lips to still her speech. He was so close that Isabella was aware of the smile that touched the corners of his mouth and his glittering eyes, seemingly more piercing than usual. She felt like she was drowning in his gaze and another frisson of sensation ran through her.

'Say no more now,' Hal whispered, 'it is too soon, but you can feel what is happening between us: I saw it in your eyes earlier. I will try to be patient for your sake – I sense you are concealing some terrible hurt or anguish – but please, do not shut me out, Isabella. I promise you will come to trust me one day and then there will be no secrets between us.'

Stunned by his words, she gave him a wide, questioning look. Then, she tensed … he was tracing the outline of her lip with one fingertip while tilting up her chin with his other hand. Dear God, he was going to kiss her and to her amazement, she could utter no protest and felt only delicious anticipation.

He bent his head and Isabella, aware solely of Hal and the pounding of her heart, closed her eyes, but when he took her hand to press a soft, warm kiss into her palm, her lids flickered upwards and she exhaled on a soft sigh of disappointment.

Lifting his head, he smiled into her eyes. 'It was delightful to hear you laugh spontaneously earlier,' he said huskily. 'I shall take my leave now, but we shall meet again very soon.'

With another lingering look, he left, leaving behind a bewildered Isabella.

Chapter Eight

AFTERWARDS, Isabella sat alone in her room; her emotions, repressed for six long years, were now chaotic.

She had tried to use an ill-judged prejudice to fight her attraction to Lord Bramwell, but, having glimpsed the real man behind the reckless Corinthian that society thought him, Isabella admitted that she had failed. Through his kindness to Dominic, his sense of humour, his intelligence and his warmth, he had found his way relentlessly into her thoughts and dreams, and into her heart. Attraction jumped across the space between them like a lightning bolt whenever he came into the room. She had only known him a few weeks, but her feelings for Hal bore no resemblance to the temperate regard she had once felt for Edward Vane; it was like comparing fire with ice.

And now she must deal with the consequences. While she might be attracted to Lord Bramwell, she was afraid to trust him. Isabella's lack of trust had been hewn from the painful ravages of her marriage and it could not be dismantled easily, but his words today had lit a spark of hope, and she needed to discover what lay behind them. If Hal was everything he appeared to be then perhaps the prize was worth the risk. If he was not, then she must escape from London before too much damage was done, even though the thought of opening up the deepest part of her soul and thereby risking it being split asunder made her feel sick with apprehension.

What would Hal say when he knew the circumstances surrounding Edward's death? Would he believe her account of that fateful night, or would he judge her harshly? The terror she had endured was still vivid in her memory, as was her shock and revulsion. Touching a small scar on her right hand, a shudder ran through her – it was a tiny, but tangible reminder of those terrible hours. Isabella knew the truth and was not ashamed of it, but it would take all her courage to reveal what had happened.

She needed to be certain that Hal was an honourable, trustworthy man; she could not afford another error of judgement because Dominic's future also depended on her decision.

Isabella sat with these thoughts and was so engrossed that she jumped when Mary came in to light the candles; dusk was already creeping into the room and she had not realized it had grown late.

Across Mayfair in Half Moon Street, Lady Portland was inspecting her new gown. She twirled this way and that in front of the full-length mirror in her dressing-room, pleased with what she saw. The diaphanous cloth which sparkled in the candlelight clung to her figure, the low-cut bodice displaying her breasts to advantage. If such a gown did not break Hal's resolve then she really was losing her touch. She watched her reflection smile artfully; she was enjoying the challenge and considered it only a matter of time before he agreed to an affair.

She had intentionally run her hand over Hal's arm when they met in Hyde Park and that brief contact had left her shivering with restless anticipation. Having made discreet enquiries about his movements, she had now contrived several meetings but this was not enough – she wanted to see Hal alone, somewhere she could remind him of the delights hinted at eight years ago and which were now his for the taking.

Julia's forthcoming ball was the talk of London and although Lady Bramwell would never send her an official invitation, Felicity planned to attend anyway with her friend Lady Cumberland. Etiquette and propriety could go to the devil if they prevented her from snatching a few moments alone with Hal.

Portland would not notice her absence; he went to his club every evening and Felicity had even had to insist that he reserve a box at Drury Lane on Friday instead of going to Watier's again. However, she knew she would soon welcome Portland being away from home as it would provide her with more opportunities to enjoy Hal's virile company. She smiled, this time with satisfaction, as she began to search her jewel box for a necklace and ear-rings to match her gown.

'I wonder why Hal decided to book a box for us at the theatre?' asked Julia, as she sat waiting for her brother in the drawing-room.

'It is rather odd,' mused Lady Bramwell. 'He was most particular that it must be tonight too.'

'Perhaps this has something to do with Isabella – Hal seems animated recently.'

'I had noticed.' Marguerite looked at her daughter and added, 'I have also noticed that you have been subdued since Freddy's visit.'

Julia gave a weak smile, but said quietly, 'We quarrelled and it was partly my fault. I – I want to apologize and have sent Freddy a note asking him to call.'

'I'm afraid it must wait a little longer, Julia: Hal tells me that Freddy has gone to the Newmarket races. He was in high dudgeon, it seems, and wanted no company.'

'He did not tell me he was leaving town,' said Julia, startled at this news.

'If you have quarrelled, that might explain his sudden departure.' Lady Bramwell had a good idea of what had passed between her daughter and Mr Isherwood; Julia was a vivacious but headstrong girl and Freddy was as much in love and jealous as any young man could be. She studied Julia from under her lashes, and continued, 'However, he will definitely be attending your ball next week. Hal made him promise to be there so you can speak to him then.'

Julia's expression brightened. 'I am relieved to hear it – I dreaded hearing that he would not come.'

Hal, who came into the room at that moment, raised his brows in surprise on seeing his sister. 'So you are here already, Julia. I thought you would need at least another hour to finish dressing – indeed, I was sure we would miss the first act.'

Julia was obliged to laugh. 'Wretch! I am quite ready, as you see.'

'What is a sister for, if not to tease a little?' replied Hal, wryly. He kissed his mother on the cheek and said, 'Do not wait up. We will be late, so you shall hear our review tomorrow.'

'Enjoy your evening and take care to acknowledge everyone of our acquaintance,' said Lady Bramwell.

They set off for Drury Lane, and Hal was not surprised to see the crush of people there. The theatres provided another arena for social display, and the play usually came a poor second to the gossip. Hal had no time for the flirting and chatter that were, for most of the *ton*, an essential accompaniment to the performance, but he wanted to be here this evening after overhearing that Sir Seymour had booked a box. He was desperate to see Isabella again and also admitted that he was jealous of Dinny enjoying her company.

Hal had suffered moments of doubt in the last two days. He meant every word that he had said to Isabella, but he was afraid that he had spoken out too soon. She might even refuse to see or speak to him again, a situation he could not bear to contemplate because she had become integral to his life. However, he could not help declaring a little of how he felt and hoped that in doing so he had not frightened her away. Isabella was like a spring flower emerging in the sun; some terrible hurt had caused her to retreat from the world and now her feelings were slowly beginning to unfurl.

He and Julia went through the entrance hall and climbed the elegant staircase to find their box. Chandeliers hung from the domed roof, illuminating the crowded pit and, as they took their seats and waited for the performance to begin, Julia scanned the faces among the audience. She tipped her head in acknowledgement to a few and suffered the openly admiring glances of the men in the pit before suddenly clutching Hal's arm.

'Why, there is Isabella, Harriet and Sir Seymour,' she said in surprise, looking at a nearby box, and then smiling and waving. 'Look, Hal! Dinny is wearing the most extraordinary pink and yellow waistcoat and his shirt points are so starched that he can hardly turn his head.' Julia laughed. 'He rivals our most famous dandies this evening and if he were not such a pleasant fellow, he would be a complete figure of fun! Oh, and Isabella looks so beautiful in that gown – but how on earth did Dinny persuade her to attend the theatre? I was never so surprised to see—' She stopped and turned to stare accusingly at her brother. 'You knew she would be here, didn't you?'

Hal gave his sister a guilty look. 'I should have told you that there was an ulterior motive, Julia.'

'You don't need to apologize,' she replied, eyes twinkling. 'Isabella is the dearest girl and I am anxious to speak to her myself.' Her expression changed when she glanced across to the occupants of the adjoining box. 'Oh! But there is someone else here who you may not wish to see – Lady Portland and her husband are sitting next to us. We must acknowledge them, I suppose, but I hope that she will not think of coming to our box! How does she contrive to be at almost every event where we are?' Julia acknowledged Lady Portland's greeting before looking away quickly.

Hal, his annoyance evident in his brooding expression and his rigid shoulders, observed Felicity Portland smiling at him seductively. Damn the woman! Had she no restraint in her manner?

Isabella, who had been half-listening to Sir Seymour's conversation with Harriet on the relative merits of comedies and tragedies, started in surprise when she saw Julia and Hal. She had not considered exactly what she would say to Hal when she met him again. Now he was here and would no doubt come to their box in the interval. How could she begin to explain her hopes, her fears and the state of her heart to him? She was apprehensive, yet also exhilarated at being near him once more. At least, thought Isabella, I feel alive again since meeting him, and she revelled in the sensations coursing through her as he smiled in greeting.

Sir Seymour cut across her thoughts by announcing that the play was about to begin. Edmund Kean's reputation as a fine Shakespearean actor was well deserved and he had been hailed as remarkable since his debut as Shylock the previous year. Isabella was surprised to discover that his stature was small, but his portrayal of tragic emotions was masterly. However, in spite of the magic Kean was weaving on the stage, Isabella found herself under a different spell. Her eyes wandered constantly back to Hal. Whenever he looked at her and smiled, she reciprocated and consequently spent most of the first act with a smile on her lips and fighting to contain relentless waves of desire.

Isabella had also noticed the strikingly beautiful redhead in the box next to Hal's. She was dressed in a satin gown which clung to her voluptuous figure, and was watching Hal in such an openly admiring and speculative way that it made Isabella blush. She wondered if the older man who was the lady's companion was indeed her husband, since he made no attempt to curb her provocative behaviour, or even seemed to notice it. Isabella had no idea who the lady was and what connection, if any, she had with Hal.

The first act complete, the interval had barely begun when Hal and Julia appeared in Isabella's box.

After uttering a general greeting, Hal added, 'Are you enjoying the performance?'

'Yes, very much,' said Harriet. 'Sir Seymour has been most informative; he is a keen patron of the theatre, you know.'

Sir Seymour gave a self-deprecating cough. 'Always happy to support artistic endeavour even though my health precludes too many late evenings.'

'How charming you look this evening,' cried Julia, as she clasped Isabella's hands. 'You must have been quizzed by all the men in the pit.'

'They mean no real harm,' explained Hal. 'It is common practice to ogle the ladies in the boxes and meanwhile, the dowagers will take note of what you are wearing, your jewellery and even try to guess what we are speaking of at this moment.'

Isabella laughed at this. 'Gracious! I thought I was visiting the theatre, not undergoing an inspection.'

'Have you and Mrs Forster received your invitations to my ball?' asked Julia.

'We have, thank you, and—'

'You are coming?' interjected Julia anxiously.

'—we will be most happy to attend,' concluded Isabella, with a smile.

'And you too, of course, Sir Seymour,' said Julia.

'Indeed!' he said, nodding as much as his shirt points would allow. 'The new waltz may be beyond my constitution, but I should be able to enjoy one or two country dances.'

Some conversation on the excellence of the play followed until Julia said, 'Hal, we had best return to our box – the second act is due to begin.' Opening a silk and ivory fan, she fanned herself and observed, 'Goodness, the heat in here is stifling!'

As Julia was taking her leave of Harriet and Sir Seymour, Hal moved to Isabella's side and whispered earnestly, 'I came here tonight to see you and to ask if you will accompany me on a drive in the park tomorrow afternoon, Isabella.'

Answering from the heart, she murmured her agreement. He nodded, a gleam of pleasure in his eyes, before kissing her hand and joining his sister outside. Isabella knew there was no turning back now – falling in love with Hal would be easy, but it would be far more difficult for her to trust him. Time would be needed for that trust to grow and to tell him about her past, but, for the first time since the death of her father, she felt cared for and protected. Colour rushed to her cheeks as she recalled the touch of his lips against her skin.

'Julia was right – it is hot in here,' she remarked, 'I'll step outside for a moment where the air is a little cooler.'

'Would you like me to accompany you, Lady Vane?' enquired Sir Seymour politely.

'No, thank you. I only intend to go a little way.'

Isabella opened the door and stepped out into the passageway. She paced to and fro for a moment, fanning her heated complexion and glancing at the people hurrying to take their seats. Suddenly, she halted; further down the passage and unaware that they were being watched, were Hal and the striking redhead whom Isabella had noticed earlier.

The lady was so close to Hal that her hair brushed his shoulder and she smiled as she tilted her head in a coquettish manner. Isabella could not see Hal's expression, nor could she hear any conversation, but she watched as one of the lady's hands reached up to caress his cheek. Then, his strong fingers covered the small hand and curled around it. Shocked, Isabella turned away quickly and returned to her box.

As she sat down again, Harriet was remarking, 'There are so many people here this evening – half the city must have crowded in.'

'If you prefer not to stay for the whole performance, we may leave after *Macbeth* – I believe *Aladdin* is the second item on the programme,' replied Sir Seymour.

'*Aladdin* and *Macbeth*,' exclaimed Harriet. 'A strange combination for one evening's entertainment. What do you think, Isabella? Shall we stay?'

But Isabella could offer no immediate reply; she felt too shaken and stunned by what she had just witnessed.

Chapter Nine

IN the heat of the passageway, Hal gripped Lady Portland's fingers and removed them brusquely from his cheek. He was relieved that his sister had gone on ahead and did not believe Lady Portland's appearance here was mere chance; Felicity would be audacious enough to follow him. Her green eyes gleamed in the subdued light and the heavy, jasmine-scented fragrance that she had always favoured filled the humid air.

'What the deuce do you think you are doing?' Hal recoiled and put her hand away from him.

'Come, Hal, admit you are not indifferent to me,' she purred, smiling. 'Do not fight it; you only have to say the word.'

'Why have you come back, Felicity?' he demanded.

'Portland wanted to return because of Napoleon's escape, but I had my reasons too; I was bored and thought there might be interesting diversions here. You are an even more attractive man than you were eight years ago, Hal.'

'Don't waste your breath – you made your choice then and I have been glad for it ever since,' he said curtly. 'Besides, you seem to forget that you are married, or is that a trivial consideration?' Hal's tone was glacial. Felicity had always been bold and confident, but even he was shocked by this brazen approach. Once a look or word from this woman had aroused a sentiment that Hal had mistaken for love; now he felt only distaste.

She gave a brief, elegant shrug of her shoulders and murmured, 'The past is done, but the fact that I am married need not be an obstacle. Portland can be cuckolded with ease and we would find each other most … enjoyable.'

He listened with disbelief; she was offering an affair with as much nonchalance and sang-froid as if she were inviting him for afternoon tea. His lip curled. He was always polite to women, but Lady Portland was testing his civility to the limit. She had not changed – in fact, she was even more of a cold hearted jade now and he wanted to escape her presence. A nerve twitched in his jaw as he struggled to contain his disgust.

'You seem to think I will be delighted to be chosen for this role,' he replied, in a low, even voice. 'Well, you are mistaken. Save your request for someone who is foolish enough to listen. Please excuse me, I must return to my sister.'

He walked away and Felicity watched his retreating figure with surprise. While she had not expected instant agreement – he was too much of a gentleman to agree readily to an affair – she had not anticipated a blunt refusal either. Anger and indignation welled up in her breast. She had offered herself to him and he had tossed her aside like an unwanted gift. No man had ever treated her in that way.

And yet Hal's refusal only made Felicity want him more. She was used to instant surrender in those she singled out for her favours and the fact he was spurning her advances made him even more attractive in her eyes. She remained confident that she could eventually seduce even a principled man like Hal. Given a little more time and persuasion, he would change his mind and her heart beat faster as she considered his many attributes: he was a prize worth striving for. Her quest had started with a spark of desire, but Hal's lack of response had fanned it to an insatiable fire of sexual yearning, the like of which she had never experienced before.

Taking her fan from her reticule, Felicity cooled her warm cheeks before making her way slowly back to her husband.

The Honourable Theodore Cavanagh arrived unannounced in Berkeley Square the following afternoon, and had anyone been able to observe his profile as he rang the bell, they would have remarked that he was a great deal like his elder brother. He had the same strong features, although his hair was lighter and his eyes were dark like his sister's, with the twinkle of amusement that was a common denominator in the Cavanagh siblings. After a less than sedate journey down from Oxford, he had leapt up the steps with youthful energy and, ringing the door bell with far more enthusiasm than necessary, gave his hat, driving gloves and coat to the bemused butler when he answered it, exclaiming, 'Where is everyone, Jennings? I thought this place would be a hive of activity but it's as quiet as a tomb!'

'We were not expecting you, sir,' replied the butler, with admirable understatement considering his expression. 'If you had sent word ahead, your room would have been prepared but—'

'No matter,' interpolated Theo, waving a hand dismissively. 'Any room will do – I'm not in my dotage yet and shan't need a hot brick to warm the sheets.' He straightened his cravat in the mirror in the hallway and asked, 'Where are my mother and Julia? Are they at home this afternoon?'

'They are in the drawing-room, sir. Lord Bramwell is out at present.'

'Then I'll announce myself,' he replied briskly, 'I can't wait to see their faces when they see me. Oh, and bring up some tea and cake will you, Jennings? I'm ravenous.'

A few moments later, Theo opened the door to the drawing-room. 'Well, if this isn't a poor welcome for a family member.'

Julia looked up in astonishment. 'Theo!' she cried, rushing over to embrace him.

'Hello, Ju,' said her brother, grinning.

'We are pleased to see you, Theo,' said Lady Bramwell, as he kissed her cheek in greeting. 'When did you arrive?'

'Just now – I've driven straight here from Oxford. I suppose Hal has told you what happened?' Theo tried to look downcast but the amusement in his gaze said that he was anything but sorry for his misdemeanours.

His mother nodded. 'It was a very foolish thing to put cows on the college green. Why on earth did you do it?'

'To enliven things a little, Mama. Latin and Greek are tedious and, more to the point, Giles Templeton bet me five guineas I wouldn't do it. I couldn't ignore such a challenge, could I?' asked Theo innocently.

'No Cavanagh could resist,' said Julia, laughing. 'How long have you been banished for?'

'A month. I tried to extend my absence, but my tutor pithily replied that my Latin essay must be submitted before I left Oxford. He thought that a month would be long enough to contemplate my folly and finish the damnable essay. Lord knows when I'll complete it when there are so many things to do in London.' Theo looked at his sister. 'I suppose I am obliged to attend your come-out ball, Ju?'

Julia raised her brows and said, 'If you must, but don't expect me to dance with you – my poor feet could not stand the punishment.'

'Thank the Lord for that!' he observed blithely. 'I'll retire to the card room where there is proper entertainment to be had.'

'You could always finish your essay instead,' replied Lady Bramwell with a smile.

Theo shuddered. 'No, thank you. It may surprise you to know I would choose an evening in Julia's company over Latin verbs.' After studying his sibling closely, he said in a more serious tone, 'Is there something wrong, Sis? You look peaky and your eyes are suspiciously red-rimmed.'

'Julia and Freddy have quarrelled, but I'm sure it will all be resolved soon,' explained his mother.

'Quarrelled with Freddy?' echoed Theo, amazed. 'I thought you two love-birds would be engaged by now. Freddy's a fine fellow and really up to snuff. What did you find to argue about?'

'Don't, Theo!' pleaded Julia, 'It was a stupid quarrel. Freddy has gone to Newmarket, but I am determined to put matters right when he returns.'

Theo, seeing that she was in earnest, resolved to tease her no more on the subject, adding only, 'Well, I'm sure it's all a misunderstanding – if ever there were two people made for each other, it's you and Freddy.' He picked up the newspaper and began to flick though the pages. 'Now, where has Hal got to, Mama? I fancy he has gone to Long Acre to look at that new tilbury he was interested in.'

'He has not gone to Long Acre,' said Lady Marguerite. 'He has gone to call upon Lady Vane.'

'Who?' asked Theo, still scanning the print and only half-attending.

'Lady Isabella Vane,' repeated his mother patiently. 'She is a widow, newly arrived in London from Yorkshire.'

'Ah! He must have known her husband, I expect, and wishes to give his condolences. It's not like Hal to visit old ladies in person though – he would normally expect you or Julia to accompany him.'

'No, Theo,' replied Julia with a chuckle. 'Isabella is a charming young woman with a six-year-old son called Dominic. We think Hal is very fond of Lady Vane; he has taken her for a drive in the park this afternoon and has escorted her and Dominic all over London in recent weeks.'

Theo lowered the newspaper slowly, staring over it at Julia with a gaping mouth until his mother reminded him to stop imitating a fish. Discarding the journal, he exclaimed, 'So Hal's showing serious interest in a lady at last! I never thought he would after that business with Felicity Portland.'

'It appears so, Theo,' said Lady Bramwell. 'Hal will have to work hard to earn Lady Vane's trust, but, as Julia says, she is a charming girl in spite of her reserve. Her son is a dear little boy who thinks the world of Hal.'

Theo contemplated this news in silence before observing, 'Hal must be smitten if he is prepared to entertain a small boy and drive Lady Vane around the park for everyone to see.' He sighed and, blissfully unaware of events which were about to unfold, added, 'Well, as Hal is otherwise engaged, it seems I shall be having a quiet evening after all.'

*

When Hal arrived in Curzon Street to collect Isabella, he sensed at once that there was something very wrong. Silwood's normally serene features were etched with concern and a frown creased his forehead. The servant greeted Hal, but his voice was so sombre that it prompted Hal to ask, 'Is something wrong, Silwood?'

Silwood hesitated until his concern overwhelmed his training. 'Indeed there is, my lord. It is not my place to give you details, except to say I am glad you are here because I believe Lady Vane will be in need of your counsel. She is in the saloon, with Mrs Forster and her maid.'

Hal looked at him in surprise, but asked no further questions, merely nodding and saying, 'I will announce myself.'

He climbed the stairs two steps at a time and paused for a moment outside the door; the sound of weeping could be heard from within.

When he entered, he was aware only of Isabella at first. She was sitting on the chaise and her complexion was deathly white, her eyes fearful. Sitting down beside her, he took her trembling hands firmly in his. 'Dear God,' he murmured, 'what has happened, Isabella?'

Her troubled gaze registered his arrival. 'Dominic ...' she replied. 'He has gone.'

From where she stood beside the fireplace, Harriet spoke through her tears. 'Thank goodness you are here, Lord Bramwell! A terrible thing has happened and we are desperately worried.' She turned to Mary, Isabella's maid, who was also in the room and crying bitterly. 'Mary, tell his lordship what happened this morning! Do not omit any details; he will know what we must do.'

'Oh, my lord, the most awful thing,' began Mary, sobbing. 'I took Master Dominic for his walk this morning. As usual, he was all excitement as we set off to the park with Aesop – he is most attached to that dog and won't go anywhere without him, you know. We played various games until Aesop took it into his head to chase another dog and Master Dominic set off in pursuit. I shouted for him to come back, but either he didn't hear or he chose to ignore me, because he kept running after the dog and I was struggling to keep up. He ran right out of the park. I was out of breath and had to stop for a moment, but by then, I had lost sight of him.'

Mary gave another sob and dashed fresh tears from her cheeks, 'I didn't know what to do. I tried not to panic, but neither Master Dominic nor the dog was anywhere to be seen. I hoped he might just be lost and so I asked passers-by if anyone had seen them. No one had, until I found a rough-looking fellow who said he had seen a boy of Dominic's description being led away by an older boy. The man considered it a little odd because Dominic was protesting and Aesop was barking, but he thought they must be brothers having a quarrel. When I had heard all this, I asked the man if he knew the older boy, and he said no, but he fancied he might be a flash-house boy on account of his ragged appearance and artful way. I didn't know where the flash-house was, my lord, so I came straight back to tell Miss Isabella.'

'Are you sure he said "flash-house"?' asked Hal.

'Oh y-yes, Lord Bramwell,' stammered Mary, 'I listened carefully to what he said.'

When his expression became grave, Isabella asked in trepidation, 'Do you know where he might be?'

'I cannot lie to you, Lady Vane,' he replied. 'Dominic is in danger and we must act quickly while there is still a chance of finding him.'

'But surely there cannot be many houses in London called Flash House,' said Harriet. 'Why can we not go to it directly?'

He shook his head, grim-faced. 'It is not the name of a particular house, Mrs Forster. Flash-houses are the colloquial term given to places of ill repute – they are at once brothels, drinking places and centres of criminal intelligence. There are many such houses in London and some are kept exclusively for the young.

I fear Dominic has been abducted: the keepers of flash-houses train hundreds of young boys and girls to thieve and beg, providing their masters with a thriving illicit business in stolen goods, and sometimes worse.'

Isabella's shocked expression changed to one of horror. 'Oh God,' she said in a constricted voice. 'I must find him.' She tried to stand, but swayed alarmingly and slumped back against the cushions.

'Mrs Forster, fetch some cold water and vinaigrette,' said Hal, reaching out to take Isabella's arm. 'Mary, go and prepare your mistress's bed – she will need to rest.'

'Yes, of course.' Harriet brushed aside her tears. 'Poor Isabella! Can you stay with her for a moment, Lord Bramwell?'

'I shall not leave her, but be quick.'

Harriet thanked him before hurrying out of the room with Mary.

When they had gone, Hal touched her cheek. 'Isabella … can you hear me?' He watched as Isabella's eyelids fluttered open, her pupils dilating as she focused on his face only inches from her own. She nodded, shivering violently with shock.

'There is no time to lose. You must stay here while I make enquiries—' he began.

'No!' she interjected, attempting to sit up. 'Let me come with you. I cannot bear to think where he might be at this moment.'

Pushing her back gently, he said in a firm voice, 'No, stay here so that you can send word to Berkeley Square if, by chance, Dominic does return. My mother will come and keep you company.'

'But I cannot rest until I know he is safe,' she cried. 'Dominic is all I have in the world. He is … he is … oh, dear God.' She stopped and burst into uncontrollable sobs.

Hal gathered her into his arms. 'I understand how you feel, my love,' he murmured. 'Dominic is very dear to me too, but I promise you I will find him.' She had been weeping into his shoulder, but looked up at this and her pleading, tearful look clawed at his heart. Clasping her hands between his, he kissed them, letting her go only when her aunt opened the door.

After quickly explaining his plans to Harriet and giving Isabella a final reassuring glance, he left to begin the search.

Chapter Ten

HAL negotiated his carriage back to Berkeley Square and considered grimly the task before him. If Dominic had indeed been taken to a flash-house, it did not augur well for finding him. The notorious rookeries of crime where the flash-houses could be found were in cramped passageways and alleys and almost impenetrable except to the thieves, prostitutes and destitute souls who lived there. They were rarely inspected by any officers of the law, and those who did visit were bribed by the landlords not to report them to magistrates.

Hal had some knowledge of flash-houses and the exploitation of children in the criminal underworld because, unknown to anyone but his close family and friends, he funded three philanthropic institutions in London. He was not a man to advertise his role as a benefactor, or claim to have an answer to the exigencies suffered by so many children, but he had wanted to put some of his wealth to good use and to play a small part in reform. So he had chosen to fund three charitable refuges instead of wringing his hands over the iniquity of youth or, worse still, ignoring what was happening scarcely a mile from his door, but which was never discussed by the majority of the *ton*.

The refuges usually helped children whose sentences for stealing had been commuted from transportation to imprisonment and, rather than be sent to the infamous Newgate prison to mix with hardened criminals, the refuges offered to rehabilitate them from their life of crime. Hal was not involved in their day-to-day running, but he had visited often and seen and heard enough to know about the nurseries of crime and the terrible poverty and suffering of even very young children living in the London underworld.

He had not dared tell Isabella the extent of his concerns, but he was afraid for Dominic's safety and for what he might have been exposed to. He pushed aside these fears, forcing himself to approach the search methodically and mentally listing the flash-houses he had heard of and their location.

His mind was still engaged in this when, as he walked into the hallway and gave his hat and gloves to Jennings, his brother appeared.

'Hal! Good to see you,' said Theo, 'I decided to visit London, so I'm afraid you will have to endure my presence for a while. I was wondering where you had got to—' He stopped suddenly, looking at his brother's expression. 'What the deuce is wrong?' he asked, frowning. 'I've never seen you look so queer in the attic. Are you foxed?'

Despite his mood, Hal answered with the ghost of a smile. 'At four o'clock in the afternoon? Certainly not, Theo. Something very unfortunate has occurred and I am in great need of your help. Go and change – put on some dark, unobtrusive clothing, nothing that looks too expensive – and bring a loaded pistol. You may need it because we are going to search some of London's most unsavoury areas tonight.'

Theo looked at his brother in astonishment. 'The devil we are! What are we looking for?'

'A small boy who is in danger, but I'll explain everything when we are on our way.'

Theo nodded. His brother's anxiety was evident and that was enough – Hal never indulged in hyperbole. Theo hurried away upstairs, calling out over his shoulder, 'I'll be ready to leave in five minutes.'

The cold water she splashed on her face revived Isabella for a moment. Her hands shook as she dabbed away the moisture and looked at her reddened eyes in the mirror. Fear had made her physically sick; never, even in the darkest days of her marriage, had she felt as afraid as she did now because this time her fears were for her son and not for herself. Her head ached terribly, but she was determined to stay awake. She had at last persuaded a distraught and exhausted Harriet to rest for a while, with a promise to waken her if there were any news.

The mood of the whole household was sombre. The servants, in particular Mary who was still blaming herself, were mechanically going about their duties but their anxiety was palpable. Even Dominic's pets seemed subdued and listless in his absence and for Isabella, the hope that he was simply lost and looking for a kindly soul to return him home was diminishing by the hour.

To try and take her mind off the horror and frustration of receiving no news of Dominic, she allowed her thoughts to turn briefly to Hal.

She had thought about what she had seen at the theatre a great deal until receiving this afternoon's terrible news. Isabella was relieved when Sir Seymour and Harriet had agreed to return home; after what she had witnessed, she had no inclination to enjoy the comedy that was to follow. She did not see Hal or Julia again before they left and she had lain awake that night, reasoning that it was foolish to draw conclusions, but also acknowledging that a seed of doubt had been planted in her mind.

Isabella was torn – her heart wanted to trust Lord Bramwell, but her head screamed to take care. Her self-confidence had been damaged by her poor judgement in the past and then trampled under the oppression of her marriage; consequently, she had little faith in her ability to read Hal's character.

But his tenderness and concern this afternoon were now branded on her memory – she could not forget the touch of his lips, his embrace, nor the way his presence and calm manner had offered her some comfort. Hours later, her hands still felt sensitized where he had kissed them and she could never confuse this visceral passion with her tepid fondness for

Edward. Indeed, she felt half-ashamed of the dreams she had indulged in about Hal last night and blushed to recall them.

Perhaps what she had seen at the theatre had a reasonable explanation, but now answers to her questions would have to wait. Whatever happened in the future, Isabella would always be indebted to him for trying to rescue her son.

She jumped when there was a knock at the door and Silwood announced Lady Bramwell.

'Ask her to come in.' Hope flared in Isabella; there might be word from Hal.

Marguerite entered moments later and, with hand outstretched, said, 'My dear, what a dreadful thing to happen! How wretched you must feel.'

As Isabella took the proffered hand, she struggled to contain fresh tears. 'I am wretched – you, as a mother, will understand my feelings – but tell me, is there any news?'

Marguerite shook her head. 'None yet, I'm afraid, but you must trust Hal to do his best for Dominic. He has more knowledge of the poorer areas of London than you might think. He dispatched several notes before leaving the house, and has also sent servants to make enquiries. My younger son Theodore, who arrived in Town today, has accompanied Hal and Julia sends her love – she would have come here too, but I asked her to stay at home in case Hal and Theo returned.'

'I cannot thank you and your family enough, Lady Bramwell. If I had no one in London to turn to at this awful time then I don't know what I would have done. Even Sir Seymour has written to his friend, Henry Grey Bennet, as he believes he could help. But,' concluded Isabella sadly, 'all I want is news that Dominic is safe.'

'That news will come, Isabella,' said Lady Bramwell, squeezing Isabella's hand reassuringly. 'Dominic is a bright little boy who will stand out among the poor, ragged children who roam London. Hal has posted a reward for his safe return and there are many who will want to claim it. Now, have you eaten since this morning?'

'I'm not hungry.'

'I quite understand – Julia and I ate little food this evening either – but you must have something to keep your strength up. Let me at least ring for some tea, and I will keep you company as long as you wish.'

It was three o'clock in the morning and Lord Bramwell and his brother were sitting in the corner of a tavern, the three footmen and two burly jarveys, who accompanied them, nearby. Neither Hal nor Theo attracted much attention from the other customers; their hats were pulled forward to shade their features and they were dressed not in their normal coats of blue superfine, but in unremarkable drab overcoats.

They had spent hours searching unsuccessfully for Dominic in some of the most vice-ridden areas of the city. The labyrinthine rookeries were wretched, squalid places: slum dwellings towered over alleys full of filth and putrid air; men, women and children of all ages and description lived in cramped conditions and this, coupled with the easy availability of gin and corrupt and inadequate policing, all led to children being exploited for crime. Barefoot and ragged, with matted, lice-ridden hair, they wandered the rookeries, fighting, thieving and begging for their very existence and it was a salutary experience for Hal and Theo, who were not easily shocked, to see the London underworld at such close quarters.

Theo, when told of the circumstances surrounding Dominic's disappearance, was inclined initially to be hopeful: the boy was most likely lost or, if he had indeed been taken, he would soon be found and they would be back in Berkeley Square by ten o'clock enjoying a fine dinner. But within an hour of their search beginning, his hopes had been dashed. Their task was an unenviable one; there were more than 200 flash-houses in London and looking for one six-year-old boy in this morass of profligacy was like searching for the proverbial needle in a haystack. It was dangerous, too – the rookeries were ruled by thieves, beggars, prostitutes and outlaws and Hal was well aware of the risks they were taking in penetrating these slums.

At one flash-house, Hal had been making enquiries when the landlord suddenly became hostile. In St Giles's Greek cant, he said they were queer culls and demanded to know if they were the law. A crowd had gathered and only when Hal, Theo and their henchman had produced their pistols were they able to escape the drunken, fractious mob.

Now, after no success in finding Dominic or receiving word of his whereabouts, neither Hal nor Theo was in an optimistic mood.

'This is a rum business indeed,' said Theo gloomily. 'There's no sign of the little fellow so far, in spite of blunt you've handed over for information. Do you think he was singled out and deliberately abducted?'

'No, I believe it was pure chance that Dominic was taken,' said Hal. 'Remember that the children who are forced to steal for these flash-houses are very young, not much older than Dominic, and the boy who took him probably thought he would be rewarded for acquiring a new recruit. He may even have just wanted his clothes – they alone would be worth more money than these children see in a year.'

'I've heard of them before, of course, but to see the rookeries and flash-houses at close quarters is shocking. They are a damned disgrace and to think most of the law turns a blind eye to their existence.' Theo shook his head. 'The landlords who exploit these children deserve hanging.'

Hal agreed, adding, 'Let's hope our visit to Bow Street pays dividends soon. Word that there is a sizeable reward should spread rapidly and we must hope someone will be tempted by the sum on offer.'

'There must be hundreds of these places. Where do we try next?' asked his brother.

'Most are in the St Giles area. We'll continue there before moving on to the Black Horse in Tottenham Court Road, then eastwards. We must hope the reward will tempt whoever is holding Dominic because it would take us months to visit all of them in London. He is a well-cared-for child who will stand out against the malnourished wretches and that too will act in our favour. I just pray that he has not been harmed.' Hal rose to his feet, ready to resume the search and determined to find Dominic.

Dawn was breaking in Curzon Street, but neither Isabella nor Harriet noticed the first rays of daylight or the birds singing.

'You should rest, Isabella,' said Harriet, looking at her niece in concern.

Isabella closed her eyes and rubbed her temples. 'Only when I know Dominic is safe,' she murmured. 'What time is it?'

'Almost five o'clock.' Harriet groaned and added, 'Time is passing so slowly! I wish we could do more, but thank God for Lord Bramwell's help, and Sir Seymour's. How considerate of him to write to Grey Bennet and to stay with us for two hours last night.'

'It was a kind gesture,' said her niece. In truth, although Isabella was very grateful for Sir Seymour's help, she had found his chatter annoying. He meant well and had no doubt had talked of inconsequential matters to ease the tension, but although Harriet seemed to have taken comfort from this, Isabella had wanted to scream: she had no wish to discuss trivia when Dominic was missing.

Isabella lifted her gaze once more to the clock. Dear Lord, every minute seemed like an hour, every hour an eternity. How much longer before there was any news?

At the same time in Berkeley Square, Hal was stripping off his shirt. He and Theo had returned briefly to wash and for a change of clothes. Hal felt physically and metaphorically dirty after searching the rookeries, but he had no time to contemplate the moral corruption and poverty he had seen – they needed to leave for Bow Street as soon as possible.

There was a tap at the door and Whittam, Hal's valet, entered. 'My lord, there is a person downstairs who wishes to see you. She says she will speak with no one else.'

'She?' queried Hal in surprise. 'Is it Lady Vane, or Mrs Forster?'

'No, my lord. I have never seen this person before. Mr Jennings was undecided whether to admit her at first, so dirty and thin as she is – he thought she might steal something – but when she said she had news of Lady Vane's son, we thought—'

'Why did you not say so at once, Whittam?' cried Hal, grabbing a clean shirt. 'Send word that she is not to leave – I will be down directly. Where is she?'

'Mr Jennings asked her to wait in the library,' replied Whittam.

'Very well. Ask my brother to join us as soon as he is able.'

The valet left to do as he was bid and Hal wiped the remains of the soap from his face, desperately hoping that whoever was waiting to speak to him downstairs had information about Dominic's whereabouts.

But when he entered the library, he felt a pang of surprise. He had expected an older woman, but a young girl, no more than twelve or thirteen, sat in the chair by the fire, stretching out bare filthy feet and hands towards the flames. She was thin and undernourished and her clothing, if it could be called such, consisted of rags. Her cheeks were pale and sunken, and a pair of brown eyes looked up nervously when she realized she was no longer alone. She jumped to her feet and shrank against the wall.

'I won't hurt you,' murmured Hal.

The girl said in a guarded voice, 'Are you the smart cove that's Lord Bramwell?'

'I am.'

'Do you live 'ere?' she asked, scanning the room with eyes as wide as saucers.

'Yes, this is my house,' he answered with a smile. 'Sit down again if you wish. What is your name?'

'Sarah,' replied the girl, staying by the wall and shaking her head. 'I run all the way here to talk to you, 'cause your friend Dominic asked me to get to you right and tight. 'E said you were full of juice as well as being a lord, an' as fine as ninepence. 'E promised me that if I came and told you where 'e was, you would rescue 'im and give me a guinea. I weren't sure whether to believe 'im but 'e was certain that you could do it.' Sarah added after a shrewd, assessing gaze, 'Looking at you, 'e might be right about that after all.'

'Is Dominic safe?' asked Hal quickly.

''E were when I left. Hid 'im in the one of cupboards and told 'im not to make a peep 'til I got back, nor that dog of 'is. I sneaked out the back way and came straight 'ere.'

'A very brave thing to do, Sarah. And Dominic must have been afraid.'

''E was,' she replied, nodding. 'He cried and cried, an' his dog barked and tried to bite 'em. Dominic screamed at everyone that 'is friend was a lord and they'd be sorry. Chivers, who runs the flash-'ouse, flogged John for taking him there, but by then, Chivers was worried because 'e believed what Dominic 'ad said – 'e could see that the boy was a well-dressed young gentleman, and knew that there could be trouble from the law for this. Chivers an' 'is wife argued over what to do with 'im. Dominic seemed to like me, so they told me to take 'im to Mother Jackson – that's where I live, see?'

Hal raised his brows. 'And who is Mother Jackson?'

'Why, everyone knows Mother Jackson!' said Sarah, clearly astonished that Lord Bramwell had never heard of her. 'She got a shop in 'olborn that sells rum clouts—'

'Rum clouts?'

'Silk 'andkerchiefs, but she gets us to steal 'em first. Then we get rid of the marks from the silk before she puts 'em in the shop. She's been doing it for years an' never got caught, even though the officers come and check. She'd kill me if she knew I'd come 'ere though,' finished Sarah, a quiver of fear in her voice.

The door opened, startling her again.

'What the Lord is going on, Hal?' muttered Theo, his gaze falling on the girl as he came in.

'Sarah, this is my brother Theodore. He has been helping me

to search for Dominic and I give you my word that he will not harm you.'

Sarah eyed Theo warily. ''E's not so big as you.'

'No,' agreed Hal with a smile. He explained to Theo what Sarah had said, then, turning back to the girl, he enquired, 'Where is Mother Jackson's shop, Sarah?'

'Field Lane, sir.'

'And does anyone else know where you have hidden Dominic?'

'No. I managed to squeeze 'im in the small cupboard upstairs without any of the others knowing. Mother said she'd send 'im out with us to learn 'ow to snatch rum clouts, otherwise 'e'd 'ave no food today either. We'd better 'urry – she'll be looking for 'im soon.'

'Not you, child,' said Hal. 'You have done enough already. Where are your parents?'

''Aven't got any. They died, and that's when I went to live with Mother Jackson.'

'You have no relatives at all?' he asked, frowning.

Sarah shrugged. 'There's just me.' Tears welled up in her eyes, but she dashed them away in a pragmatic fashion.

'Poor child,' murmured Theo.

'Theo, take Sarah to the kitchen and ask them to take care of her until we return.' Hal then addressed the child again, 'You will be well looked after here so do not be frightened.'

''Ere, what about my guinea?' she said, indignantly. 'Dominic promised you'd give me some blunt.'

Hal put his hand in his pocket and pulled out a guinea. He walked over to Sarah, who looked at him in suspicion and shrank further away, but he reached out, took her hand and folded her thin fingers around the coin. She stared at the gleaming coin as if unable to believe it was real. Then, she looked up and grinned, the smile lighting up her thin, filthy features.

'Dominic was right – you're a fair gentleman, all right and you'll pull Mother Jackson's cork if she causes you trouble,' declared Sarah gleefully, enjoying the prospect of Mother Jackson being brought to account.

Theo chuckled. 'Let us hope we don't have to pull her cork to get to Dominic. The law can administer her punishment.'

The girl shuddered. 'I don't want nothing to do with the law.'

'You won't, I promise you,' replied Hal.

'Don't I 'ave to go back to Field Lane then?'

'No, never. You will live somewhere more pleasant and you will not have to steal handkerchiefs again.'

Sarah's eyes widened at this and she stammered her gratitude.

Hal brushed aside her thanks, declaring that, on the contrary, they were in her debt. After explaining precisely where she had hidden Dominic, and for Hal's future reference telling him the name and location of the flash-house Dominic had originally been taken to, Sarah was taken down to the kitchen by Theo.

Hal collected his overcoat, hat and pistol, scribbled brief notes to Isabella, his mother and one to Bow Street, before joining Theo, who was waiting outside in the growing daylight.

Chapter Eleven

WHEN Theo and Hal arrived in Field Lane by hackney carriage, Hal, who had chosen the sturdiest coachman he could find, asked him to wait at the end of the street.

'Are you sure you wanted to be brought here, sir?' queried the driver, raising his brows at their surroundings.

Hal nodded. 'We will not be staying long, I hope, and there's an extra guinea or two if you don't abandon us to our fate,' he said with a wry grin.

The driver laughed and gave a wink. 'I'll plant a facer on anyone who tries to make me move.'

Field Lane was the misnomer for a stinking, unprepossessing alley off Holborn, in the crawling thieves' district bordered by Saffron Hill and Butcher's Hall Lane, with the fetid Fleet River at its rear. Field Lane was covered with filth and detritus that abounded in much of London, but in curious contrast, freshly washed silk handkerchiefs hung on strings across the alley. Hal and Theo were eyed with mild suspicion by its inhabitants, but, as their clothing suggested that they were men of only modest means, they were able to make their way unhindered to Mother Jackson's shop. A group of thin pallid-faced children stood near the doorway and watched as they entered.

The dingy interior was not an improvement on the exterior. The floors were filthy, there were a few badly fitting shelves and an old door had been pressed into service as a counter. The goods on offer, however, were of the finest quality. Handkerchiefs of every colour and size hung in the window and were arranged around the shop.

A woman was screaming obscenities through a door at the rear as Hal and Theo entered. Her hair had escaped from the grubby lace cap she wore and hung about her face in lank tresses. Her dress was stained and her face bore evidence of the ravages of gin. Bloodshot blue eyes squinted myopically at her visitors and, clearly shocked to have customers this early in day, she stopped her vociferous cursing and hid the bottle she was holding. She straightened her cap and smiled, showing a set of carious teeth.

'Good morning, gentlemen. How can I help you?' she began, trying and failing to disguise her East End vowels. 'Would you be looking for a particular sort of handkerchief today?'

Hal replied with another question, 'Are you Mother Jackson?'

Her smiling benevolence vanished; customers did not usually ask for her by name. 'Who wants to know? You ain't the law, are you?'

'No, but neither are we here to buy handkerchiefs,' answered Theo.

'Well, if you ain't the law, and you don't want to buy any rum clouts, what do you want?'

'A young boy whom we believe is on your premises,' explained Hal, 'and we will look for him, with or without your permission.'

'You can't search my house – it's not proper,' she cried. 'I run a legal business.'

Theo shook his head. 'It might appear so, but the way you acquire your goods is most certainly illegal; you train children to pickpocket and beg, and treat them cruelly if they do not.'

Mother Jackson feigned outrage. 'The children here I've taken in out of the goodness of my heart! Orphans, most of 'em, and I feed and clothe 'em at great expense—'

'Madam,' interrupted Hal, in a bored voice, 'I do not intend to argue with you when I have not even breakfasted. You are what is commonly referred to as a fence, or, in your own parlance, a fencing cully, a receiver of stolen goods. Your army of pick-pockets returns with the booty, then you remove the owners' marks from the silk before putting them on sale as legitimate goods. Do not insult my intelligence by suggesting otherwise, or we shall be forced to call upon the law officers who are waiting at the end of the street.'

'Bow Street has been watching you for some time,' remarked Theo, taking Hal's lead. 'They simply require enough evidence to punish you.'

She swallowed, eyeing them nervously and then muttered, 'It's true they've been 'ere a few times, but they can't prove anything.'

'If you assist us, we shall not immediately inform them. However, if you continue to be obstructive ...' Hal's voice trailed away, leaving the implicit threat hanging in the air.

Mother Jackson, realizing she had little choice but to co-operate, snapped, 'Who are you looking for?'

'A blond-haired boy, about six years old. We believe he was brought here last night,' said Hal.

'Him!' she spat fiercely. 'I knew there was something queer about that boy – he was too well fed to be from the streets. Trust Chivers to send trouble my way! The brat cried so much that he made my head ache and I would have drawn his claret if I could have got past his damn dog. Search if you like but you'll 'ave no luck – he's nowhere to be seen. Reckon he must 'ave skipped off. I can't find Sarah either and when I get my hands on 'er, I'll flog 'er to within an inch of her life.'

'We shall look for ourselves, and thankfully, you will never treat Sarah in that despicable manner again,' replied Hal curtly. 'Theo, watch Mother Jackson in case she tries to call for help.'

'With pleasure,' said his brother with a grin. He leaned his broad shoulders back against the wall and, arms folded, prepared to wait.

As Hal pushed open the door into the rear of the shop, he kept his fingers curled around the pistol hidden in his overcoat pocket. Mother Jackson might have a husband, a lover, or other male company on the premises and he needed to be prepared. Sarah had told him where she had hidden Dominic, so Hal worked quickly. He passed through a room where at least twenty children were squabbling over a loaf of stale bread, presumably the objects of Mother Jackson's earlier wrath. They looked up in surprise as Hal entered, but when he gestured for them to remain quiet, there was no dissent; they assumed that he was an associate of Mother Jackson and knew better than to question her acquaintances.

Ignoring the foul-smelling, grim surroundings, he hurried on, climbing two narrow flights of stairs until he stood on a dingy landing at the top of the house where, directly above his head, there was a trapdoor.

He placed the nearby rickety wooden ladder against the ledge above and climbed the steps, testing each one to ensure it would take his weight. Cautiously, he lifted the door with one hand, holding his cocked pistol in the other. There was no resistance as it creaked open, so he pushed it back fully and peered into the darkness. As his eyes adjusted to the gloom, he could see handkerchiefs strewn around the tiny attic. 'Dominic?' he said, 'Are you there?'

A sob came out of the shadows and a plaintive voice cried, 'Hal!' Suddenly, Dominic's dirty, tear-stained features appeared as he crawled out from behind a wooden chest.

Isabella was elated when she received Hal's note. The missive was brief and did not explain how Dominic's whereabouts had been discovered, but for now Isabella was content to know that her son would soon be home. She had told Harriet, who had wept with relief before replying that she had always known Lord Bramwell would find him. She had then hurried away to write to Sir Seymour to inform him of the good news.

As she waited, Isabella paced the saloon, alternately looking at the clock and then through the window to the street below. From her vantage point, she saw a hackney carriage pull to a halt outside and, after a moment or two, Hal's unmistakable tall figure emerged. Isabella watched him reach up to lift Dominic down, and then Aesop jumped out of the carriage, followed by another man, whom Isabella did not know. With a cry of joy, she wrenched open the door and ran down the stairs, coming into the hall just as Silwood opened the front door.

'Dominic!' she cried, a catch in her voice.

Dominic was clutching Hal's sleeve, but he let go as soon as he saw his mother and ran to her, putting his arms around her as she picked him up and hugged him. Aesop, meanwhile, barked and wagged his tail.

'Don't be angry with me, Mama. I'm very sorry – I should never have run away from Mary.'

Isabella, laughing and crying simultaneously, said, 'I'm not angry, just glad that you are safe. Are you all right?'

'Yes,' murmured Dominic into her shoulder, 'thanks to Hal and Theo. And Sarah of course. I've been to some horrible places, but now I'm tired and hungry.'

He concluded with a yawn and, through her tears, Isabella noted that although he was dirty and dishevelled, he appeared otherwise unharmed. She hugged and kissed her son again, still unable to quite believe that he had returned home safely. Isabella did not know who Sarah was, but she hoped Hal would explain. He stood nearby with the other man and he smiled as he met her gaze.

He introduced his brother and Theo declared with a friendly grin, 'I'm pleased to make your acquaintance, Lady Vane. These are strange circumstances to meet under for the first time, but fortunately the outcome is a happy one.'

'How can I ever thank you?' she declared warmly.

'It's Hal you should thank more,' observed Theo. 'He did most of the work.'

Mary bustled into the hallway and cried, 'Oh, praise the Lord – you are back, Master Dominic!'

'Go with Mary now, Dominic,' said Isabella. 'Take a bath and have something to eat; you can tell me what happened before you go to sleep.'

He rubbed his eyes, tiredness rapidly overtaking him. 'Must I have a bath, Mama?'

Isabella gave a little laugh as she set him on his feet.

Crouching in front of him, she smiled, saying, 'You will feel much better if you do, love. Mary will help you, and take Aesop too.'

Dominic gave his rescuers a grateful and slightly sheepish look from under his lashes as he thanked them.

'Be good now, Dominic,' said Hal. 'At least allow me to have breakfast before involving me in any more scrapes!'

'I will,' he replied, giving another huge yawn.

'And look after that fellow,' added Theo, pointing at Aesop, 'he's an excellent guard dog.'

Mary and Dominic left with Aesop trotting behind and Theo, with a glance at his brother and Isabella, said, 'I'll wait for you in the carriage, Hal. Lady Vane, I'm pleased that your son is safe – I've only been in his company for a short while, but he is a delightful little boy. Pluck to the backbone too: he's not complained for a minute about his frightening experience. I look forward to seeing him when he has recovered and to meeting you again at my sister's ball.'

'Oh yes, of course. Thank you again – you have been so kind.'

Theo nodded and went out through the front door, leaving Hal and Isabella alone.

Isabella saw him clearly for the first time that morning and her heart leapt with longing and with love. Hal looked incredibly handsome to her eyes. He was tired and unshaven, but the stubble covering his jaw only added to his appeal. His cravat had been removed and, underneath his overcoat, the open neck of his shirt revealed a hint of dark chest hair.

Swallowing hard, Isabella tried to regain her composure. She desperately wanted to walk the short distance between them and beg him to take her in his arms. Instead, she said quietly, 'Please come into the library for a moment, Lord Bramwell.'

Once there, Hal apologized for his appearance, adding, 'I wanted to bring Dominic home at once, but I fear you will consider me a loose screw.'

'Oh no! Indeed, no. How can I begin to express my gratitude?

If any harm had befallen Dominic, I do not know what I would have done. And if y-you had not h-helped m-me, th-then I—' Overwrought with emotion, Isabella drew in a ragged breath and bit her trembling lower lip, unable to continue.

Seeing this, Hal stepped quickly towards her. 'My dearest girl, don't distress yourself any more. Dominic is safe and, having questioned him carefully, I am convinced he has come to no real harm. No doubt he will tell you what happened when he is able and so shall I, but first I think you need to sleep and to spend some time with your son.' He ran his palm over his jaw and gave a soft, rueful laugh. 'I had better leave – I am in dire need of a shave and if I am seen like this, I shall never live it down.'

'You look very fine to me,' she said, shyly.

Hal smiled in surprise at her unguarded comment and looked into her eyes. To his amazement, and joy, he saw a plea in their depths. Should he follow his instincts and answer it? He hardly knew if it was right to do so, but he found it impossible to resist. Her glorious hair was swept into a simple chignon from which several tendrils had escaped to caress the curve of her cheeks, and from underneath dark, lustrous lashes, her brilliant eyes gazed back at him steadily. He hesitated for a heartbeat, then bent his head and touched his lips to hers. It was the lightest of kisses, a mere brushing of his lips against hers, and it demanded nothing in return at what he knew was a difficult time for Isabella. It was a kiss that offered love, reassurance and comfort; it was also a fleeting glimpse of the heaven that Hal yearned for.

Reluctantly, he pulled away, afraid he had gone too far and that the trust he had been trying to build between them would be shattered by that kiss. He was also unshaven and unkempt, and Isabella's emotions were fragile after the tumult of recent hours – what would she think of him?

But when he looked down into her lovely countenance, now delicately tinged with colour, her eyes shone and a smile hovered on her lips. Hal stifled a groan; he was desperate to kiss her until she understood just how much he loved her, but for now this had to be enough.

For Isabella, that fleeting kiss had left her breathless. She had wanted to deepen the kiss, to slide her hands under his shirt and let her sensitive fingers trail over the muscles beneath. She was in awe that the merest touch from Hal could elicit such an intense reaction and, having tasted this seductive and addictive drug, she felt bereft now that it had been taken away. Isabella sensed that he was anxious: their kiss had been brief, but it went completely against propriety. However, she did not care for the proprieties now, nor could she dredge up her concerns; the last few hours had unlocked another door in her heart. Laying her hands against his chest, she reached upwards to press her lips to his. Again, it was the briefest of kisses, feather light and tentative, but she needed to take this step, to take the initiative. Although she closed her eyes as their lips touched, every other sense was heightened: she felt the warmth of his body and the fine texture of his shirt, she recognized the faint clean scent of soap on his skin, and even the taste of him seemed comfortingly familiar.

He made a low sound of protest when she ended the kiss.

'Oh!' she murmured, blushing. 'Pray do not think ill of me – I-I had to kiss you again.'

'I could never think ill of you,' whispered Hal. 'What must you think of me for taking advantage of you at a time such as this? Forgive me.'

Isabella shook her head. 'There is nothing to forgive, Hal.'

His gaze ran over her and he smiled. 'That is the first time you have called me by my name and it thrills me to hear you say it. I thought I might have offended you with that kiss, Isabella, but it was truly not something I intended to happen when I arrived.'

'I know. And I do not want you to think afterwards that I kissed you out of gratitude because you would be quite wrong,' she replied. 'I wanted to show you how I feel, not just for what you have done for Dominic, but for all you are coming to mean to me—'

'My darling–' he began, taking her hands between in his.

There was a look of apprehension in her eyes as she continued, 'But I must ask you to be patient, Hal. My emotions have been suppressed for so long, and it is not easy for me to deal with other feelings – unfamiliar, powerful, overwhelming feelings that I never knew I possessed until you awakened them.'

'I shall try not to rush you, even though my passion for you is so intense it is almost a physical pain,' he murmured, caressing her cheek with his fingertip. 'But there is something I want you to understand … I desire you not only physically, but in every way imaginable and because of that I want no barriers between us. I want to know you – every charming nuance, every wonderful detail – however long it takes. I promised that one day soon there would be no secrets between us and we have already begun to share our souls.' After a pause, he added, 'I wish I could show you how deeply I feel, Isabella, but the moment is not right. Your emotions are still raw and I will not insult you by capitalizing on that. When the time comes for you to reveal your secrets, there must be nothing else to distract us; I would not have it any other way.'

'Yes,' she murmured, 'just the two of us, in the right setting and with time to talk.'

'Then, for now I must content myself with this….' he said, before kissing her again, this time more ardently. Afterwards, as his lips brushed across her forehead and temples, he muttered in a husky voice, 'I should leave now, but I give fair warning, Isabella: I'll call on you tomorrow to take you for the drive in the park we had planned.'

Smiling into his eyes, she nodded her agreement and they went back into the hall, where they were met by Sir Seymour who had just hurried in.

He greeted Isabella and then seeing Hal, said, 'Well done, Bramwell,' as he shook him by the hand. 'I'm very glad to hear Dominic is safe. Your brother outside has told me some of the details – Dominic was abducted in broad daylight, eh?' Sir

Seymour shook his head in dismay. 'London is a dangerous place these days. Something must be done and I shall speak to Grey Bennet on the matter, you may be certain of that.' Then, he peered at Hal through his quizzing glass. 'Bramwell, I know there are extenuating circumstances, but you must go home and shave immediately! Not at all the thing to be calling upon ladies in a less than perfect state of dress.'

Hal laughed and looked at Isabella, amusement and love lurking in his eyes. 'Quite right, Sir Seymour. I have apologized for my appearance to Lady Vane, but she has been most understanding and says it will not weigh against me.' Then, he departed to join Theo outside.

Harriet came downstairs and begged to be told all the news about Dominic, but Isabella explained that she could not enlighten her further yet and excused herself, leaving Sir Seymour to Harriet's care.

Later, having heard her son's alarming story, Isabella sat in the chair next to his bed watching him sleep. Her gratitude towards the unknown Sarah, Theo and, of course, to Hal was boundless. Dominic had been in mortal danger; the underworld was a harsh, unforgiving place, and if it had not been for Hal's determination and the bravery of one young girl, she might never have seen Dominic again. A shudder of fear ran through her at the thought and she vowed to ask Hal what had happened to Sarah, and how she could repay her kindness.

It was hours since Hal had left, yet Isabella still felt ablaze with desire. Edward had accused her of being a cold witch and eventually, because he had flung the epithet at her so often, she had believed it to be true. But Hal had proved Edward's bitter denunciations wrong and Isabella knew now that she did possess sensual feelings where Hal was concerned. She was attracted to him with an intensity that shocked and frightened her.

Then Isabella remembered the flame-haired lady at the theatre and a cold flicker of doubt entered her heart; her love and desire for Hal would be worthless if she could not trust him.

Tomorrow she must discover the lady's identity, and find out what her connection was to Hal.

Chapter Twelve

THE following day, Julia and Lady Bramwell were taking a late breakfast together in the morning-room used for the purpose in Berkeley Square. Sun streamed in through the window, holding out the promise of fine weather.

'Hal seems happy this morning,' remarked Julia, as she spooned blackcurrant conserve on to her plate.

'With good reason,' said her mother. 'Dominic is safe, but matters could have turned out very differently. The providential outcome was due in part to a girl called Sarah, who, Hal tells me, is no more than eleven or twelve years old. She hid Dominic and made her way here alone to raise the alarm.'

Julia raised her brows. 'That was a courageous thing to do. What has happened to her now?'

'She is being cared for of at one of Hal's refuges.'

'I see,' said Julia, nibbling thoughtfully on a slice of bread and butter. 'The hours when Dominic was missing must have been awful for Isabella.'

'Indeed. As a mother, I know I would have been similarly distraught. It is fortunate that everything ended well and there is no lasting harm done.' Lady Bramwell sipped her coffee and observed with a percipient smile, 'Hal tells me that he is taking Isabella for a drive this afternoon.'

'I believe they are falling in love, Mama.' Pushing aside her plate with a sigh, Julia leaned on the table and cupped her chin in one hand. 'I hope I shall soon be as content.'

Marguerite, glancing across the table at her daughter's

despondent expression, said, 'Have you received word from Freddy?'

'Only an impersonal note to say he will be attending tomorrow night – nothing more.'

'Try to be more cheerful,' urged Lady Bramwell. 'Freddy will be anxious to make amends now he has had time to think.'

'He might still be upset with me,' said Julia sadly.

'I would be surprised if he is,' observed her mother. 'Freddy is normally amiable and more than a little in love with you.'

Julia made a sound of frustration. 'I wish he would tell me so.'

'He will,' declared her mother. 'Now, shall we indulge ourselves with some shopping this morning?'

The door opened and Theo came in. Overhearing this comment, he protested, 'I hope you don't require my company – I'd rather finish my essay than go shopping.'

'It will be difficult, but we will endeavour to manage without you, Theo,' replied Lady Bramwell, amused.

'I'm relieved to hear it.' He sat down and took the cup of coffee his mother passed across the table. 'After searching the gin dens and flash-houses last night, even I crave a quieter time of it today.'

'So, will you be working on your essay then?' prompted his sister, arching a mischievous eyebrow.

'Most definitely not, Ju,' he said with a shudder. 'I plan to dine with Hal at White's and enjoy a hand or two of cards.'

'The *tabula rasa* awaits, Theo,' teased Julia.

Theo groaned in disgust. 'Don't start sounding like my tutor – the essay can go hang!'

Despite her responsive laughter, melancholy shadowed her eyes and Theo, observing his sister over the rim of his cup, frowned when he saw this. Freddy Isherwood was an excellent fellow, but Theo had no doubt he had mishandled his courtship of Julia. The unhappy couple obviously needed some assistance and Theo decided it was high time he gave this problem his consideration.

*

When Hal reached Curzon Street, he jumped down from his carriage and instructed a waiting footman to walk his horses. Shortly afterwards, he was shown into the saloon where Harriet and Dominic were waiting.

Leaping to his feet and scampering over to embrace him, Dominic said, 'I've been expecting you.'

'Hello, troublesome cub!' Hal grinned and lifted him into the air, making Dominic squeal with delight. 'Have you recovered from your adventure?'

'Mostly. I had a bad dream last night about Mother Jackson, but Mama came and sat with me until I went back to sleep.' Dominic then regarded Hal gravely for a moment. 'I want to know what has happened to Sarah.'

'She's safe, Dominic. Sarah won't have to return to Field Lane; she will live somewhere else instead and have a more comfortable life.'

'Shall I see her again?'

'If you would like to,' said Hal, with a smile. 'Sarah will go eventually to my home in the country, Chenning Court. She can go to school and then learn how to be a lady's-maid, or whatever she wishes to do.'

'I'm pleased that Sarah is safe – I liked her.'

'There is something else you would perhaps like to see when you visit Chenning – Theo and I built a tree house in the woods when we were young. It's not very big and perhaps it needs repairing now, but I would enjoy showing it to you.'

'A tree house,' cried Dominic, his eyes dancing with excitement. 'I would like to see that.'

'Then I shall make arrangements with your mother soon.'

Harriet, who had been listening and watching this exchange with interest, said, 'You have been so kind, Lord Bramwell. Indeed, I do not know what we would have done without your family's support and I know that Isabella is very grateful too. She will be here in a moment; even the promise of a visit from Sir Seymour could not tempt her to miss driving with you today, so I am obliged to entertain him. Ah, here she is!'

Isabella came in, dressed in a blue and white jaconet muslin gown and a dark-blue spencer decorated with epaulets. She smiled when she saw Hal, drawing confidence from the frank admiration in his gaze. Refreshed after a good night's sleep, Isabella felt excited, nervous and a little shy at the prospect of an hour or so alone with Hal. The touch of his fingers when he handed her into the carriage sent the now familiar rush of anticipation through her and, as they set out in bright sunshine for Hyde Park, she covertly studied his profile and watched the deft way he took the reins and handled his horses, quite unlike the brutal treatment Edward had meted out to his thoroughbreds.

'Dominic seems to have recovered from his frightening experience,' began Hal once he had negotiated the worst of the traffic.

'Yes, I believe he has. Hal, I should tell you at once that I have had a change of heart—'

He pulled his horses abruptly to a halt, ignoring the loud protestations of the driver of the tilbury behind who had almost collided with them. Searching her face, he echoed in alarm, 'A change of heart? Not where your feelings for me are concerned, I hope?'

Isabella, clutching the side of the carriage as it bounced to a stop, blushed. 'No. Indeed, after yesterday they are even more profound, but,' she added with a little laugh, 'take care because if you pitch me into the gutter, I cannot say what I may think of you then.'

A smile spread across his features. He flicked his whip and set off again, saying, 'I apologize for my impatience. Please continue – what were you about to say?'

'Only that now Dominic has told me how Aesop protected him, I cannot send the dog away and have agreed that he may stay in London, as long as he is kept well away from Sir Seymour.'

'I fear neither Dinny's wardrobe nor his nerves could withstand further attention from Aesop,' he replied, amused. 'Has Dominic explained about Sarah?'

Isabella nodded. 'Dominic said Sarah had a terrible fear of Mother Jackson.'

'Like many in the underworld, Mother Jackson is brutal, unfeeling and has no compunction at using orphaned, destitute children for her own gain. I have seen to it that she will face punishment and the other children will be taken care of.' His expression grew grim as they entered the park by the Stanhope Gate and he explained, 'The flash-houses are a disgrace; they are well known to law officials, but many are paid to turn a blind eye to their activities. I hope the scandal of their existence will lead eventually to pressure for change and demands that they be closed down.'

'But where has Sarah gone? I would like to thank her.'

'Before I tell you, I should explain that I fund a number of charitable refuges,' said Hal. 'With the level of crime and corruption in London, they can only rescue a few from the thousands who are being exploited, but they provide the hope of better prospects for those few. Most of the children are rescued from Newgate after their sentences have been commuted from hanging, even though their crimes are usually no more heinous than stealing a loaf of bread or a handkerchief. That our laws can sentence a child to hang for a petty crime, often one committed simply to stay alive, is appalling.'

She turned to study his profile, her eyes wide with shock. 'Is that where Sarah is – at one of your refuges?'

'Until I can make arrangements for her to go to Chenning. Sarah is an orphan and more than happy to leave the city behind. Unfortunately, there are many more children like Sarah.'

'Indeed, it is dreadful,' said Isabella in a sombre voice. 'I had no idea of the extent of crime and poverty here. Hal, I insist on contributing towards the cost of Sarah's education. It is the least I can do in recompense of what she did for Dominic.'

'Very well, if you insist. We can discuss the details another time.' Hal was uncomfortable with Isabella shouldering this undertaking, but he did not argue; he hoped that soon he would bear all her burdens, financial and otherwise. 'There is something you could help with now – Sarah needs suitable clothing.'

'Then let me obtain some dresses, boots, gloves and such like.'

'She is about twelve years old, but very thin and undernourished,' said Hal.

'My maid has a niece of similar age, so I have a reasonable notion of what is required.' Colour rose to Isabella's cheeks as she admitted, 'I – I did not realize you funded refuges, Hal. I am ashamed to say that when we first met I thought you an utterly reckless, inconsiderate creature.'

He raised his brows quizzically and chuckled. 'Was that one reason why you were so cold towards me then? Society may think me devil-may-care, Isabella, but I was never truly such. My sporting wagers sprang from boredom and frustration, not from any desire to break my neck. I have recently declined Lord Dryburgh's challenge to a curricle race to Newmarket and several similar requests; since meeting you, my time is much more agreeably occupied and the only way I shall be impetuous in the future is in loving you. As for the refuges, I wish I could do more. The living conditions of the poor is not a subject which concerns the vast majority of the *ton* – you, my family, a few close friends and those who run the refuges are the only people aware of my philanthropic interests. You see,' he concluded, 'I didn't want my efforts to be seen as a wealthy man's idle hobby because I view it more seriously than that.'

By now, they had threaded their way along a crowded Rotten Row, past numerous stylish high-perch phaetons, elegant barouches and sporting curricles, all of whose occupants had stared at Lord Bramwell and his companion with ill-disguised curiosity.

Hal knew that his appearance here with Isabella at this most fashionable of hours would cause a stir. This would be seen as a statement of his serious intentions towards Isabella – a precursor to a proposal of marriage – and he was more than content for society to see it as such. 'Shall we walk a little now we have escaped the crush and the attentions of the inquisitive?' he said.

'But what about your horses?'

'As you see, my groom has caught up with us.' Hal indicated the man approaching on horseback. 'He will walk them while I enjoy your company without having to concentrate on driving through these crowds.'

When the groom had taken the horses in hand, Hal helped Isabella alight from the carriage. There were few people in this quieter area of the park and, as they began to stroll in the warm sun, Hal drew her hand through his arm.

'Tell me about your family,' said Isabella. 'I envy you – I have always longed for brothers and sisters.'

'My father died suddenly five years ago. He was a fine man and it was a terrible time for us all, but especially my mother: their marriage was very much a love match,' he began. 'Julia is as she appears – headstrong, vivacious, but also extremely loyal and loving. We are hoping that she and Freddy will recognize soon that they are made for each other.'

Isabella looked at him in surprise. 'Oh, I had not realized that was the way of things. I am very fond of Julia, and agree they would make a charming couple.'

'Theo, whom you have met briefly, is boisterous and outspoken, but good-hearted. He causes no real trouble apart from the occasional scrape. Lukas and Hugo are twins, and still at school. They are enthusiasts for the latest scientific inventions, and we have to listen to their schemes for building some contraption or other when they come home.'

'They sound delightful,' she said wistfully, 'I wish I had such a family.'

'They will all love you almost as much as I do, Isabella.' Admiring her profile, he added, 'Do you wish to tell me anything of your family?'

'It is painful for me, Hal. I want you to know, but I have kept it to myself for a long time.'

'Then tell me only as much as you feel comfortable with.'

'Very well,' murmured Isabella. She took a breath and began, 'I had a contented but lonely childhood. My mother, whom I can only remember vaguely, died in childbirth when I was three years old. The baby – a boy – was stillborn. My father was not a rich man and with her great beauty and reasonable dowry, my mother had been expected to marry a wealthy and titled man. Instead she chose to elope with my father, to the bitter disappointment of her family who disowned her when they heard of the marriage.'

'That must have been difficult for your mother.'

'Yes, but she had anticipated their disapproval and she and my father were very much in love. He never truly recovered from her death. He became withdrawn afterwards, although he still went into society occasionally and ensured I was allowed the company of other children. He was a fond and doting father, but he never entered into the lively pastimes that a young child craves. I therefore grew up with a vivid imagination, spending hours weaving tales of love, adventure and excitement to amuse myself in my solitude. Perhaps that contributed to my later problems.'

'In what way?' he asked.

'I think that I imbued my late husband with some of the chivalrous traits of my imagination, rather than discovering more about his character.' Isabella paused for a moment, lost in thought, and then continued, 'When my father became gravely ill, he grew concerned for my welfare after his death; he felt strongly that I needed the protection of a husband. Edward Vane's estates were ten miles distant to our land. He was generally talked of as a handsome young man, albeit slightly wild, and my father had respected Edward's father who had died some years earlier. On his few visits to us, Edward gave no indication of his true nature and perhaps my parent, in his anxiety to see me taken care of, saw only the face that Edward wished us to see.'

'What did you think of Edward?' Hal was anxious not to say too much and stem the flow of information.

'I was seventeen and had little knowledge of the world. In nursing my father through his last weeks, I spent only a short time in Edward's company and then always with a chaperon or my father. Edward seemed genuinely to love me; he fêted my beauty and told me he was desperate for us to marry as he had fallen in love with me on sight. He said we would see London after our marriage and he would strive to make me happy in the future. It was exactly what I wanted to hear when I felt so vulnerable.' She shook her head and added quietly, 'Much later, I saw that I should never have married him. However, I agreed to it then, in part to give my father some peace in his final days, and also to stem Edward's desperate pleas that his life would be blighted if he could not make me his. With my youthful optimism and romantic notions, I thought Edward and I would deal well enough together, but I could not have been more wrong. I blamed myself – never my father. I was not forced into marrying Edward so no one else was culpable. It was my poor judgement that was responsible for the circumstances I found myself in afterwards.'

'Isabella, do not judge yourself so harshly,' said Hal. 'You were very young and could not have been expected to make a judicious decision when your father was dying. And no doubt Edward was also an accomplished actor.'

'He was and I was completely fooled by him. Dominic's birth was the only bright moment during those dark years and as for how Dominic came to be ... it – it was not how I would have wished it.'

Hal noted that the fingers which rested against his coat sleeve were trembling. He covered them with his hand, raised them to his lips and said tenderly, 'Tell me more when you feel able – I shall not press you further now. What happened between us yesterday meant more to me than I can put into words and if I told you how much passion is in my heart, I am half afraid you will run away.'

'And I was afraid that you would think me too forward,' whispered Isabella, looking up and seeing her smile reflected in his eyes. 'My feelings have been stifled for so long, yet it is you who have brought them to life, Hal. I feel happier, and more loved and protected than ever before because of you.'

'That is all I need to hear for the moment, my love,' said Hal, feeling both joy and satisfaction to know that he was responsible for sparking her emotions back to life. Gazing intently into the sapphire brilliance of her gaze as the breeze toyed with a stray curl which caressed her cheek, he added in a husky voice, 'We had better walk back to the carriage because you are looking at me in such an adorable fashion that I am sorely tempted to kiss you again for everyone to see.'

They retraced their steps back to where the groom was waiting. After Hal handed her back into the curricle, they returned to the more crowded area of the park and Isabella noticed another carriage coming towards them. It was a luxurious phaeton and its passenger was the beautiful redheaded woman Isabella had seen at the theatre. The older man who had been her companion that night and whom Isabella assumed was her husband was driving the phaeton. The lady flashed a beguiling smile at Hal before directing a look of dislike at Isabella.

Shocked at this venomous glare from someone she did not even know, Isabella tensed. She looked under her lashes at Hal, wanting to observe his reaction, but he acknowledged the occupants with an almost imperceptible nod and fixed expression.

Isabella forced herself to ask nonchalantly, 'Who is that lady? I saw her when we were at the theatre – she and that gentleman were in the box next to you, I believe.'

'Lady Felicity Portland. The gentleman is her husband, Lord Cedric Portland,' he replied. 'They have lived on the Continent for several years and only recently returned to London.'

'You are obviously acquainted with Lady Portland,' she prompted.

'I was once engaged to be married to her.'

'Oh! I – I did not know,' she replied, stammering in her confusion. 'I am sorry for causing any distress.'

'You have not caused me distress,' said Hal with a shrug. 'It happened a long time ago. When I was twenty-one I became infatuated with a woman who, even at the age of eighteen, knew precisely how to excite a slavish following. I was blind to her faults – like you with Edward, I saw the beautiful and gracious icon of my imagination rather than the real woman, in spite of my parents' efforts to advise me otherwise. I made an offer of marriage in a rash moment which was accepted. Another offer followed quickly after mine, and Felicity, deciding that she needed a husband with a larger fortune, eloped with Lord Portland. It caused a scandal at the time and nothing else was talked of for a whole week.' His last few words were spoken in a voice heavy with sarcasm. Hal then added, 'For a while, I thought my life had been blighted forever until I recognized my lucky escape. I have not seen her since until a few weeks ago and, while she has every right to come back to England, I wish that she had stayed away.' After a pause, he gave a short laugh as if to lighten the mood. 'But that is enough – we should not spoil a fine afternoon by discussing Lady Portland.'

So that was it, thought Isabella. Now she knew who the woman was, but doubt still gnawed at her. If Hal had once been engaged to Lady Portland, could he still care for her? He had said that he was devastated when she left and when Isabella had observed them at the theatre, they had appeared intimate. Perhaps he still admired Lady Portland but could not admit to it. She was very beautiful and sophisticated, after all, but Hal seemed too principled to dally with a married woman while courting another. He had also just spoken movingly of his feelings for her and surely an honourable man would not dissemble at such a moment or during their tender exchanges of yesterday? Suddenly, she wished she had asked Hal to explain what she had seen at the theatre, but now the opportunity had slipped away – they were almost back in Curzon Street and Hal's conversation had been confined to general matters.

Her lips compressed as she made her decision. It was Julia's ball tomorrow and she would ask Hal then about what she had seen at Drury Lane. She would also tell him the full details of her marriage, Edward's death and, most importantly, how much he had come to mean to her.

When they arrived outside Isabella's house, he said with a wicked grin that she should be prepared to have her attentions monopolized by him tomorrow evening. Then, he brushed his lips over her knuckles, climbed back into the curricle and with a wave of his hand, drove away. Isabella watched his tall figure until it disappeared into the distance.

In Hyde Park, the thrill that had run through Lady Portland when she realized it was Lord Bramwell in the approaching carriage had been swept away by jealousy when she saw the beauty beside him. Here was proof of his interest in someone else, and to see him enjoying another woman's company was like rubbing salt into the open wound of her lack of success.

If his companion had been his mistress, it would have been difficult enough to accept, but feminine intuition told Felicity that the lady was not a high-class piece of muslin and the thought that he might be in love filled her with anger. She did not crave Hal's love, but she did covet his undivided attention and an *affaire de coeur* would make the task of securing him more complicated. She needed to know, and who better to ask than her husband who heard all the latest gossip at his club.

'Portland, who was the lady with Lord Bramwell?'

'Diamond of the first water, ain't she?' acknowledged Lord Portland. 'That is Lady Vane – she is the talk of the clubs, where she is referred to as the Ice Angel because of her beauty and reserve. There are bets being taken as to how long it is before Bramwell offers her marriage – the *on dit* is that he is much taken with Lady Vane and here they are, driving in the park for all to see.' He chuckled. 'I'll enter an extra fifty pounds in the wager book on the banns being read within two months – the odds are still worth having at five to one.'

Lady Portland mulled over this information. If Hal was indeed on the cusp of marriage, there seemed little hope that he would agree to being her cicisbeo at present. But Felicity was not yet willing to admit defeat; he might see her offer as the last opportunity for a liaison before marriage, and she was very willing to be the partner in an adieu to his bachelordom. She decided she must find a way of seeing him alone in order to offer herself to him again. His capitulation was now essential – her lust demanded satiation and made her reckless.

Chapter Thirteen

THEODORE surveyed the crush of people in the ballroom; at least 150 people had been invited this evening and it seemed that most were already here. The room, situated at the back of the house, had been liberally decorated with flowers and greenery, the best musicians had been hired for the evening and the chandeliers sparkled in the candlelight. In the adjoining rooms, tables struggled under the weight of cold ham, beef, roast quail, truffles and pheasant pie, while the finest wines, champagnes, jellies, tarts, soufflés and other confectionery delights had been supplied by Gunther's.

Hal, Julia and Lady Bramwell were still in the hall greeting arrivals and Theo, relieved to be excused from that duty, mingled with the guests and spoke to several acquaintances. Reaching the corner where the formidable array of dowagers was sitting, he was unable to avoid Aunt Jane, who motioned for him to join her. Aunt Jane was hard of hearing and for that reason alone, a two-way conversation would have been difficult, but she also had a never-ending flow of inconsequential chatter about the recent warm weather, Lady Sefton's jewels and Eliza Hennefer's flirtatious behaviour. As well as this, she insisted on calling him Hal and, recognizing he was fighting against an irresistible current, Theo gave up his feeble attempts to respond and merely smiled as Aunt Jane told him for the sixth time what a sweet boy he was. It was therefore with great relief when Theo noted Freddy's entrance into the ballroom.

'Dear Aunt Jane,' he said in a loud voice, jumping to his feet, 'you must excuse me because Mr Isherwood has arrived and I have a pressing matter of business to discuss with him.'

Aunt Jane blinked in surprise. 'One should not discuss such things at a ball!' she said, indignant. 'You young men are forever rushing about and scarcely have time to draw breath. Oh well, go if you must, but before you do, I must tell you about my rheumatism—' She stopped when she realized she was speaking to thin air: Theo was already heading across the room.

Theo disliked seeing his family or his friends miserable and, moved by the unhappy state of affairs between Julia and Freddy, he had spent at least a quarter of an hour that afternoon considering how to bring about a reconciliation.

He surmised that until they had quarrelled, Freddy would have visited almost every day, eager to accompany Julia on outings, shopping expeditions and even to that most tedious of places to Theo's mind, Almack's. Julia had no doubt given Freddy to understand that she wanted him to behave in this way, but Freddy did not know Julia as well as he did.

Theo loved his sister dearly but she was like other females: contrary creatures who said one thing and meant another. He had experienced Julia's contradictory behaviour in the past – if he told Julia a gown suited her, not five minutes later she had changed it for another; if she said she wanted Theo to drive her out to enjoy some fresh air, she actually wanted him to take her shopping. For Theo, all women, including his sister, never said exactly what they meant. With this in mind, and helped by some other specious reasoning, Theo had hit upon the notion that Freddy could solve the impasse with his sister by altering his tactics.

In Theo's opinion, Freddy should be less eager this evening. He should only admire Julia from afar; he should only indulge in conversation with her when the evening was well advanced and even then, give no indication of his feelings; he should only dance with other ladies and, finally, Freddy should wait before renewing his addresses. This behaviour would be the opposite of what Julia was expecting and, piqued that Freddy had not followed her slavishly, Julia would then snap out of her melancholy and beg him to marry her. All this seemed very reasonable to Theo; really, he thought, it was fortunate that he was here to smooth true love's path.

What was needed now was a quiet word with Freddy to convince him of the merits of this course, so Theo made his way through the crowd and cried, 'Freddy! Over here, if you can get through this crush.'

Freddy grinned in response and came over. 'Damn it, it's good to see you, Theo,' he said, shaking his hand, 'how are you? I heard about your lark up at Oxford.'

'Oh, that!' Theo gave a mischievous wink. 'Just high spirits, Freddy – you know how it is.'

'I know exactly – in my day, I had trouble with a travelling fair,' replied his companion, looking sheepish. 'These things blow over eventually.'

'I've been obliged to rusticate until the fuss dies down which is why you see me here this evening.'

'Hal has told me what happened with Lady Vane's son,' said Freddy. 'By God, I wish I had been here to help. You should have sent for me at Newmarket; you know I always stay at The Red Lion.'

Theo shook his head. 'There was no time. Luckily, we received help from an unexpected source and thank the Lord we did. However, all is now well and as this evening looks a sad crush, it will go down as one of the season's successes. It seems Ju is very popular.'

'She is,' agreed Freddy, with a sigh. 'I haven't been able to get near recently, no matter how hard I've tried – Hearn and Dryburgh are always in the way. We quarrelled, and I've been licking my wounds.' His expression brightened as he added, 'But I intend to make amends this evening.'

'Have you spoken to Julia yet?' asked Theo, in an urgent voice.

'No, she was engaged when I arrived so I spoke to Hal and

came straight in here. As soon as I can have a moment with Julia, I'll apologize and tell her exactly how I feel.'

'Then I'm glad I've managed to catch you first. If you take my advice, Freddy, you'll tell Julia no such thing.'

'Eh? Why on earth not?' said Freddy, puzzled. Then he added in concern, 'Damn it all, has she confided in you?'

'She told me that you had quarrelled, but no more.'

Freddy, his brow clearing, heaved a sigh of relief. 'Thank God! I thought you were going to tell me she hates me now. But then why the devil shouldn't I tell her how I feel?'

Theo patted him on the shoulder in a confiding gesture. 'Call it brotherly intuition, Freddy. Ju has been looking rather peaky in your absence, and having given the matter a great deal of thought, it struck me only today that she might need more time before you declare yourself. You know how females are.'

'No,' said Freddy, looking bemused. 'Frankly, I have no interest in other females, only Julia, so if you have any advice where she is concerned, tell me what it is.'

'Well, ladies always want you to do entirely the opposite to what they say,' explained Theo in a low voice. 'If Julia gives the impression she wants your company this evening, ten to one she means you should stay away from her. She's young and enjoying her first season; all the invitations and adoration she's had have probably turned her head a little. I've only recently arrived, but if I know you, Freddy, you've spent the last few weeks dangling after Julia like a love-struck numbskull.'

Freddy looked decidedly guilty at this and Theo nodded in satisfaction, pleased that his assumption had been correct. 'I knew it!' he said triumphantly. 'Now, my reasoning is if you crowd Julia tonight, you'll just annoy her. On the other hand, I'll lay you odds that if you stay in the background and give her the impression that you are nonchalant about the whole thing, she will be throwing herself on your chest and begging you to marry her just as soon as you can get a special licence.'

'Be nonchalant,' murmured Freddy, staring at his companion in amazement.

'Exactly!'

'... stay in the background,' continued Freddy.

'That is what I advise,' agreed Theo, nodding.

'... and don't crowd her!' concluded Freddy, his voice rising in disbelief.

'Must you keep repeating everything?' said Theo, testily. 'It is quite simple – staying away from Julia this evening will have the effect you desire and afterwards, my sister will want to drag you down the aisle as soon as possible.'

Freddy considered this for a moment or two in moody silence. Before he arrived, he had been perfectly clear what he should do next. Now, after Theo's words, he was undecided.

He had found the argument with Julia deeply upsetting and wondered if he had indeed been too possessive of her time since she had arrived in London. He was normally a sensible man and yet where Julia was concerned, sensible thought seemed to abandon him. Perhaps he had behaved like a jealous idiot, but while he was willing to beg her pardon for being too possessive, he could not and would not apologize for the strength of his love which had led him to behave so. He had come here tonight intending to ask for her hand in marriage, but Theo's advice had succeeded in putting doubts in his mind and Freddy began to wonder if he had settled on the right course.

He eyed Theo dubiously. 'Are you certain about this, Theo? It is not what I had planned. I intended to make a push this evening.'

'You see, Freddy,' observed Theo, with smiling satisfaction, 'just as I thought, you are all eagerness to claim Julia – understandable considering how madly you are in love with her – but if you will listen to me and appear indifferent, I'm certain that will be just the thing. In any event, most women prefer a lengthy courtship and are happy to drag things out a little.'

Still not entirely convinced, Freddy replied ironically, 'You seem to know an awful lot about how ladies' minds work, Theo. I cannot for the life of me imagine how you do because they are a complete mystery to me.'

'Having a sister helps – I've experienced the mysterious ways of Julia's mind many times,' replied Theo, grinning.

Freddy could not argue with this – he had only a younger brother – and with his resolve now beginning to crumble in the face of Theo's reasoning, Freddy simply muttered, 'Hmm,' in response. After a moment or two, he added in a bleak voice, 'Well, you must know your own sister so I suppose I had better take your advice.'

'Excellent! I knew you would rely on my judgement.'

During their conversation, Freddy's expression had changed from jovial to melancholic. He now observed the occupants of the ballroom with gloomy indifference, saying frankly, 'This will be deuced difficult. I want nothing more than to pour my heart out to your sister and I'd rather not stand around like a moon-ling if I can't. What should I do?'

'Why, keep me company at the card tables of course,' said Theo. 'Have a country dance or two with other damsels, just for appearance' sake, and then go to the card room.'

Freddy's jaw dropped. 'What! Hell's teeth, I shall be damned jealous anyway, and if I cannot have at least one dance with Julia ...' His voice trailed away and he shook his head at the prospect.

'Oh, very well,' said Theo, in a grudging tone, 'but do not engage in too much conversation.'

'This evening is not going to be anything like I imagined,' acknowledged his companion grimly.

When Isabella arrived, Lady Bramwell thought how lovely she looked. She was wearing a primrose silk gown with short full sleeves, a border of tulle trimmed with blonde lace decorated the hem and a fine shawl was draped over her arms. Contrary to the prevailing fashion, Isabella's jewellery and other acces-sories were minimal: she wore drop pearl ear-rings, while her golden hair was dressed high upon her head in a simple knot adorned with faux pearls and fresh flowers. Her beauty, always startling, was truly sublime this evening, with her cheeks delicately flushed and the sparkle of anticipation in her eyes.

Marguerite could not blame Hal, who stood to her right, for catching his breath audibly when he saw Isabella. As they exchanged greetings, each seemed to have eyes only for the other and Lady Bramwell smiled, thinking nothing would give her greater pleasure than for Isabella and Hal to find love.

Taking Isabella's hand, she said simply, 'You look charming, my dear.' After greeting Harriet, who was also looked attractive in a Pomona-green gown trimmed with lace, Marguerite continued, 'Let us go in together; most of the guests have already arrived and Jennings can deal with any latecomers.'

They went into the ballroom, Marguerite talking to Harriet, Julia searching the throng for Freddy, Isabella and Hal following closely behind.

'You look very beautiful this evening,' he murmured.

'I wanted to look my best tonight,' replied Isabella. 'I feel quite different lately and that is your doing.'

'Oh? What am I responsible for?'

Colour rose to her cheeks. 'You have made me aware again that I am a woman, Hal. I want you to find me attractive, not in a conceited way, but to please you, and only you.' She blushed deeper still and added, 'Oh dear, I'm not explaining myself very well, am I?'

'You have explained yourself perfectly, my love,' he said, his eyes fiercely intent upon her face. 'Dance with me, Isabella. I need to feel you in my arms, and dancing is the only way I can achieve that in these surroundings.'

He took her hand and she allowed Hal to lead her out to complete the set that was forming, no longer shocked by her immediate sensual reaction to him. It felt natural to have him near, to feel the solid strength of his body close to hers and she compared this to the revulsion that Edward had invoked. Until she had a quiet moment to ask him about Lady Portland, Isabella determined to enjoy herself.

This she did, and the next few hours passed by in a heady

whirl – Hal danced with her on three occasions, much to the obvious annoyance of many ladies present, led her into supper, procured her drinks, and showed no inclination to leave her side, thereby allowing none of the other gentlemen clamouring for her attention near.

During her third dance with Hal, Isabella noticed that Harriet was dancing with Sir Seymour, who was surprisingly light on his feet. 'Sir Seymour must have tempted Harriet to join him in another dance. How graceful he is.'

'Dinny usually puts the young beaux to shame with his elegant steps, although that lilac waistcoat is not so easy on the eye,' he replied, amusement curving his mouth.

'It is rather extravagant.'

He laughed. 'I would choose another description.'

'But his eccentricity gives no hint of his compassionate nature,' said Isabella. 'Sir Seymour was so kind when Dominic went missing and he has spoken to me since of his discussions with Henry Grey Bennet, and how they mean to do something about flash-houses.'

'Dinny is no fool,' agreed Hal. 'In spite of his foibles, he is a clever man who is willing to put some of his fortune and influence to good use. He will have my support in any efforts he makes in that direction. Does Dominic know that you have come here tonight?'

'Yes, he was disappointed that he could not come too, even though I told him he would be terribly bored.'

'Perhaps I can soften the blow: there is a balloon ascent in Hyde Park on Saturday and you are all invited to witness it from my barouche,' said Hal. 'Dominic will enjoy it, I'm sure. Theo, Julia and even my mother have expressed a wish to attend and no doubt Freddy will join us if he and Julia have resolved their quarrel. However, much as I love Dominic's company, I confess to feeling selfish this evening – I want you to myself, Isabella.'

'I feel the same,' she replied softly. 'I have spent long hours thinking and planning for my family and, while I have done it without complaint, it is delightful to forget that burden for a time and enjoy myself.'

His grip on her tightened and, pulling her closer, he said huskily, 'I mean to take every burden from your shoulders, my love, and bring pleasure into your life in many ways.' Then, he added in a rueful voice, 'You are the most abominable girl! Having vowed that I would be patient, all my good intentions have flown now I have you in my arms.'

She looked up at him wonderingly. 'And I believed that I was the cold creature Edward branded me, but you have shown me that I am not.'

'You were never that to me ... even when we first met, I glimpsed the warmth under that icy exterior.' Looking down into her charming upturned features, Hal uttered a faint groan. 'I can wait no longer when you mean so much to me,' he murmured. 'Isabella, although we have known each other only a short time, there is a question that I am desperate to ask you. Perhaps you can guess what it is.'

She replied after a pause, 'I think I can.'

'You don't feel I am rushing you?' he asked, a frown creasing his brow.

'Yes, a little,' she admitted, 'but I forgive you because of the sentiments behind your haste. I can't fight what I feel for you any more – the intensity of it frightens me, but I can't go back now because you have brought my soul to life again. I have waited years to find you, Hal – I thought I never would – so I welcome your ... question.'

His frown lifted. 'Thank God,' he said, in an unsteady voice. 'I was worried you might step on my toes to punish my impetuosity.'

'There is still time – the *particular* way you are looking at me is making everyone stare,' she replied, a twinkle of amusement in her gaze.

'Let them!' declared Hal. The dance was almost over so he added, 'I am obliged to circulate a little this evening, my darling. Will you meet me, alone, in half an hour when I have done my duty?'

Her fingers clung to his, anticipation singing through her veins as she whispered, 'Where shall I find you?' A note of alarm sounded in Isabella's mind when she remembered Lady Portland, but happiness made her impulsive and she pushed it aside.

'In the garden. Leave through the doors on the far side of the room; outside, there is a walk, hedged with yew, and beyond that a small lawn enclosed by trees. I'll wait for you there. The evening is growing cool, but I promise you will not be cold, my love,' he said, a gleam of rakish devilment in his eyes.

As the music drew to a close, she replied, 'I promise I will be there, Hal.'

Neither Hal nor Isabella had yet seen Lady Portland, who had arrived late with Lady Cumberland. However, Felicity, mingling with the other guests without a shred of embarrassment, had noticed Lord Bramwell and Lady Vane dancing together and from their warm glances and shared smiles, they appeared very much in love. Resentment and jealousy flared inside her. She still intended to offer herself to Hal again: to count him as a conquest was both a searing need and a matter of pride.

Across the room, Lady Bramwell and Julia had noted their uninvited guest with astonishment.

'I cannot believe that woman has had the effrontery to come here,' said Marguerite furiously. 'Jennings confirmed that she arrived with Lady Cumberland; he had no choice but to admit her, of course.'

'Should we ask her to leave?'

'We could, but she is quite shameless and an awkward scene might ensue. Perhaps she is curious and wants to see how our family goes along without her.'

'No,' said Julia, shaking her head. 'She is determined to pursue Hal.'

'Then I shall ask Hal's opinion on what is to be done, but I feel it would be best if we just keep a wary eye on Lady Portland.

After all, the evening is well advanced and even she can do no harm in an hour or two.'

Julia shuddered. 'Don't underestimate Felicity Portland. Thank God that Hal escaped her clutches!'

'That is in the past, and what Hal does now is no business of Lady Portland's. I cannot see what she hopes to gain by coming here, but maybe after seeing Hal with Isabella this evening, Felicity will accept that he is lost to her forever.'

'I am not as sanguine as you, Mama.'

Lady Bramwell looked at her daughter with a puzzled expression. 'Julia, this is your evening, an event you have been looking forward to for months – do not let Felicity Portland ruin it. I know you too well and, despite outward appearances to the contrary, you are unhappy. Why have you danced only once with Freddy?'

'Because he only asked me once,' said Julia sadly. 'It seems that I have upset him more than I realized: he is staying well away from me and even when we danced, he was not his usual self – he was cold and distant, and seemed uncomfortable while I, in turn, was embarrassed and could not find the words for the apology I intended to give.' She bit her lip. 'Perhaps he hates me now.'

'If Freddy's love has turned to hate then he is not the man I think he is,' replied her mother, pragmatically. 'His behaviour is a little strange, but perhaps he still feels awkward after your quarrel. I am sure that you will be reconciled by the end of the evening.'

'I hope so,' replied Julia, but with no real conviction. She could not convey the depths of her disappointment, and despondency. She felt hurt by Freddy's indifference. Dressed in her new blue gown and with her hair arranged in a most becoming style, she had taken a great deal of trouble over her appearance. All her efforts had been for Freddy alone and although she had received numerous compliments from her other admirers, none of it had meant as much as a few words of praise from Freddy would have done. However, he had merely stated rather mechanically how fine she looked before returning to the card room.

She had tried to articulate her sorrow and regret at their quarrel, but for once, all her verbal skills deserted her in the face of Freddy's stony silence and the words had stuck in her throat. Julia could have cried with frustration; she loved Freddy and the notion that a silly quarrel had caused this reaction confused and appalled her.

She had even asked Theo what he thought of Freddy's behaviour this evening, only for Theo to reply that Freddy seemed fine to him. Perhaps, he had suggested breezily, Freddy was allowing her the freedom to enjoy her debut ball. Julia had made no reply, but she had wanted to scream that was the last thing she desired.

Hal paced the lawn, waiting for Isabella. It was a warm evening; the scent of honeysuckle filled the air and a light breeze rustled through the surrounding trees. Distant strains of soothing music floated out from ballroom, and the garden was dimly lit by the full moon which occasionally appeared from behind the clouds skittering across the sky.

There could be no more perfect setting for what he wanted to say to Isabella. He felt apprehensive, but anticipation pulsed through him as he tried to piece together a suitable speech, laughing softly at his ineptitude as he did so. Hearing a footfall from behind the hedge, a smile of greeting began to curve his mouth – it soon died when he saw that it was Lady Portland and not Isabella who stood before him.

Hal had been furious that she had come here without an invitation, but his mother had dissuaded him from asking her to leave, saying that Lady Portland could only harm her own reputation. Hal had capitulated in deference to his mother's wishes and because of his haste to meet Isabella. But now, seeing Felicity Portland before him, anger rose again in his breast – was this woman to spoil even this moment? He drew in a deep breath to calm his fury; Felicity could not know who he intended to meet.

'Hal,' she murmured seductively as she approached. 'I saw you come out here and followed you – there is something I need to say.'

'Then say it and let that be an end to any communication between us.'

'Do not be hasty – you may regret it.'

'I doubt that,' he replied brusquely, anxious to be rid of her. 'What do you want?'

'You,' said Lady Portland. She gave a provocative smile and moved closer, allowing her shawl to slip and reveal the low *décolletage* of her gown. Gazing up at him, she whispered, 'It was always you, Hal. I was a fool to choose Portland and I have regretted it ever since, even more so since I returned to London and saw you again. I know that we could enjoy each other's company.'

'Despite being familiar with your methods, I am still shocked by your boldness,' he said. 'Your offer leaves me unmoved.'

'Don't you care for me just a little?' she purred, running her gloved hands over his chest.

He moved away and said through gritted teeth, 'No. Let me explain in clear terms because you seem to find it hard to understand what I am saying. I never cared for you, Felicity; it was just a foolish, youthful infatuation. I realized afterwards how lucky I was that you chose Portland, and I do not want you now.' Hal, his expression bleak, enunciated each word that followed with bitter emphasis, 'You mean nothing to me. Is that plain enough?'

This time, Felicity was a little taken aback, but she replied, 'If you truly do not care for me anymore, I must accept that. However, I am still willing to offer myself without affection on your side. You see, I want you so much that my blood is burning. I can think of nothing else so I am asking – no, begging – you to quell that desire and then I will go away. Indeed, I have no shame.' She laughed, her breasts rising and falling with her quickened breathing. *"Careless lust stirs up a desperate courage"* – rather appropriate for me, is it not? You may be married soon so what harm is there in a brief liaison before then? Please, Hal,' she said, stepping towards him again, 'you must do this.'

As she did so, Felicity looked over Hal's shoulder to see Isabella watching them from a distance. Hal, who had not noticed her arrival, gave Felicity a pitying glance and her anger flared: she did not want his pity. He was going to refuse her, finally and completely – she knew it and hated him, and Isabella.

'I actually feel sorry for you—' he began in a hard voice.

But Felicity could not let him utter the refusal and, seeing her opportunity, quickly slid her arms around his neck and kissed him. From under half-closed lids, she watched Isabella turn away and leave.

Incensed, he thrust her away and wiped his hand across his lips. 'Damn you! I believe you are mad. Go, before I lose my temper completely!'

Her mouth twisted in a parody of a smile. 'Very well. Such a pity that you will not accept my offer – we would have dealt extremely well together.'

She pushed past him, but she had not finished yet. After smoothing her gown and composing herself from the exertion of hurrying back to the house, she looked for, and found, Isabella. She was alone in one of the side rooms, half hidden behind an ornate screen and Felicity noted with satisfaction her hunted, distrait expression.

Isabella watched Lady Portland's approach with trepidation. Reeling from what she had seen, she had stumbled back inside, desperate to find somewhere to be alone and collect her thoughts.

She had no wish to converse with this woman, but it seemed that she was to be left no choice as Lady Portland came straight towards her. Isabella felt her body go rigid, and the air seemed suddenly oppressive and heavy with tension.

Felicity arched a brow. 'Lady Vane, is it not?'

'Yes – I am Lady Vane,' replied Isabella, 'and I have heard

about you, Lady Portland, and your connection to Lord Bramwell.'

'Oh, but you cannot know everything about my connection with Hal. I am sorry that you witnessed our caress a few moments ago, but you should appreciate how matters stand.'

'What do you mean?' asked Isabella curtly.

'Simply that Hal and I still care for each other.'

Isabella's lip curled in derision. 'That cannot be true. Hal has told me that you mean nothing to him and he has no reason to lie.'

'Think that if it pleases you, Lady Vane, but he does have a reason,' murmured Felicity.

'I do not believe you.'

Despite this denial, Lady Portland saw the indecision in Isabella's eyes and pounced. She gave a trill of mocking laughter. 'You are so naïve – an innocent indeed – I declare it is quite endearing. Of course he has a reason: surely you know that you are referred to as the Ice Angel in the clubs, for your beauty but also for your reserve? Wagers have been lodged as to how long it would be before you thawed and allowed someone near.'

'Wagers?' echoed Isabella faintly.

'Gentlemen gamble on the slightest thing, my dear,' declared Lady Portland. 'They will gamble on one raindrop beating another down the window pane, so they will not miss the opportunity to bet on thawing the Ice Angel.'

There was silence for a moment as Isabella struggled to take in what she was hearing; a dreaded realization was slowly dawning. 'And Hal is involved in this – this wager?' she murmured.

Lady Portland gave a cold smile. 'Of course,' she snapped mendaciously. 'Why do you think he has been so persistent in his attentions? You must admire his determination. Why, he has scarcely left your side this evening – evidence enough for everyone to see that he has succeeded and now he stands to win a great deal of money.' She studied Isabella's anguish with dispassion. 'But I am shocked that you had no inkling of this when most of London knows of it.'

Isabella shook her head in disbelief. 'I must ask him if this is true.'

'Don't expect him to admit to it. In my experience, Lady Vane, gentlemen are rarely truthful and Hal is no exception. Do not take it to heart – it was only dalliance on Hal's part. He was always going to return to me after winning the wager.' She shrugged. 'Now I see that you were indeed unaware of this and are distressed, but it was very stupid of you to care for him, my dear.'

Satisfied that her words had achieved the desired effect, Lady Portland swept away to demand that her carriage be brought immediately to the front door.

A stray tear trickled down Isabella's face and she brushed it aside impatiently. Bewildered and confused, the only thought that registered was Hal's betrayal. His professions of love had been empty, meaningless and uttered only in pursuit of winning a disgusting wager. Bitterly, she remembered how he had talked of having no secrets, yet he had used her to win a bet which was the talk of the London clubs.

Isabella recalled his reaction yesterday when he assumed she had had a change of heart. Little wonder he appeared so relieved by her answer when a moment earlier he must have thought winning was in doubt. She was a laughing stock, which was hateful enough when she had craved obscurity, but Hal's treachery was far worse. While she did not like Lady Portland, twice she had seen their intimacy with her own eyes and now Lady Portland's cruel words had the ring of truth; Isabella knew that gambling was a pastime which most men indulged in, some to excess.

Once again she had allowed herself to be deceived. This evening Hal had wanted to demonstrate to society that he had succeeded and, like an unsuspecting fool, she had complied. No doubt he had arranged to meet her in the garden to tell her that she was of no further interest.

She had to leave – she didn't want to see Hal ever again.

Finding her way to the hall through the library and then the morning-room to avoid meeting Hal or any of his family, she told Jennings that she was going home because she was unwell. Agitated, Isabella then stepped outside to wait for her carriage, where she met Mr Isherwood.

He seemed distracted, but peered carefully at Isabella. 'Are you all right, Lady Vane?'

Isabella could not deny her distress. 'No – something has upset me and I will be leaving London very soon.'

'Sorry to hear that,' said Freddy, who was the worse for drink and trying to marshal his thoughts. 'When?'

'First thing tomorrow, if it can be arranged,' she replied, her tone bitter.

He shook his head sadly. 'I've had the most abominable evening too – came out here to get away.' Freddy, looking up, observed, 'Lady Vane, I don't like the idea of you travelling alone. Can I assist in any way?'

Isabella murmured, 'No, thank you – I will have to organize everything myself. Oh, where is my carriage?' She turned back to Freddy, who was once more asking to help with her journey. 'What about Lady Julia? You can't leave London, for her sake.'

Freddy grimaced and set his jaw pugnaciously. 'That's where the trouble lies and I'm dam— deuced if I'm going to stay here to see her fêted by Hearn and Dryburgh when I can't do a thing about it.'

He persisted in his offer and, as her carriage had now arrived, Isabella had no time to argue further. She capitulated and asked him to meet her in Curzon Street at an agreed time, after making him swear that he would not breathe a word to anyone, particularly Lord Bramwell, about her destination.

Freddy, watching her carriage move out of the square, decided to go home too. He had endured the most difficult evening of his life and felt depressed as well as drunk. He did not normally drink to excess, but he had been driven to it by unhappiness. Julia's sad looks in his direction had made him feel wretched and he wondered if Theo had been mistaken in his advice.

Freddy knew now that he could no longer bear to be away from Julia and needed to see her as soon as he had shaken off the effects of his potation. Suddenly, his befogged brain remembered his promise to Lady Vane. Putting a hand through his hair, he groaned aloud. There was nothing for it but to be as good as his word and accompany Lady Vane on her journey. He would be out of town for a day or two at most and must lay his heart at Julia's feet when he returned.

While Freddy was reaching this decision, Hal was still waiting for Isabella in the garden.

Chapter Fourteen

HAL felt incredulous at Lady Portland's shameless proposition. Felicity had always prided herself on her ability
to attract a man's attention and obviously she could not
comprehend that she had failed with him. He had toyed with
returning to the house to demand her departure, but,
knowing Isabella would arrive soon, he had decided to wait
and let the balmy evening air soothe his anger.

But when Isabella did not appear, Hal grew anxious.
Something must have happened because he did not believe that
she would stay away without good reason. Then, his anxiety
began to merge with suspicion; he had seen the vicious look
Felicity Portland had directed at Isabella in the park and she
had seen them together again this evening. Felicity must have
recognized by now his relationship with Isabella was serious.
His mind racing, Hal considered another possibility, one that
appalled him ... perhaps Isabella had come outside earlier. That
would explain why the damned Portland woman had thrown
herself at him. Pushing his hand through his hair in agitation,
he strode towards the house, all the while cursing himself for a
fool: if what was he was surmising was true, it was imperative
he find Isabella.

He ran the final yards and searched the ballroom and the
side rooms, soon realizing that Isabella was nowhere to be
seen. Instead, he sought out his mother, who was in the hall
with some departing guests and, drawing her aside, he
demanded, 'Have you seen Isabella? We had arranged to meet

in the garden, but she never appeared and now I cannot find her.'

'Jennings has this moment informed me that she left a short while ago,' replied Lady Bramwell. 'She left a message that she was feeling unwell, but it seems she did not say goodbye to anyone.'

A frown creased Hal's brow. 'I don't believe she is ill. She would have sent word to me if she was. I fear Lady Portland has spoken to her and, by God, if she has upset Isabella, I swear I will deal with her harshly.' He turned to leave, but Marguerite laid a detaining hand on his arm.

'Wait, Hal. Lady Portland also left – shortly before Isabella, according to Jennings.'

'Devil take her!' muttered Hal fiercely. 'The woman is mad with spite and jealousy, and I should have guessed she would cause trouble somehow.'

Lady Bramwell had not connected Isabella and Lady Portland's sudden departures, but seeing Hal's turmoil she was also growing concerned. 'What could she have said to make Isabella leave, Hal? Lady Portland is spiteful, but Isabella is too sensible to be affected by comments about her dress or her place in society.'

'I don't know, but I intend to go to Curzon Street and find out.'

'But if you are mistaken and Isabella is ill, you will not be able to see her until morning.'

Hal shook his head, knowing instinctively that he was right. 'I'll lay my life that she has left because of Lady Portland.'

'It is two o'clock in the morning,' said his mother. 'If Isabella has been upset by that woman, you can talk to her first thing tomorrow and put matters right.'

At that moment, Hal would have gladly broken the hinges off the elegant front door of Lady Bingham's town house to speak to Isabella, but, much as he hated to acknowledge it, it was too late to see her now.

Just then, a flustered-looking Harriet appeared with Sir Seymour following close behind. 'Lady Bramwell, I have just heard that Isabella is ill and has sent the carriage back for me,' said Harriet. 'How strange – she seemed perfectly well earlier. Perhaps it is a sudden headache brought on by the stress of Dominic's disappearance.'

'It would be understandable if that is the case,' said Sir Seymour.

'Would you give Lady Vane a message from me, Mrs Forster?' said Hal in an urgent voice.

'Of course. I'm sure that she is sorry at having to return home unexpectedly.'

'Will you tell her … can you ask her not to believe—' Hal hesitated, frustration etched on his face and then he sighed, raking his fingers through his hair once more and muttering under his breath, 'No, it is useless. I cannot explain without seeing her.' He looked up and spoke again to Harriet. 'Tell Lady Vane that I will call in the morning and that I wish to speak to her as soon as possible.'

Harriet smiled reassuringly, thinking Lord Bramwell's concern was for Isabella's health. 'I am certain that she will have recovered by then, Lord Bramwell. Call as soon as you wish after breakfast – we shall be at home.'

'Will ten o'clock be convenient?'

Harriet nodded. 'Ah, here is the carriage! Thank you for a most enjoyable evening, Lady Bramwell.'

'Please give Isabella our best wishes,' she replied.

Sir Seymour, moving forward and bowing low over Harriet's hand, said, 'Goodnight, Mrs Forster. If I may, I shall also call tomorrow morning – that is, I would like to enquire about Lady Vane's health.'

'We shall look forward to it,' replied Harriet with a smile, as she wrapped her shawl around her against the night air.

Hal watched Harriet's departure with an unseeing gaze. Convinced that Lady Portland had unleashed her spite, he did not know whether she had slandered him or Isabella, but either way, there was nothing else he could do this evening.

Lady Bramwell, who had been watching painful emotions flit

across Hal's features, saw Julia come into the hall. She noted that her daughter looked pale and had abandoned all pretence of enjoyment.

'Has anyone seen Freddy?' asked Julia.

Hal raised his brows. 'Not this past hour. Is he in the card room?'

'No, he finished his last game some time ago.'

Her mother suggested, 'Perhaps he is with Theo.'

'Who?' asked Theo cheerfully, joining the family gathering.

'Freddy,' explained his sister. 'I can't find him anywhere.'

'Do you know, it's a deuced strange thing, but I can't find him either. He was a trifle foxed – been drinking a bit too deep and was as moody as a bear – so I think he may have gone home. He knew I wanted another hand of piquet before he left, too,' said Theo.

Jennings, until now an interested but silent observer of these events, decided to speak at this juncture and addressed Lady Bramwell in a low voice, 'If you will pardon my intrusion, Lady Bramwell, Mr Isherwood has indeed left – I saw him depart after Lady Vane.'

Overhearing this, Julia declared in a faltering voice, 'Oh! Then m-my evening is ruined.'

'That is unlike Freddy,' said Hal.

Theo nodded, adding cryptically, 'Knew you would react that way, Ju.'

'What are you talking about?' demanded Julia, eyeing Theo with suspicion through moist eyes.

'Oh, nothing … I'm sure you'll see Freddy soon.'

Lady Bramwell intervened. 'Oh dear, it seems everyone's affairs are in a tangle. You had best go to bed, Julia. Don't despair – Freddy will receive a note inviting him to take coffee with us tomorrow and I will ensure you are left undisturbed until you have sorted out your problems.' She turned to her eldest son. 'Perhaps you should go to bed too, Hal.'

He shook his head, his mood sombre. 'I cannot sleep – I'll be in the library.'

'I understand. Theo and I will stay with our remaining guests.'

'Oh, Lord,' said Theo, uttering a groan. 'If I have to endure another conversation with Aunt Jane, I won't get to bed until five o'clock!'

When Harriet arrived back in Curzon Street and observed the glow of candlelight under Isabella's bedroom door, she was surprised; she had assumed Isabella would have retired to bed. However, as Harriet opened the door, it was clear that Isabella was not asleep, nor even in her nightgown – she was fully dressed and placing clothes into a portmanteau. She glanced up as Harriet entered, but continued with her task.

Harriet, having looked on in silent astonishment for a moment, asked, 'What are you doing?'

'Packing,' replied Isabella. 'We are leaving London first thing tomorrow.'

'Leaving London?' echoed Harriet faintly, 'To go where?'

'Haystacks.'

'But Haystacks is not ready yet—' began Harriet. Then she saw the shimmer of tears in Isabella's eyes. 'Oh, my dear, what has distressed you?'

Isabella bit her lip. 'I would rather not explain now, Harriet. There is little time if we are to be ready.'

'But I do not want to leave London,' said her aunt. 'We are comfortable here and are not due to go to Sussex for several weeks. Has your decision something to do with Dominic? If so—'

'No,' interjected Isabella, pausing to look up. She drew in a deep breath and said, 'It has nothing to do with Dominic.'

'Then why? It is unfair of you to do this without a word of explanation.'

'You are right – it is selfish to expect you to come with us,' said Isabella. 'Stay, if you wish, but I will have to swear you to secrecy as to my whereabouts.'

Harriet sighed. 'That was not what I meant, Isabella. If you believe it is necessary to leave London, then I would not dream of letting you go alone, but tell me what is behind this sudden decision.'

'Lord Bramwell has betrayed my trust,' she murmured. 'I have discovered that he does not care for me and has only courted my affection to win a wager.' As Isabella observed Harriet's shocked expression, she added bitterly, 'Apparently, I am known as the Ice Angel in every gentleman's club in London and listed in their betting books. Lord Bramwell took up the challenge to thaw me and tonight, he has won his hateful wager in full view of society. I never want to see him again and that is the reason for my haste. Please do not ask me any more now because I cannot bring myself to speak of it.' She ended on a sob, and covered her face with her hands.

Harriet, her tender heart stirred, embraced her niece. 'Isabella, I hate to see you like this ... hush.' When Isabella's tears had subsided a little, Harriet ventured, 'It seems impossible to me that Lord Bramwell could act in so dishonourable a fashion, but you obviously believe this to be true. Indeed, I had wondered if you were beginning to care for him and now I see that you do.'

'I love him, Harriet, and that makes his betrayal even more painful,' replied Isabella, wiping her remaining tears away angrily. 'What a fool I've been! I believed everything Lord Bramwell said, in spite of an insistent doubt, but after what I have seen and heard this evening, I must listen to my head rather than my heart.'

'Shouldn't you speak with him before we leave?'

Shaking her head, Isabella returned to her packing. 'He would deny it anyway. Dominic will be upset, but he will recover.' Then, she added in a whisper, 'My heart will not.'

'It seems incredible that Lord Bramwell could be involved,' said Harriet. 'I hoped that you cared for him because—' She hesitated, and then, collecting herself, added, 'Perhaps that explanation is also for another time. My dear, I would like to stay in London, but I cannot bear to see you unhappy again so we shall all leave tomorrow. Have you ordered the carriage?'

'I have asked for it to be brought to the door at six.'

'Then we shall be gone before Lord Bramwell arrives. When he realized you had left without saying goodnight, he seemed agitated.'

Isabella started in alarm. 'Does he come here now?'

'No, he thought better of it, but he said that it was imperative he talked to you so I suggested he called at ten o'clock tomorrow – you see, I had no idea what had happened.'

'I'm sorry, but my one thought was to get away. Harriet, Mr Isherwood is to accompany us.' Isabella explained how this had come about, then continued, 'I agreed, albeit reluctantly, but I made him promise not to speak a word of this to his friend.'

Harriet nodded and sighed. 'Running away is not the right thing to do in my opinion, but it seems I cannot persuade you otherwise at present. Work at Haystacks will not be finished so we must make the best of what we find there.'

Harriet left Isabella shortly afterwards, bearing instructions for the staff and a parcel, addressed to Lord Bramwell, which was to be delivered to Berkeley Square after their departure.

For Lord Bramwell to have sought Isabella's attentions merely to win a wager sounded nonsensical to Harriet. However, she alone knew the details of her niece's marriage and the circumstances surrounding Edward's death, both of which had resulted in Isabella's insecurity and lack of trust. While Harriet did not agree with her decision to leave, she understood why to do so would be Isabella's instinctive response. But how to address her own affairs? After some thought, Harriet wrote a letter which she gave to a footman before returning to her own packing with a heavy heart.

The following morning, Mr Isherwood's valet Simpkins pulled back the curtains in his master's bedchamber to reveal a fine dawn. He placed a steaming cup of coffee next to the bed and said, 'Sir, it is five o'clock.'

After a few minutes, his master stirred. However, he did not speak, but instead buried his head underneath the pillow so Simpkins tried again, 'You have an appointment in one hour, sir.'

Freddy moaned. He emerged from under the pillow, opened one eye and grimaced; even that movement caused hammer blows to fall inside his skull. Regarding his valet balefully, he mumbled, 'Simpkins, you are mistaken – I have been asleep for half an hour at most. For pity's sake, go back to bed.'

Simpkins, who had been in his master's employ for several years, grinned as he recognized the after effects of overindulgence in drink. 'I am sorry, sir, but that is the correct time. In fact, it is now five minutes past five. There is coffee on the table if you would care to take some.' After a diplomatic pause, he continued, 'May I suggest that the coffee would ease your dry mouth?'

Eyes closed, Freddy growled in a menacing fashion. 'No, you may not. You and the damned coffee will be consigned to the fiery reaches of Hell if you do not leave me in peace.'

Valiantly, Simpkins did not flinch. 'Such sentiments are understandable considering your ... er ... delicate constitution this morning, but you were insistent that you be woken at this time, in spite of, if I may be so bold as to use your words, sir, "whatever insults I might throw at you".'

Freddy, his eyes now fully open despite the pain, looked bemused. 'Did I say that? Now why on earth—?' Suddenly, he recalled the events of the previous evening. 'Good God, I promised Lady Vane!' He sat up, clutching his head between his hands and groaning again as more hammer blows fell. 'Now I remember – I had a terrible evening, and took refuge in the bottle.'

Following this speech, Freddy moistened his dry lips and owlishly eyed his valet. Through the fog of pain, and struggling with a mouth and tongue which felt as if they belonged to someone else, Freddy noticed that Simpkins was trying, and failing, to keep his expression impassive. Freddy considered the woeful picture he must be presenting and his lips twitched.

'Simpkins,' he began, in a sardonic, threatening voice, 'I need to have shaved, dressed, written a note of instruction to my groom and present myself in Curzon Street, looking respectable and lucid of mind, within forty-five minutes – preferably less. You will assist me to achieve this, or you will receive not only more insults, but the contents of this cup aimed at your head. You will also be looking for new employment. Is that clear?'

'Perfectly, sir,' came the reply. As he moved away to fetch some hot water, the valet's shoulders shook with silent mirth.

Chapter Fifteen

LADY Portland was sitting up in bed when her maid delivered the message, '*Madame! Madame!* You have a gentleman visitor.'

'What nonsense is this, Celeste?' replied her mistress in irritation. 'It is half past ten – no gentleman calls upon a lady so early.'

Celeste threw out her hands, saying indignantly. 'I tell the truth, *madame*. Your visitor is in the library and he says he will not leave until he has spoken to you.' She looked slyly under her lashes at her employer. 'He is very handsome – I should be pleased to see such a man at any time.'

Felicity looked up. 'Who is it?'

'Lord Bramwell, *madame*.'

A slow smile curved Felicity's lips. 'So, he has changed his mind and prefers me to that milk-and-water miss after all.' She scrambled out of bed and added, 'Hurry, Celeste! Help me to get dressed. I shall wear the dark-green muslin – no, wait – it must be the blue silk: it is more becoming. Where is Lord Portland?'

'Still in his bedchamber, *madame*. I understand he returned late from his club and has not yet called for his valet.'

'Excellent. Tell the other servants that Lord Bramwell and I are not to be disturbed.'

'Of course, *madame*,' said Celeste, with a knowing smile.

A short while later, Felicity went downstairs and opened the library door. Hal stood at the window, his tall figure silhouetted against the sun as he looked out on to the street. He turned round and for a moment, she could not see his expression because his features were in shadow.

She walked towards him with hands outstretched, saying, 'I knew you would think again and come to me—'

Felicity stopped abruptly when she saw his face. His features might have been carved out of stone, so grim and merciless was his expression. Narrowed eyes and the set of his shoulders spoke eloquently of towering rage, but this was different to the anger she had witnessed in him last night. It was implacable, unyielding and, for the first time in her life, Felicity felt vulnerable and a little afraid of being alone with a man.

He had not uttered a word and, in an effort to break the tense silence, she said, 'I thought you had decided to accept my offer, but I see now that is not the case.' His mouth tightened, but still he did not speak and she gave a nervous laugh. 'Have you lost your tongue, Hal?'

'Don't play games, Felicity,' he said tersely.

Clasping her hands together, she stammered, 'I – I have not the least idea why you should come here, other than to accept my offer.'

'I know that you said or did something to upset Lady Vane last night and I swear by the Almighty if you do not tell me – at once – what you have done, I will choke the truth out of you.'

Her eyes widened in shock and, in an involuntary action, she put her hand to her slim, white throat. His low tone made her shiver and Felicity did not doubt he meant every word. She hesitated, then said, 'I recall now that I did speak to her briefly.'

His eyes glinted. 'I await the details with bated breath.'

'We – we talked of you.'

'That much I had guessed,' he snapped. 'Continue.'

'Well, I … that is, I told her that we still cared for each other,' said Felicity.

His lip curled in derision. 'A complete lie. What else?'

Lady Portland shrugged. 'Does it matter?'

'Yes – what else did you say?'

Goaded by his manner, Felicity abandoned all pretence and

with a note of exultation in her voice admitted, 'I said that you had courted her only to win a wager – a wager running in the gentlemen's clubs to thaw the Ice Angel. Stupidly, she believed every word. It was easy enough to convince her, especially as I made certain that she saw me kiss you in the garden – she was watching us.'

'My God,' he muttered under his breath, moving towards her. 'Your lies have done more damage than you know. I hope you are satisfied.'

She flinched under his blazing gaze, but shrugged her shoulders again. 'Not particularly. I have still not obtained what I really wanted – you – but it was worth it to see the shock on Lady Vane's face at your supposed perfidy. Her love for you must be great indeed if she can be so easily persuaded.'

Hal's arm shot forward and his long fingers fastened around her wrist. Jaw clenched, he hissed, 'I would knock you to the ground if you were a man,' before releasing her and turning away.

Lady Portland rubbed the skin where his fingers had gripped. Realizing he was controlling himself only with visible effort and that she had pushed him to the limit, she tried to assuage some of his anger. Giving a trill of laughter, she exclaimed, 'What a mountain you make of this! If you and Lady Vane are so much in love, you can tell her that you were not involved – that it was all a lie, invented by me and what she saw in the garden was not what it seemed. If you think it necessary, I will write a letter, or even see her in person, to admit what I have done.'

He turned back to face her. 'How magnanimous of you to offer help after instigating the problem,' he replied sardonically. 'And how conceited of you to think that we would need or desire your intervention.'

Flushing, she retaliated, 'I know I am spiteful and shallow – it is my nature – but that need not worry you because I shall stay out of your way in future. Go to your Isabella! I wish both of you joy.'

'I called in Curzon Street before I came here – she has already left Town and I have no idea where she has gone,' he said in a bitter voice.

She gave him a look of astonishment. 'Surely the servants know?'

'I had already considered that,' he flung back in disgust, 'but either they do not know or have been sworn to secrecy. However, I will find her and afterwards, we shall have the kind of happiness you can only imagine. As for you ... if you ever interfere with me or my family again, Lady Portland, you will discover what invoking my wrath will bring down upon you.'

Felicity was growing to hate as well as fear his low-pitched even tone. 'I am a respectable woman, married to a wealthy man of good standing – how could you hurt me?' she asked warily.

'You are tolerated if your affairs do not become food for gossip. However, I could ensure that your behaviour becomes common knowledge, that you are discussed in every drawing-room, gentleman's club and ballroom in London until you are no longer welcome in London society, and perhaps elsewhere. You would be shunned and receive no invitations or morning calls from those whose company you have been enjoying the past few weeks. Have you any idea what it would be like for someone of your character to be an outcast, completely ostracized by polite society?' She shuddered but made no reply, and he smiled mirthlessly. 'I thought the prospect would not appeal. You have gone too far and your lies have touched someone dear to me. Stay away or I swear that you will regret it until the end of your days.'

He strode to the door and Felicity breathed a sigh of relief, glad that this extremely uncomfortable interview was drawing to a close.

Then, he turned back. 'I almost forgot to mention it – do not attempt to attend Almack's again.'

'Why ... what have you done?' she asked, startled by this cryptic comment.

'I was prepared for your treachery. Last night, I composed a letter to the patronesses which, following this conversation, they will receive within the next half an hour. I will not trouble you with the exact contents, but suffice to say I have mentioned your scandalous appearance at Julia's ball and also hinted that when you lived on the Continent, your sympathies, both moral and financial, lay with Napoleon rather than with Wellington and his allies.'

Felicity gasped as she realized the import of what he had said. 'But that's not true!'

'Oh, nothing is stated as fact; I have merely alluded to your guilt. The patronesses will not mention it outside their circle, but with matters reaching another crisis across the Channel, any hint of disloyalty will mean your exclusion.' His lips twisted into a sinister smile. 'There will be whispers and conjecture, of course, and you will have to live with the constant fear of exposure, but perhaps this will stop you interfering in other people's affairs once and for all.'

'Damn you, Hal!' she cried, but he made no reply as he left the room.

Lady Portland stared blankly ahead. To be denounced for scandal was bad enough, but to be branded, albeit in whispers behind cupped hands, as a traitor was quite another and she swallowed nervously, knowing that anti-French feeling was running high in England.

She sank into a chair and remained there for some time until she decided that breakfast might steady her nerves. She was still lingering over her coffee and musing on whether to accept Lord Taylor's amorous advances after all, when her husband entered the breakfast parlour. The vision of Lord Portland, ruddy of complexion and grimacing at his gout, seemed oddly comforting for once and Felicity went to him, throwing her arms around his neck. 'My dearest, I have been waiting for you.'

He did not return her embrace. 'Have you?' he replied. 'Well, that is most gratifying, since my valet informs me you have been entertaining Lord Bramwell.'

She looked at him from under her lashes and, seeing his sullen expression, decided to make light of it. 'Really, Portland,' she replied with a tinkling laugh. 'I am a married woman. There is no scandal in me receiving a gentleman in my own house, in full view of my husband and servants.'

His expression did not change as he asked in a brusque voice, 'What did he want, Felicity?'

'Oh, nothing to speak of,' she said, nonchalantly. 'He enquired after our health and asked about the Continent – he has a mind to take his new wife there, if events will allow it.'

'Hmm, that sounds implausible, but let us leave that subject for the moment while you explain why you went to Lady Julia Cavanagh's ball without an invitation?'

Felicity was taken by surprise; she had not expected to be questioned by her placid and malleable husband. 'Do not be angry with me, Portland. It was Lady Cumberland's fault – she convinced me to go with her against my better judgement.'

'You should have refused, madam,' he said, grimly. 'Indulgent I may be, but I do not appreciate being made a damned laughing stock! Dryburgh told everyone at the club how you appeared uninvited at Berkeley Square. I was furious to hear my wife being discussed in that manner, but I was forced to remain silent – your actions were indefensible.'

'Oh! Please, do not—'

'And now I find you have transgressed again by meeting Lord Bramwell alone this morning,' continued Lord Portland inexorably. 'I suspected that you have cuckolded me for some time, but I was prepared to tolerate it as long as you were discreet. However, now we are back in London, I find you behaving like a hoyden, holding morning assignations with a former admirer, and making me the butt of ribald jokes at my club – it is the outside of enough and I shall act.'

Real tears now stood in Felicity's eyes; she had never seen her docile husband aroused to such fury and there seemed no way to soften his mood. 'What do you intend to do?' she asked.

'Go to Harrogate.'

'Harrogate!' echoed Felicity in astonishment.

'The waters there will be beneficial to my gout, and you will accompany me. We shall be away from London for several months.'

'But Harrogate is in the north,' she said, horrified. 'There will be no society and nothing to do.'

He gave an unsympathetic shrug. 'Excellent – a period of quiet reflection is exactly what you require.'

'Can't we at least go to Bath?' she pleaded.

'No, I am set upon Harrogate and will brook no further discussion on the matter. Please make the necessary arrangements for our departure. Until your behaviour improves, I have also decided to limit your allowance and cease purchasing those expensive gifts you delight in; I will not tolerate being embroiled in scandal.'

'You cannot cut my allowance as well, Portland – it is too cruel.'

'I can and I will, madam.' Unmoved by her tears, he narrowed his eyes and added in a biting tone, 'And let me warn you that if I am given further reason to question your conduct, you will be banished to Portland House in Devonshire, where you will have ample opportunity to practise your needlework and nothing else.'

Lord Portland then limped to the door, slamming it shut behind him.

Lady Bramwell found her son in the library. He sat in the chair beside the fireplace, frowning into the embers, tiredness and sorrow carved into his features.

'Have you spoken to Isabella?' she asked.

He did not look up, but shook his head. 'She left London early this morning with Mrs Forster and Dominic.' Hal then recounted his visit to Lady Portland, adding quietly, 'No doubt there are some wagers concerning Isabella – it is the way of things in London – however, I know nothing of them.'

There was a long pause until Marguerite said, 'So Felicity lied out of spite to cause problems between the two of you?'

Hal nodded. 'Whether it was her intention or not, she has

succeeded in driving Isabella away and I don't know where she has gone.' There was a note of desperation in his voice.

'You must find Isabella and tell her the truth,' said his mother firmly.

'But why couldn't she trust me? It pains me that she believed Felicity's lies so readily and considered me capable of such a thing.'

'Hal, I do not usually interfere in your affairs, but I must make an exception and ask you this: do you believe Isabella loves you?'

He gave a half-smile, remembering the tender moments they had shared. 'Yes, I know that she cares.'

'Then that is all that matters,' replied Lady Bramwell. 'We both know that Isabella has been hurt in the past – that is why she is insecure and needs your love. She is probably already regretting leaving without speaking to you, and Mrs Forster, who is an eminently sensible woman, will also be trying to convince her to return.'

He stood up, dragged both hands through his hair and gave a deep sigh. 'You are right, ma'am. I was angry that Isabella could not trust me, but I should have known better – I have seen how fragile she still is. But where do I begin to search for her?'

There was a tap at the door and Julia entered, looking pale and wan but with a glint of determination in her dark eyes.

'I'm sorry to interrupt, but I wanted to know if you have sent the note to Freddy, Mama?'

'It was dispatched a short time ago.'

'Good, because nothing is going to stop me resolving our differences today.' Julia then eyed her brother thoughtfully before asking about Isabella.

Having explained and listened to his sister's scathing opinion of Lady Portland, Hal continued, 'I need your help, Julia. Can you think of anything – a word, a phrase or passing reference which may give us any clue to Isabella's destination?'

'The first time we called in Curzon Street, Isabella remarked on their new house in the country, but I cannot recall the name.'

Hal's dark brows were drawn together in concentration. 'The house was called Haystacks.'

'But that doesn't help much,' said Lady Bramwell. 'It could be anywhere in the country.'

'Dominic told me that his Great Uncle James had left the house to his mother and it was near the coast,' said Julia.

'At such short notice, Isabella must have gone to her own property,' said Hal. 'Now we know that the property is called Haystacks, it was left to her by a relative and is near the coast, but it is still not enough information to find her.'

There was another knock at the door and Jennings entered. 'This package was delivered by Lady Vane's footman, my lord.'

Hal took it and, when the butler had left, tore off the wrapping.

'What is it?' asked Julia eagerly.

Disappointment was clear in Hal's voice as he replied, 'Only a brief note from Isabella, explaining that these are the items she had purchased for Sarah and that her agent will contact me regarding payment towards Sarah's education. There is nothing else.'

'So Isabella kept to her word, despite her anguish,' murmured Marguerite.

Hal put the clothes aside and stared at the note in his hand as if it were his last remaining link with Isabella.

'Hal, I have been thinking,' mused Lady Bramwell, 'you mentioned that Isabella's house was called Haystacks and it was not far from the coast. This may not be connected, but Lady Pargeter told me about an elderly gentleman whose estate in Sussex ran parallel with her own property there. He was something of a recluse and there was surprise locally when it emerged that he had left his property to a female relative. Lady Pargeter told me that the relative was a young widow with a small son who lived in Yorkshire with her aunt.'

'So you think the relative could be Isabella?' asked Julia.

'It is possible,' replied her mother. 'I had not made the connection until a moment ago – Lady Pargeter said the house was not large and had fallen into disrepair, but I distinctly recall it was called Haystacks and it was five miles from the coast, near the village of Swanborough, just outside Lewes.'

'It must be the place,' said Hal. 'There are too many coincidences.'

The door opened and Theo poked his head into the room. 'So this is where you're all hiding – I have some news.'

'Come in, Theo,' said Lady Bramwell.

He did so, observing, 'Some very odd things are happening this morning. I didn't think it was worth going to bed at five o'clock, so I went for a ride along Rotten Row and what should I see during my journey home? A coach and four trundling out of Curzon Street with, of all things, a parrot in a cage strapped to the back.'

'A parrot,' echoed Hal and Julia in unison.

'A parrot, I tell you,' said Theo, nodding. 'Strangest thing I ever saw! For a moment, I thought I must have drunk too deep myself last night.' He grinned suddenly. 'Surprised the creature didn't wake the whole of Mayfair: I could hear it repeating "bacon-brained gudgeon" from the other end of the street!'

Lady Marguerite, Hal and Julia looked at each other, apprehension dawning as to the significance of what Theo had seen.

'It appears you have unwittingly observed Lady Vane's departure from London. You see, Dominic numbers a parrot called Jemima among his menagerie,' explained Hal.

'A-ha, does he indeed?' said Theo, glad to have this mystery solved. 'Then it must have been Lady Vane's carriage. Didn't know she was planning to leave London, mind you. However, there's something else: a rider was accompanying this carriage – a gentleman, tall figure on a big brute of a chestnut horse. He was too far away for me to see him clearly, but both he and the horse looked familiar and I have only just realized who it was – Freddy!'

'*Freddy!*' cried Julia. 'Freddy has accompanied Isabella! Oh, all this is my fault! Our stupid quarrel has driven him into the arms of another woman and I cannot bear it.'

'Julia, do not be so dramatic,' said her mother reprovingly. 'Freddy is besotted with you. Most likely he has gone with Isabella because he offered his assistance, although how he discovered what her plans were, I cannot imagine.'

'Jennings told us that Freddy left shortly after Isabella. If Freddy encountered Isabella and her distress was evident, he would offer to help,' said Hal.

'Well, I suppose that must be it,' said Theo, 'but when I advised Freddy to stay away from Julia last night to help his cause, I hardly thought he would take my advice to the extreme and quit London at dawn. I expected him to be here this morning so you could throw yourself on to his chest with relief, Julia. Trust Freddy to get a maggot into his head and go too far!'

By the time Theo had finished this enlightening speech, a hush had fallen over the rest of the assembled company. Julia, rising from her chair, broke it by saying in an ominous tone, 'What did you say?'

Puzzled, Theo asked, 'Which part, Ju?'

'About your advice to Freddy. Did I hear correctly? You advised him to stay away from me last night?'

'Oh, that! Er – yes, I suppose I did,' began Theo hurriedly, observing Julia's rising temper and narrowed eyes, 'but only because I thought it might help matters. Now, there's no call for you to look daggers at me, Ju – I was trying to help.'

'Help!' she retorted in disdain, her fingers closing around the Sévres china figure on the nearby table.

'Julia! Put that thing down … damn it all, there's no reason for you to get so annoyed,' pleaded Theo, eyeing her nervously.

'I could murder you right now, Theo,' she muttered and, with alarming accuracy, she threw the figure at Theo, who moved just in time for the Sévres to smash against the wall.

'Well, of all the ungrateful—' declared Theo.

'That is enough,' said Lady Bramwell. 'You are worse than when you were children. Theo, what possessed you to interfere and offer Freddy such advice? It was badly done, and I will be interested to hear your reasoning and your apology later. For now, let us try to be more constructive. Hal, what are your plans?'

Hal, who despite being abstracted had watched the preceding scene with some amusement, replied, 'I intend to go to Lewes. I don't want to wait until Freddy returns to discover where Isabella is, and it seems the best chance to find her quickly. I'll travel on horseback – I have suitable horses posted along the London to Brighton route and, although I won't overtake them, I should arrive by evening.'

'That seems the best course of action,' agreed his mother.

'Well, I'm not staying here for the whole day without speaking to Freddy,' said Julia bluntly. 'Theo, you must take me to Lewes in Hal's curricle.'

'Me!' he expostulated. 'Can't do it: I'm engaged to go to Tattersall's with Barnaby Tume.'

'No, you can escort me to Haystacks instead. It is the least you can do after offering your helpful advice to Freddy.'

'I advise you to comply before you have more china thrown at your head, Theo,' said Hal.

His brother hunched a grudging shoulder. 'Oh, very well, but I hope I won't have to suffer your recriminations for the whole journey, Julia.'

Julia replied sarcastically, 'I may just refrain from boxing your ears.'

'Theo, you can change the team if necessary. You should make good time that way,' said Hal.

He nodded in agreement. 'At least this gives me chance to try out your curricle.' With a wicked grin towards Julia, he added, 'You had better hang on to your bonnet, dear sister.' Theo then looked at Lady Bramwell. 'What are you going to do, Mama?'

'Enjoy a quiet day here, of course. I have no intention of dashing down to Lewes and hopefully, you can all sort out your affairs without my assistance.' Marguerite chuckled. 'The drawing-room at Haystacks could become rather crowded this evening.'

*

Sir Seymour, meanwhile, had arrived in Curzon Street shortly after Lord Bramwell had departed. He rang the bell and idly studied his new blue and white striped waistcoat while he waited, thinking with satisfaction that his tailor had excelled himself this time. Silwood opened the door, but when Sir Seymour asked to be announced, Silwood replied that both Lady Vane and Mrs Forster had gone out of Town.

Dinny goggled at the butler in astonishment. 'What was that? Gone out of Town! You must be mistaken.'

Silwood raised his brows. 'I assure you that they left early this morning, Sir Seymour.'

'How very odd,' muttered Sir Seymour, before asking rhetorically, 'What am I to do now?'

Silwood then handed Sir Seymour a letter, saying, 'Mrs Forster asked that this be given to you when you called, sir.'

'Ah, at least there is a letter,' observed Sir Seymour eagerly, taking the note and removing the single sheet. As he read it through his quizzing glass, his mouth fell open in surprise. With no further word to Silwood, he pocketed the note and hurried back down the steps.

Climbing back into his carriage, he addressed the coachman, 'Stop dawdling, Thomas – we are leaving for Sussex at once.'

As the coach left the courtyard of The Black Swan in Redhill, Isabella reflected that all her travelling companions seemed to share her sombre, reflective mood. Harriet, who was seated next to her in the carriage, gazed silently out of the window. Mary sat opposite, dozing, with a sleeping Dominic resting against her arm, his blond head jolting whenever the wheels travelled over rough road. Joshua, the kitten, was asleep in a wicker basket and even Aesop lay in the crook of Dominic's arm, regarding the sun-drenched fields of sheep and cattle with uninterest. Freddy rode alongside on his chestnut gelding, but his expression was fixed and offered no relief from the gloomy atmosphere inside the coach.

When they had stopped at the inn, Freddy procured a private room for breakfast, but no one had been inclined to much conversation. Isabella had been wondering if Freddy knew of Hal's involvement in the wager and she felt anger and embarrassment at the thought of the Ice Angel providing private amusement for Hal and his friend. However, when she touched on the subject of wagers and gentlemen's clubs over coffee, Freddy had evinced no reaction at all – it seemed he knew nothing of what Hal had done.

Isabella was grateful for Freddy's help; the journey had gone more smoothly due to his presence because, like most of the top-sawyers, he stabled his own horses on the route. All the landlords knew him and provided the best parlours and refreshments for Mr Isherwood and his companions. However, the normally gregarious Freddy was morose and Isabella did not think this could be entirely attributed to his delicate constitution this morning. She wondered what had caused his unhappiness. At any other time, she might have tried to coax the details from Freddy, but with her own sadness weighing heavily, she felt unequal to the role of confidante.

Isabella's most difficult task had been to tell Dominic about their change of plan. When he had discovered they were leaving London, he had not seemed too disappointed, saying, 'I wanted to see more of London, but I'm looking forward to exploring our new house.'

'You will make many exciting discoveries there, Dominic,' replied Isabella.

'Will Hal come to Haystacks tomorrow, Mama? I should like to show him too.'

'No, Dominic,' she replied, 'Hal will not be coming to see us tomorrow.'

Dominic looked quizzical. 'When will he come then? Soon, I hope.'

Isabella exchanged a meaningful glance with Harriet, knowing that the inevitable moment of truth had arrived. It was hard enough dealing with her own wretched feelings without giving disappointment to her son, but she could not lie to him. 'I'm sorry, Dominic, but you will not be seeing Hal again.'

'Not see Hal again?' he asked in a tremulous voice. 'Or Julia, or Theo?' When she shook her head, he began to cry. 'I like Hal and it is unfair to have to go away and not see him or my other new friends again, Mama. I did not even say goodbye.' Dominic raised his gaze to hers hopefully. 'But I will still be able to see the tree house at Chenning, won't I? You promised me that I could.'

Isabella felt as if her heart were breaking in two. She placed her arm around her son and said, 'No, love – you cannot go to Chenning after all. I know this is hard for you to understand, but Hal has done a bad thing which has upset me very much and that is why you will not see him again.'

'I – It's not true,' he faltered, sobbing. 'Hal would never do a bad thing – I know he wouldn't – and now you've broken a promise and that's a bad thing to do as well.'

'I'm truly sorry, Dominic, but it could not be helped.'

He had continued to cry, but she had spoken soothingly to him until he had fallen into an exhausted sleep. Isabella felt both physically and emotionally exhausted too. She hoped that given time Dominic would forget Hal, but she knew she would never forget him despite what he had done. Resolutely, she pushed these melancholy thoughts away, knowing that it did no good to dwell on what might have been.

Isabella had not yet discussed last night in detail with her aunt, but, with Dominic and Mary asleep, Isabella felt the time was right. She touched Harriet's arm and asked quietly, 'Harriet, do you wish to hear how I learned of Hal's betrayal?'

Harriet turned, her gaze resting on Isabella's pale features. 'Yes, I do.'

'Then I'll explain – you have been so good and I owe you that much – but first, why didn't you want to leave London?'

'Are you certain that you want to hear the reason?' replied Harriet, with a queer smile.

'Of course. Was it because we had not visited all the sights yet?'

Harriet sighed. 'Nothing so trivial, I'm afraid. I did not want to leave London because' – she paused, then hurried on – 'because Sir Seymour has asked me to marry him! I was hoping to discuss it with you last night, so I might feel comfortable when he called in Curzon Street today for my answer. However, events overtook my plans and it was entirely inappropriate to mention it afterwards. You see, Isabella, I wanted to accept his offer.'

Isabella stared and said nothing for a full minute; she was staggered by what Harriet had told her. Eventually, in a constrained voice, she replied, 'Oh, what have I done? Harriet, I am so sorry – I have been blind as well as selfish, and now I have ruined everything for you!'

Chapter Sixteen

HARRIET took Isabella's hand and said gently, 'I didn't tell you last night because I didn't want to add to your distress.'

Isabella, still reeling from Harriet's announcement, shook her head as she admitted, 'I feel utterly stupid. I – I had no idea that you and Sir Seymour had grown so close.'

'You would not have noticed because we scarcely knew what was happening ourselves until we were in the midst of it,' replied Harriet. 'I should explain how this has come about. Of course, neither Dinny nor I had any thought of it when we met – you will recall that he was overwhelmed by your beauty, Isabella.' She chuckled and added, 'He is embarrassed to admit now that he was dazzled by you, but I was not surprised at all. You see, you are very lovely and yet you have no conceit; I was proud and pleased to see you so admired.'

'You drew me back into the world even though I was unwilling.'

Harriet smiled. 'And you began to enjoy yourself.'

Isabella agreed, but Harriet noted the sadness that clouded her niece's features. 'I am sure you are thinking about Lord Bramwell and I want to talk to you more on that subject in a moment. However, to return to Sir Seymour, I knew that you were the main reason for his visits, but there were many subjects we enjoyed discussing and I always felt comfortable with him. Whenever you left the room, there was no awkwardness between us. Indeed, and I blush to mention this, we often did not notice that you had gone because we were deep in conversation.'

'You were always able to put Sir Seymour at ease,' said Isabella.

'Yes; whenever he arrived in Curzon Street to find you not at home, Dinny said it seemed natural to ask for me instead. I know he can appear a little eccentric, but he is a dear man, and very knowledgeable.'

'There is no need to convince me of his qualities, Harriet. Sir Seymour was very kind when Dominic disappeared.'

'He was, wasn't he?' replied her aunt, with indulgent pride. 'He comforted me during those terrible hours. By then, it seems we had both realized how we felt, but each was afraid to speak of it – Dinny thought that I would consider him a libertine for transferring his attentions. In turn, I could not imagine that he would prefer me. We did not admit to our feelings until Dominic returned home. You had been in the library with Lord Bramwell and then wanted to see Dominic, so Dinny and I were left alone. Do you remember?'

'How can I forget,' whispered Isabella. Remembering the kisses she and Hal had shared that morning brought a hint of colour to her cheeks. With vivid clarity, Isabella recalled the feel of his body beneath her fingertips, his mouth moving slowly over hers, the way she had longed for more.... Pushing the image away, she denounced herself inwardly for a fool.

'It was then Dinny found the courage to tell me how he felt,' observed Harriet, smiling at the memory. 'I was so happy, Isabella – I never thought that I would wish to marry again, but Dinny has proved me wrong. I told him that his feelings were reciprocated. However, I did not know what to do next.'

Isabella gave her a quizzical look. 'Why? What do you mean?'

'I was not certain that you loved Lord Bramwell. He seemed to be in love with you, but I was not sure how you felt. You keep your emotions well hidden, Isabella,' said Harriet. 'I knew that you did not love Sir Seymour – you were fond of him, of course, but you did not look at him in the same way. There was always something else in your eyes whenever you looked at Lord Bramwell.'

'I thought it must be obvious how much I had come to care for him,' said Isabella.

'I assure you that it was not, my dear. When Dinny asked me to marry him, I explained that I could not marry him immediately and leave you alone. Dinny was most understanding – I have told him a little about your unhappy past, my dear – and we agreed to wait until it became clear if you were in love with Lord Bramwell or not. Of course, at Julia's ball, you and Lord Bramwell appeared very close and affectionate, so I decided to talk to you when we returned home and explain afterwards about Sir Seymour and me. However, events made that impossible and it was not the right time to speak of my happiness.'

'You are so generous, Harriet; I hope Sir Seymour appreciates your true worth,' said Isabella warmly. 'But I have ruined everything. Sir Seymour will not know where you have gone, and he will be angry or upset – probably both.'

'He will be neither because I wrote to him last night to tell him of our destination, and, briefly, the reason for my departure. As soon as things are more settled, I shall return to London, or ask him to come to Sussex so that we may sort out our affairs.'

'But you must still marry him,' cried Isabella. 'We shall still see you often, and Dominic and I will do very well on our own.'

'Of course you will, my dear – you will marry Hal, I shall marry Dinny and we will all be happy.'

Isabella gaped at her aunt. She laughed incredulously, hurt and disbelief on her face. 'You must be mad to even suggest that when you know what he has done.'

'But I do not know, Isabella. Lord Bramwell would not behave in that way in my opinion. Tell me, how did you hear of his involvement?'

Isabella proceeded to tell Harriet everything: how her initial attraction to Hal had grown into love, what she had witnessed at the theatre and in the garden, Lady Portland's revelation that she and Hal still cared for each other, and of Hal's involvement in the wager.

When Isabella fell silent, Harriet declared bluntly, 'She was lying. If you had told me earlier that Lady Portland was responsible for this, I would not have let you leave London.'

'You cannot know she was lying.'

'Isabella, she is a spiteful, designing harpy who would use any means to destroy your relationship with Lord Bramwell.'

'B-But I saw her kissing him,' said Isabella. 'And are you aware that they were once engaged?'

'Yes. Lady Bramwell, who was extremely angry that the woman had arrived at Julia's ball uninvited, told me all about Lady Portland. When Felicity jilted her son and married Portland instead, Marguerite was very relieved. She also told me that Hal realized long ago it was nothing more than a youthful infatuation.'

'This much I already know – Hal has told me himself,' acknowledged Isabella.

'Then perhaps you should believe Lord Bramwell rather Lady Portland,' retorted Harriet drily. 'Did you know that Lady Portland has been pursuing Lord Bramwell since returning to London, but he would have none of it? From what you have said, you did not see Lord Bramwell kissing Lady Portland – you only saw her trying to kiss him.'

'But the wager—' began Isabella faintly.

'Don't be naïve, my love,' interjected her aunt. 'You know that wagers are commonplace. Indeed, there may be wagers surrounding you, but that does not mean Lord Bramwell is involved in them. Of course, only he can confirm that Felicity Portland was lying, but I advise you to compare the sincerity of his words and actions with her reputation. A predatory woman like Felicity Portland would sense your vulnerability and use it to her advantage.'

'She was very convincing, but now I don't know what to think.' Isabella turned her troubled gaze to her aunt, 'If you are right, then Hal must hate me now for doubting him.'

*

Sir Seymour was making good progress. He was travelling in his private post-chaise, emblazoned with his coat of arms and equipped with luxurious velvet upholstery. Occasionally, he leaned out of the window to instruct his postillions to not slacken their speed, but, an hour from Swanborough at a sudden sharp turn in the road, the carriage lurched violently and came to a halt at a drunken angle.

Sir Seymour stuck his head out of the window. 'Why have we stopped, Thomas?'

'Looks like we have a wheel trapped in a rut, sir,' came the reply. 'You'll have to get out while me, Carter and Fielding try and release it.'

'Deuced bad luck!' grumbled Dinny in annoyance. 'Can I help?'

'Thank you, sir, but this will be a muddy job. Best stand clear and let us deal with it.'

'This is no time to worry about mud,' replied Dinny, stepping out of the chaise and trudging to the rear to inspect the trapped wheel with his servants. 'If we lift the axle, Carter can go to the horses' heads and lead them forward. Hurry, man!'

Thomas looked up in astonishment and tried to remonstrate again with his employer. 'But Sir Seymour – your boots will be filthy afterwards.'

'To hell with my boots!' declared Sir Seymour roundly, 'I need to get to Swanborough. Now help me with this axle!'

Meanwhile, some miles behind Sir Seymour's stranded carriage, Julia and Theo were making rapid progress.

'For God's sake, Theo, have a care!' cried Julia, as her brother swung the curricle expertly around a bend. 'If you throw me into a ditch after your helpful advice to Freddy last night, I will never speak to you again.'

Theo grinned. 'Is that a promise, Ju?' he asked, urging the high-stepping bays to even greater speed. 'If it is, I'll make sure I throw you into a ditch.'

'You are incorrigible – I pity the poor girl you fall in love with.'

'No need to,' replied Theo affably, turning to look at her. 'Whoever it is, I won't throw her into a ditch either – even Hal says I can drive to an inch.'

'For goodness' sake, keep your eyes on the road!' shrieked Julia, gripping the side of the carriage as the lightly sprung curricle bounced over a bump. 'I want to arrive uninjured.'

'Do you want me to spring 'em faster?' asked Theo, with a chuckle.

Julia groaned. 'No! This pace is perfectly acceptable, but I would be happier if you concentrated on your driving.'

'Then stop talking to me,' he said, laughing mischievously.

Exasperated, she observed, 'I'll never understand why Freddy listened to you last night.'

'As to that, it seems to me everything will turn out fine – you're off to see Freddy, throw yourself on his chest, blame me for everything and declare your love. In response, he will gather you into his embrace, blame me for everything and declare his love – very simple, really. It just happens that this reconciliation will take place in Sussex instead of London.'

'Oh, you're quite impossible, Theo,' said Julia, unable to smother a chuckle.

At three o'clock in the afternoon, Isabella's carriage turned into the narrow lane that led to Haystacks. They had stopped briefly at The Plough so that Freddy could order a room for the night, and then moved on again, past the church, out of the village for another mile and a half until they had reached the lane. It was little more than a dirt track with deep, water-filled ruts and the coachman negotiated it with care to prevent the carriage getting bogged down.

Isabella could see the roofline of the house against the afternoon sky. Gables and chimney shafts rose over a stone-tiled roof, underneath which nestled a compact, two-storey Elizabethan brick building incorporating bays with mullioned windows and a projecting porch. This idyllic image was spoilt somewhat by the air of neglect which surrounded the property, evidenced by the occasional missing roof tile and overgrown garden.

They climbed out and Dominic and Aesop ran around the gravel drive, stretching their cramped legs while Isabella went to ring the bell. When there was no reply, she rang it a second time, saying to Harriet, 'I hope Mr and Mrs Johnson will not be too shocked to see us. They live in quarters off the kitchen, at the rear of the house, so it will take some time for them to answer.'

Eventually, the heavy front door swung open to reveal a wizened servant, who stared in surprise at the collection of people on the doorstep, and the carriage laden with portmanteaux and a bird cage sitting in the drive.

'L-Lady Vane,' he stammered. 'We were not expecting you for another month at least. Oh, Lord – the missus will be in such a panic; there's not much food in the house and no fires lit.'

'Don't worry, Johnson,' replied Isabella, walking through into the musty, oak-panelled hall. 'Our departure was hasty and I had no time to send a message on ahead. We shall manage somehow.' She introduced Harriet, Dominic and Freddy and explained that they would need beds made up for the night, but Freddy would be staying at The Plough.

'It's creepy here, Mama,' said Dominic, who had been eyeing the gloomy interior.

'It will seem more welcoming when we have settled in, love,' said his mother. 'Johnson, if it is convenient, I shall have the room that I stayed in on my previous visit.'

'The bed will need airing, Lady Vane – it's fearful cold and with all the repairs, the place smells of damp plaster.'

'Then our first task must be to light fires in here, in the bedrooms, in one of the parlours, in the dining-room and the drawing-room.'

Mrs Johnson, who was as round as her husband was thin, came bustling in to see who was at the door. After expressing as much surprise as her spouse at the arrivals, she announced, 'Some of the rooms can be prepared in a trice. The lad who works in the stables can go and get my niece to help us. There is a good supply of wine in the cellar – the late master was never close-fisted with his drink – but I'm worried about what you will have for dinner, Lady Vane. I've only a ham and a couple of chickens, and you and your guests will be used to far better fare.'

'That will be acceptable,' said Isabella. 'Mr Isherwood, would you like to take your horse to the stables? They are in reasonable condition and should prove adequate.'

'I'm sure they will, Lady Vane,' replied Freddy with a smile. 'Could I have a word with you in private first?'

Isabella agreed and, after asking Harriet to supervise the unloading of the luggage and suggesting Dominic and Aesop went to the kitchen with Mrs Johnson for a glass of milk, she led the way into the small front parlour. 'I have been most grateful for your help today,' she said, adding teasingly, 'You kept your promise, even though it was clear that you were not at your best.'

He grinned. 'No, my head ached like the devil, although I should not complain when my discomfort was self-inflicted.'

'I expect you will travel back tomorrow?'

'Yes, I am sorry that I cannot be of more use, but I wish to return immediately,' said Freddy.

'To see Lady Julia?' she ventured.

'Yes.'

Blushing, Isabella admitted, 'There are ... difficulties between myself and Lord Bramwell and that is why I left London suddenly.'

'When my head had cleared, I knew that something must have happened; I saw how upset you were last night.'

'I'm sorry, but I can't discuss it at the moment,' she said, biting her lip. 'I hardly know what to think anymore and I need to reflect.'

'Of course, Lady Vane,' replied Freddy, 'I don't wish to pry. I would advise you, however, to beware of Lady Portland. She is a spiteful, heartless creature.'

'Those are almost the same words that Harriet used to describe her.'

'Lies fall from Lady Portland's tongue as easily as the truth,' he said.

Isabella stared back at him for a long moment. 'Thank you for the advice.'

After a pause, Freddy remarked quietly, 'You realize that it is only a matter of time before Hal finds you – I cannot lie to him about your whereabouts.'

'I would not ask you to, but he may never wish to see me again.'

Freddy shook his head. 'No, he will still search you out – Hal is not a man who gives up. I hope matters between you can be resolved.' She made no reply, so he said, 'I'll be off to the stables. Shall I take Dominic and keep him amused for an hour or two?'

'That would be helpful,' said Isabella, with a grateful smile. 'It will cheer him up to be in your company – you are one of his new heroes, you know.'

He laughed at this and went out to find Dominic. An hour and a half later, the house looked more welcoming. Fires had been lit in most of the rooms and, although the house still felt cold despite the warm late spring weather outside, there was enough cheer in her surroundings to make Isabella feel, physically at least, more comfortable. Mrs Johnson had produced tea and cake and, after Freddy had ensured that the horses had been attended to, he had busied himself chopping firewood. Stripped to the waist, he wielded the axe so effectively the pile of firewood at the side of the barn soon doubled in size. After returning to the house to wash and replace his shirt and coat, he was now taking Dominic on a tour of the house. Shrieks of laughter could be heard from upstairs as they played hide and seek, while Harriet and Isabella sat in the drawing-room.

Isabella considered that the drawing-room could be very pleasant when the decorations had been replaced; it was not large, but it faced south and looked out on to the lawns. Two large windows let in the afternoon sun and threw a more cheerful hue on the dilapidated furniture and wall coverings. There were a few chairs, some worn rugs and two sofas arranged around the fireplace. A bookcase full of mildewed volumes ran along one wall, and card tables sat against the walls either side of the fireplace. The air of disuse and damp that permeated the room had not dissipated, but at least the fire created an impression of warmth.

Now the initial bustle of their arrival was over, recent events were once again occupying Isabella's thoughts. She relived continually what Lady Portland had said last night, as well as the image of her kissing Hal, but then she would recall Harriet and Freddy's advice and her resolution wavered. Harriet was convinced of Hal's innocence and Freddy, notwithstanding his natural allegiance to his friend, had warned her about Lady Portland. She could not banish Hal from her mind and could not escape the ever-growing conviction that she had made a terrible mistake.

Harriet, who had been observing her niece's troubled expression, said, 'The repairs are progressing well, but it will be uncomfortable here for some time yet. The chimney in the hall is smoking badly.' Harriet looked under her lashes at Isabella. 'Have you considered what I said to you this morning?'

'Yes,' murmured Isabella.

'And what are your conclusions?'

'I am beginning to doubt Lady Portland's words – even Freddy said she is an inveterate liar – but, if I was wrong to listen to her, it makes no difference now because the damage is done,' said Isabella. 'Hal must hate me for not giving him a chance to defend himself.'

'You could return to London and ask Lord Bramwell yourself if you want to get to the truth.'

Isabella looked at her aunt, a glimmer of hope in her eyes. 'Do you think he would see me?'

'I'm certain of it,' replied Harriet. 'He must be very worried about you, Isabella. Last night, you made no allowance for the constancy you have seen in Lord Bramwell. His love for you was no act, but if you still have doubts, consider how he rescued Dominic. If Lord Bramwell wanted to win a wager regarding you, he did not need to search for your son in those dreadful places. Hal did it because he loves you and Dominic, and for no other reason. He had nothing to gain by it.'

The doorbell sounded in the distance and Harriet rose to her feet. 'That must be Mrs Johnson's niece. I'll go and answer the door – it will take Johnson ten minutes to get there and he's already struggling to prepare dinner.'

Leaving Isabella in the drawing-room, she went into the hall and opened the door, but to her amazement, instead of Mrs Johnson's niece, Sir Seymour stood before her.

'Dinny!' she exclaimed.

'I had to come and find you, Harriet,' he said with a smile, before stepping over the threshold to enfold her in a tenacious embrace.

When she emerged, blushing and breathless, Harriet said, 'Oh, this is a delightful surprise! How good you are to have travelled all this way, but there was no need – I would have returned soon.'

Dinny, continuing to hold her in his arms, said, 'I know, but I intend to have your answer today.'

'You are most persistent, sir,' she replied, her eyes twinkling. 'Very well, having travelled nearly sixty miles, you shall hear it at once: I accept your proposal of marriage – that is, if you still want me.'

'If I still want you?' echoed Sir Seymour, indignant. He said no more, but he placed one finger under Harriet's chin and kissed her again, this time more slowly while she remained within the circle of his arm.

They stayed so for a time, until Harriet gave a contented sigh. 'We should move out of the hallway, Dinny. The servants may come in, or even Isabella. She is upset and confused, but I think I am making progress.'

Sir Seymour laughed indulgently, 'Now, my love, what mischief are you up to? Your note was very brief.'

Harriet told him about the events that had led up to their departure and that Freddy had accompanied them. Eventually, Sir Seymour said, 'Bramwell is an honourable man. I'd stake my life that he is not involved, more likely that Lady Portland's story was apocryphal.'

'I have spent the day telling Isabella just that, and she is gradually coming to see it herself.' Suddenly, Harriet noticed Sir Seymour's bedraggled, mud-splattered state. 'My dear, your boots … your clothes … everything – including your new waist-coat – is ruined.'

'Oh, that,' he remarked insouciantly, 'my chaise became stuck so I helped the postillions to lift the axle. However, I am not concerned – the loss of a waistcoat cannot be measured against the pleasure of becoming engaged.'

Sir Seymour's reward from Harriet for this remark was most gratifying: it led to further moments of exquisite silence.

When they were all gathered in the drawing-room and Isabella had heard the news, she said, 'Harriet, you deserve all the happiness in the world and let me be the first to congratulate you.' Isabella kissed her aunt's cheek before turning to Sir Seymour. 'You must know already how fortunate you are to have won Harriet's heart, Sir Seymour. I wish you joy.' She then bestowed an affectionate embrace on him.

'Thank you, Lady Vane,' he said, flushing darkly, 'you have been most understanding, both in relation to me and with my desire to take your aunt away.'

Isabella smiled. 'I won't listen to such nonsense. Promise me that you will indulge and cosset Harriet shamefully, and allow her to visit us often.'

'I could not have induced Harriet to accept my offer other-wise,' he replied.

'Can I offer my congratulations too?' asked Freddy, offering his hand to Sir Seymour. 'I'm delighted to hear that you are engaged.'

Dominic, who had been listening to this conversation, asked suspiciously, 'What does engaged mean?'

'It means that you have promised to marry someone,' said Harriet. 'You see, today I have promised to marry Sir Seymour.'

'Oh,' he murmured. 'Will that happen soon?'

'Quite soon, I expect,' she replied.

'And Aunt Harriet will not live with us anymore afterwards, Mama?'

Isabella knelt down beside her son. 'Well, no – but Harriet and Sir Seymour will visit us often, so you will hardly notice.'

Gloomily, Dominic disagreed. 'Yes I will.'

'Now, Dominic,' said Sir Seymour in an encouraging tone, 'I give you my word that we will visit often, and you can stay with us on my estate in Gloucestershire whenever you like. There are enough sheep, cattle, horses and ponies there even for your tastes.'

'Thank you, sir. I will enjoy that very much,' replied Dominic politely, before muttering, 'I wish that Hal was here.'

No one seemed to know what to say to this until Freddy suggested, 'Shall we go and play hide and seek again, Dominic? There are more hiding places here than in any other house I have been to.'

Dominic's expression brightened. 'Yes, please! It's your turn to find me this time.' He ran to the door and disappeared into the hall; Freddy, giving a rueful grin, followed him.

'Dinner will be in one hour,' cried Harriet. When a muffled affirmation that Freddy had heard floated back down the stairs, she added, 'Dinny and I are going to the kitchen, Isabella – the Johnsons are struggling to cope, so we have offered our assistance. Would you like to help too, or stay here until dinner is ready?'

'If you don't mind, I would like to be alone for a while,' she replied.

Harriet nodded and went out with Sir Seymour, and Isabella sat down on one of the threadbare sofas, glad of the silence and an opportunity to think. She decided she had much to be thankful for. There was her property, such as it was; she had a comfortable income and could provide for her son; Harriet was happy and settled; and she had the emotional and financial independence she had craved for during her marriage. Why, then, did she feel so empty? Her heart told her why – she missed Hal. Isabella found she wanted to believe in him, to give him the chance to defend his honour and prove his love. As a handsome and wealthy *nonpareil*, he would always be admired and coveted by other women, but it was wrong to assume that he would succumb to that temptation. Not all men were like Edward and if she did not go to Hal and ask him for the truth, she could be allowing her past to ruin her future.

Grappling with this and a hundred similar thoughts, Isabella was unaware of the bell being rung for the second time that afternoon and, when the door of the drawing-room opened a short while afterwards, she assumed it was Harriet and did not look around. 'Having thought about everything a great deal, Harriet, I have decided I must speak to Hal.'

There was no immediate reply, until a deep and familiar voice said softly, 'I'm very glad to hear it.'

Chapter Seventeen

ISABELLA thought that she had made Hal's voice materialize by the intensity of her yearning for him. She was afraid to look, knowing he could not be there and yet she had heard him so clearly. Slowly, she rose to her feet and turned; Hal stood in front of the closed door, watching her and waiting.

When she realized that he was not an apparition conjured from her subconscious, all other considerations were set aside and she rushed towards him instinctively. 'Hal! It *is* you.'

He folded her in a crushing embrace, planting frantic kisses on her mouth, her hair, her cheeks, her eyelids, her ears, and her neck before returning to her lips; no part of her that he could reach escaped his caresses. 'Oh, my darling,' he murmured, 'you will never leave me again – I won't allow it.'

She returned his kisses until suddenly she regained a little of her senses. 'No, wait! I cannot – that is, we must talk,' she whispered, placing her hands against his chest and trying to put some distance between them.

Hal groaned, but he let her go. 'I agree that we must talk, but I would prefer to kiss you senseless first.'

She gave a tremulous smile at this. 'But I cannot concentrate if you do.'

'Then I promise I will not touch you while we discuss what has happened. However, I warn you that afterwards, you will not concentrate on anything but me for some time,' said Hal in a low, ardent voice. After removing his coat and cravat, he went to sit on the sofa on the far side of the fireplace and leaned forward, forearms resting on his knees, as he waited for her to speak.

Sitting opposite, Isabella could still scarcely believe he was here and her gaze absorbed every detail: the dark hair that fell over his forehead, the grey eyes now regarding her with fierce intensity, and the familiar tall, loose-limbed, muscular frame. Lack of sleep and concern was etched into his features, but his presence felt as vital and reassuring as ever and Isabella had to stop herself from reaching out to him.

She began hurriedly in an unoriginal fashion. 'How did you find me?'

Hal proceeded to explain, adding, 'The coincidences were such it seemed the best chance to locate you quickly, and yet still I have cursed my lack of speed with every expletive I know.'

'D-Did you wait long in the garden?'

'Twenty minutes perhaps. I thought at first you must be delayed, but I soon recognized that something must be wrong or you would not have stayed away.' He studied her intently. 'You must have known what I was going to ask you then, Isabella.'

'Yes,' she whispered.

'Then you can appreciate my torment. Mrs Forster said that you were ill, but I thought you might have left for another reason. It was too late to talk to you then so I had to wait until morning.' Hal pushed his fingers through his hair. 'My torment turned to desperation when I arrived in Curzon Street the following day to find you had left hours earlier. I went straight to Half Moon Street to see Felicity Portland—'

Isabella started in surprise and intervened, 'You already knew she was involved?'

'I suspected something. You see, my darling, I know her devious ways so it was logical to assume she had said or done something to upset you. Lady Portland wanted to ruin our relationship.'

'But why?' asked Isabella in confusion. 'I had never spoken to her before last night.'

'Because she was jealous and I refused to be the partner in

her next affair.' Hal, aware of her gasp, continued, 'Lady Portland is a woman with no propriety, no morals and no heart, Isabella. She is bored with her marriage and offered herself to me without embarrassment. She asked me first at the theatre when I was leaving your box after the interval. She assumed she only had to lift a finger and I would be as infatuated as I was eight years ago. Even though my refusal was unequivocal, she still behaved provocatively, trying to convince me with the methods she no doubt employs with other men.'

Isabella made an anguished sound. 'Oh, if only I had known! I watched you together, Hal – I came out for some air and saw you with her. Her hand was on your cheek … I couldn't bear to watch any longer. Afterwards, I was bewildered and upset because you had appeared very intimate.'

He stretched out his hand towards her and then, recollecting his promise, withdrew it. 'My dearest girl, why didn't you ask me? I would have explained everything; I want no secrets from you.'

'I wish I had now – what a fool I have been.' She shook her head, tears welling in her eyes. 'I did not know who she was then, but I could not put it out of my mind. A doubt remained, and somehow I could never find the right moment to mention it. Then, when I found out you were once engaged, I wondered if you might still care for her.'

'No,' he said emphatically. 'I thought I did once, but, as I told you before, I was very young and blind to her character.' Hal stopped, watching as a tear trickled down her cheek. He swallowed and said in quite a different voice, 'I cannot keep my word if you cry. God, it is purgatory to sit so near and not touch you! You will be sorry you asked me make that promise, Isabella. In fact,' he concluded, a wicked half-grin spreading across his face, 'I will spend the next thirty years making you sorry.'

Isabella gave a weak smile at this. 'I'm sorry, Hal. My only excuse is my fear of making another mistake – a sad legacy of my marriage. Did Lady Portland tell you what she had said to me?'

'After a little ... er ... persuasion,' he admitted, 'I threatened to choke it out of her.'

Isabella raised her brows, but amusement shimmered through her tears. 'You callous creature.'

'She deserved it.'

'I believed her spiteful lies,' acknowledged Isabella. 'She must have sensed my vulnerability, and she knew I had just seen her with you in the garden.'

'But I threw her away from me afterwards,' said Hal urgently. 'Isabella, I cannot lie to you – you are referred to as the Ice Angel in the clubs because of your beauty and your reserve, and no doubt there are wagers surrounding you because that is the way of things in London. However, you must believe me when I say that I am not involved.' He ended on a desperate note, his eyes searching her face and seeking reassurance.

'I do, Hal,' she replied. 'I should never have listened to Lady Portland and I was wrong to run away. I thought you'd hate me for doubting you.'

'Hate you?' He gave a wry laugh. 'I can dissemble no longer; I fear my actions when I arrived have exposed the truth – I love you to distraction. I can't think clearly; I'm eaten up with jealously if I see you talking with, or smiling at, another man, and I feel that time not spent with you is wasted. I admit that I was briefly annoyed you thought me capable of being involved, but I hardly knew what I was saying at the time. It was my mother who pointed out that there were probably reasons why you believed Felicity Portland's lies.'

'There are reasons ... painful memories which have influenced my behaviour and clouded my judgement. I want you to know what happened to leave me so lacking in trust.'

'And I want to hear everything when you are ready to tell me, sweetheart,' he said. 'By the way, I have ensured that Lady Portland will not interfere again; I felt it was justified after what she had done.' Smiling, Hal then murmured, 'I think the time for discussion is over now, my darling.'

In reply, she reached out to place her hand in his. 'I love you,

Hal. My doubts have caused you pain, but I can only say that whatever anguish you felt, mine was in equal measure.'

He stood up, pulling her gently to her feet and towards him. *"'Hear my soul speak: the very instant that I saw you, did my heart fly to your service"*,' he said, his tender gaze skimming her features. 'Will you be my wife, Isabella?'

'Yes,' she said, smiling up at him. 'I cannot live without you.'

'Let me begin to show how much I love you,' he said huskily. He lowered his head and, like a man starved of his vital life essence for too long, crushed his mouth to hers. With delight and satisfaction, he sensed her physical and spiritual release as her body relaxed completely, her hands moving to encircle his waist before gliding upwards over his back and shoulders. He moved his mouth over hers, savouring her sweetness and the exquisite sensation of having her in his arms. Her untutored, fervent response fuelled his desire and his kiss grew more compelling, more demanding until he ran the tip of his tongue across her lips.

Isabella quivered and moaned softly. Parting her lips, she opened to him, welcoming his taste and his warmth as she drowned in wave after wave of sensation. His fingers slid through her hair to cradle her closer and the rest of the world retreated – there was only Hal and, for the first time in her life, Isabella allowed her sensual instincts to guide her. She felt languid yet alive, content yet wanting more, and for long, delicious moments, Hal's lips and hands continued their odyssey.

Lingering kisses played over her throat, her neck and the delicate whorls of her ear, and Isabella gasped and closed her eyes, revelling in the pleasure. Then, as he traced the outline of her face with his lips, his hands gently stroked her body and coaxed shuddering thrills from her core. She arched towards him, a rush of need sweeping through her. Her fingertips skittered over the sculptured muscles of his chest and shoulders and she kissed the pulse at the base of his throat, his skin feeling hot and silken under her touch, before he groaned and claimed her mouth in another searing kiss.

Afterwards, they moved to the sofa, where there was no need for conversation, only whispered endearments and kisses as each welcomed the pleasure of having the other so near.

The knock at the door took some time to register. When there was a second, more insistent tap, Hal murmured reluctantly against her lips, 'At least Harriet has given us a little time, for which consideration I am very grateful.'

'I hope it won't be too long before we can be alone again,' whispered Isabella, her eyes drowsy with passion, her face tinged with colour.

He smiled and placed another tender kiss on her lips. 'Later – I promise.' Taking her hand, Hal led Isabella to the door.

He opened it to reveal Harriet, who began to apologize for interrupting until she glanced from one to the other and cried out, 'Oh, I was certain you would sort out your differences – you were too much in love for it to be otherwise!' She hugged Isabella. 'I wish you happiness, but it is clear that you don't need good wishes to achieve that.'

'We don't, but thank you, Mrs Forster,' replied Hal. 'I understand that you and Sir Seymour are to be congratulated.'

Harriet blushed faintly and nodded. 'Today is becoming quite a procession of engagements.'

'Which reminds me – we must expect Theo and Julia's arrival at any moment. Julia is very anxious to see Freddy.'

'Julia and Theo?' echoed Isabella, in surprise.

'Theo happened to witness your departure from London, my love,' said Hal. 'He did not realize it was you, but he was amazed to see a parrot in a cage strapped to the back of the coach and when he announced that he had seen Freddy accompanying this procession....' He grinned and added, 'Well, Julia was ready to murder Theo for suggesting Freddy stay away from her last night. If my brother and sister have had no delays and have not strangled each other *en route*, they should be here any minute.'

Isabella laughed. 'Freddy will be overjoyed. He has been miserable all day, and not because of his aching head.'

'Where is he?' asked Hal.

'Upstairs, playing hide and seek with Dominic,' replied Harriet. 'Dinny and I are trying to prepare dinner and if Julia and Theo are coming, we must set two more places.'

While this discussion was taking place, the bell was rung again violently. Johnson, who was used to a slower place of life and already exhausted by all the unusual activity, trudged to the door once again, opening it to reveal yet more new arrivals in the gathering gloom.

'Ah-a,' said Theo, who was standing in front of an impatient Julia. 'Good evening. Is this Haystacks?'

'Why, yes, sir,' replied Johnson.

Julia hissed irritably into Theo's ear, 'I told you this was the right place! Had you listened to me, we would have been here earlier instead of going to the other side of the village.'

'Please come in and wait in the hall.' Johnson cleared his throat expectantly and when Theo did not respond, asked, 'Er, who shall I say is calling, sir?'

'Eh? Oh, I forgot to tell you, didn't I? Lady Julia Cavanagh and the Honourable Theodore Cavanagh,' he declared, as he stripped off his driving gloves and looked about the musty hall with interest, coughing at the smoke belching from the fireplace.

'I wonder if Hal is here yet?' whispered Julia, removing her fetching straw bonnet trimmed with cherries as Johnson went out.

'He should be, Ju,' muttered her sibling. 'The landlord at The Plough must think a pot of gold has been unearthed here, with so many people anxious to reach it today. Lord, what a ramshackle place! There's only that old servant to be seen – I hope nothing has gone awry.'

'Nothing has gone awry, Theo,' said Hal, walking into the hall with Isabella. 'In fact, everything has been resolved perfectly – Isabella has accepted my hand in marriage.'

Julia, giving a cry of delight, rushed over to embrace them. 'I knew from the beginning that you were meant for each other. How I shall love having you for a sister, Isabella.'

'Thank the Lord,' said Theo, with a grin. 'I know you will make him extremely happy, Lady Vane.'

'Thank you, Theo, but please call me Isabella – I am to be your sister too. Sir Seymour and Harriet are also to be married. Sir Seymour is in the kitchen; he travelled down today from London.'

Theo's mouth fell open. 'Dinny and Mrs Forster! Well, this is a day for surprises.' He chuckled as a sudden thought occurred to him. 'I can't wait to see the waistcoat he wears at his wedding.'

'I am pleased for you both,' declared Julia, 'and for Sir Seymour and Mrs Forster, but I am desperate to sort out my own affairs.'

Isabella smiled. 'Freddy is upstairs, amusing Dominic. Go to him, Julia, and send Dominic down to us. Do you need directions to find Freddy?'

Julia, a glint of determination in her eyes, replied, 'No, I will find him.'

She hurried away purposefully, climbing the stairs which opened out into a landing. Hearing muted laughter, she walked towards the sound and found herself at the end of the long picture gallery which traversed the rear of the house. Dominic stood before her, and when he sensed someone was near, he turned around. Julia put her finger to her lips and Dominic grinned, understanding she wanted him to stay silent.

'Hello, Dominic,' she whispered. 'Have you found Freddy yet?'

He nodded, gave a mischievous smile and pointed to the long curtain at the end of the gallery. Julia murmured, 'Go downstairs – your mother has a surprise for you. Let me find Freddy.'

He mimed a whoop of excitement and tiptoed away. Stifling a giggle, Julia stepped silently across the oak boards and approached the faded, threadbare curtain. Slowly, she pulled it back. Freddy was turned away from her, looking out over the gardens and unaware of her presence. He seemed lost in thought and the broad expanse of his shoulders sagged as if he were carrying some great weight. Julia's heart leapt with longing and she took a final step forward. Sliding her arms around his waist, she pressed her cheek against his back and said softly, 'Don't ever listen to Theo again where I am concerned, my love.'

Freddy started in surprise before drawing in a ragged breath and spinning round to face her. 'Julia!' Unable to resist the temptation offered up to him, he made a low sound of ecstasy, dragging her into his embrace and kissing her roughly, which treatment Julia seemed to find highly romantic as she threw her arms around his neck and responded in kind.

They stayed locked in their embrace behind the curtain, bathed in the fading sunlight streaming through the window. Freddy's kisses allowed Julia neither the opportunity nor the inclination to speak and when eventually she did try to apologize, she was quickly silenced by another fierce kiss, after which she contented herself with looking up into his face and smiling dreamily.

Remembering her words when she had found him here, he grinned and belatedly replied, 'I won't, but I could forgive him anything just now.' Then, lifting her into his arms, he carried her to the nearby window seat, from where he did not allow her to move until he was satisfied that she understood the strength of his affections.

Hal and Isabella were in the drawing-room when Dominic rushed in. 'Mama, Julia is here—' He stopped abruptly, and then cried out, 'Hal, you are here too!' before running to hug him.

'Hello, reckless cub,' said Hal, laughing.

'How did you get here? It must be magic, 'cause I wished that you could be at Haystacks.'

'Not by magic – I came on horseback as quickly as I could.'

Dominic looked up, his brow furrowed in puzzlement. 'But Mama told me that I wouldn't be seeing you again because you had done a very bad thing.'

'I was wrong, love,' said his mother. 'It was all a mistake.'

'I told you that Hal couldn't do anything bad,' replied Dominic.

'So you did,' she admitted, giving Hal an amused glance.

After leading Dominic by the hand over to one of the sofas, Hal sat down beside him. 'We have some news for you, Dominic.'

'Julia said it was a surprise.'

'Yes, it is and I hope that you will like it,' said Hal. Then, after a pause, 'I love your mother very much, Dominic, and I have asked her to marry me. She has made me very happy by saying that she will.'

'Does that mean you're engaged?' asked Dominic.

Hal smiled. 'That's right.'

Dominic lowered his gaze. 'Oh,' he replied, his expression despondent.

'What is the matter?' said Isabella in concern, sitting down on the other side of her son. 'Don't you want me to marry Hal?'

'That depends,' said Dominic, twisting his fingers together.

'Depends on what?'

'On where I'm going to live afterwards. Aunt Harriet and Sir Seymour have just got 'ngaged and Aunt Harriet isn't going to live with me anymore. I don't want you and Hal to get engaged, if you are going to live somewhere else with Hal and not with me.'

'But you won't have to live somewhere else,' said his mother, with a smile of relief. 'You will live with us until you are grown up.'

'Always?' asked Dominic, his gaze flitting between them.

'Always,' promised Hal.

A grin spread across his face. 'Then I do want you to get engaged 'cause then I can see Hal and the tree house at Chenning.'

'You will be able to see it very soon,' said Isabella, gazing warmly at her betrothed over Dominic's head.

The door opened, and Harriet came in to announce that dinner was almost ready. 'Theo is trying to help, but getting in our way,' she added.

Sir Seymour, resplendent in an improvised sacking apron with the sleeves of his fine linen shirt rolled up to the elbows

and his cravat removed, arrived in the doorway too. He held a
large carving fork in one hand which he waved in the direction
of the kitchen as he chuckled and said, 'Harriet, my dear, we
should dine at once, before Theo devours the meat and the rest
of us have only the bones to pick over. He did manage to cut
some bread before the delights of the chicken and the wine
cellar claimed his attention.'

'Very well,' she replied. 'I hope the dining-room chimney is not
smoking too much, but I daresay it will not matter if it is – we
shall be such a happy party that none of us will notice.'

'O-ho, so Theo is here as well,' exclaimed Dominic, his eyes
growing even wider with excitement. 'This is better than my
birthday! Everyone has come to Haystacks and now we are to
have a party.'

Hal drew Isabella's arm through his and smiled. 'Let us eat,
my darling, while there are still some scraps that have escaped
Theo's attentions.'

Despite its shabby décor, draughty windows and the smoke
that issued occasionally from the chimney, the dining-room
appeared welcoming in the candlelight. Johnson served the food
and Julia and Freddy joined them shortly afterwards. Julia, her
cheeks now suffused with colour, greeted everyone and, with an
adoring look at her companion, announced shyly, 'Freddy and I
are to be married.'

A general chorus of congratulations followed before Dominic
asked in surprise, 'Are you and Freddy 'ngaged too, Julia?
Everyone is doing that today, except Theo.'

Theo, who came in holding a dusty bottle of wine, heard the
laughter that followed Dominic's final comment. 'What am I
exempt from?' he asked.

'Getting engaged, Theo,' explained Freddy. 'You are the odd
one out in our party.'

'You should consider it, my boy; I find it a most comfortable
state,' said Dinny, with an affable smile.

Theo shook his head and sat down at the table between his
brother and Sir Seymour. 'Not yet, thank you; I need someone

who talks a lot less than my sister.' He grinned and winked across the table at Freddy. 'Glad to see you've got her in hand at last, Freddy. Try a glass of this – a bottle of '94 burgundy I found in the cellar. It's a veritable treasure trove down there, Lady V— I mean, Isabella.'

'I'm pleased it meets with your approval, Theo. Take whatever you wish,' she replied.

'That's very good of you,' he said, wreathed in smiles. 'Are you sure? Finest collection of wine I've seen. Must be worth a fortune, Hal.'

'Really?' replied his brother, paying scant attention; he was intent on watching Isabella's profile as she turned to speak to Julia.

Theo laughed. 'Seeing as your interest is diverted at present, I'll take a few bottles back to London. There's plenty to celebrate, after all.'

'Julia and I have decided to return to Town after dinner. Our return will be very late, but the journey will pass quickly,' said Freddy, seeing his smile reflected in Julia's eyes.

'Ah, yes, we should all consider our arrangements for this evening,' said Sir Seymour. 'You and Julia may use my post-chaise, Freddy – I shall be putting up at The Plough for a day or two.'

'Thank you, Sir Seymour. Your chaise will be more comfortable than Lady Bingham's travelling coach,' said Freddy. 'Theo, you can accompany us if you wish.'

'What, sit with you two lovebirds all the way back to London?' Theo shook his head. 'No indeed, Freddy! I'll take your room at The Plough and travel back tomorrow in Hal's curricle.'

Freddy chuckled at this indignant reply and then turned to Hal. 'I packed a few clothes and my shaving equipment. Would you and Theo care to make use of them?'

Hal nodded. 'A kind thought, Freddy. I intend to stay at The Plough too, but, if I may, I'll give you instructions for my groom; my post-chaise will need to be brought down to Sussex and there will be plenty of other arrangements to be made in the coming weeks.'

'I suppose there will be with three weddings to organize,' mused his brother as he forked several slices of chicken on to his plate. 'Don't ask for my help though – I'm going to be busy.'

'What with exactly?' asked Hal, raising his brows.

Theo laughed again. 'Why, with my Latin essay, of course! That will be a damn sight more relaxing than having china thrown at my head, being ordered to dash sixty miles across the countryside, helping to prepare dinner for eight people *and* bringing about three engagements!'

It was almost midnight when Isabella and Hal were alone once more. After Julia and Freddy's departure, Theo and Sir Seymour had returned to The Plough for the night, but without Hal, who had arranged to join them later. Harriet had retired to bed and an excited Dominic had eventually surrendered to sleep after extracting a promise from Hal that he would be at Haystacks tomorrow.

The drawing-room was illuminated by a few candles and by the glow of the fire, the dingy furnishings lost in the resulting comfortable ambience. They sat together on the sofa and when Hal had kissed Isabella thoroughly, she sighed with content-ment and leaned her head against his shoulder.

'Happy?' he whispered.

'Very,' she replied, in a languorous voice.

'Happy as I am at this moment, I shall only be perfectly content when we are married,' he murmured. 'I hope you don't expect a long engagement, my love, or need several weeks to buy bride clothes because I cannot wait that long.'

She smiled, taking pleasure in his impatience. 'I prefer a short engagement.'

'Then we shall be married as soon as it can be arranged.' Tilting her chin upwards, he kissed her again. 'Are you ready to tell me everything now? I will understand if you do not want to taint this moment by dredging up painful memories.'

She shook her head. 'It is important that you know it all, Hal.' Drawing comfort from his embrace, she pressed closer and said in a quiet voice, 'I suppose it all began just before my father died – it was then I first glimpsed signs of Edward's true character.'

Chapter Eighteen

'My father was gravely ill,' continued Isabella. 'He was aware that he was dying and, as I told you when we walked in the park, he grew agitated, wanting my marriage to Edward to take place in his sick-room. Edward was all encouragement for this. I, however, was in turmoil – I wanted to give comfort to my father, but it did not feel right to marry Edward in such haste. In trying to relieve my father's anxieties as well as listening to Edward's pleadings, I felt under pressure to accede.

'Some days after agreeing to the ceremony taking place, I reconsidered and tentatively suggested to Edward that we should delay. My father was under the affects of the opiate and would hardly have been aware of what was happening, so I proposed that the ceremony be a mock one, carried out simply to satisfy my father. We could then arrange for the legal ceremony to take place after a suitable period of mourning. Edward's reaction was totally unexpected – he flew into a violent rage.'

When she shivered at the memory, Hal's arm tightened around her. 'What happened?' he asked.

'He said that I was a provocative little witch, that I had encouraged him to marry me quickly and now I wanted to make him wait. We would be married as arranged, he said, or he would tell my father that I was a cruel, contrary and conniving little baggage. I was barely seventeen, and confused and frightened, Hal. Horrified by Edward's manner, I pleaded with him not to upset my father because I thought it might hasten his death, and reluctantly agreed the marriage could take place as he wished. Edward's rage then abated and he persuaded me to forgive his intemperate words.'

'A disgraceful way to treat you when your father was dying,' said Hal in a constricted voice.

'I know that now,' she replied, 'but at the time I was immature and anxious to please someone whose impatience, I believed, was because of his love for me. So, in an error of judgement I have regretted a million times since, I forgave Edward and the ceremony went ahead. It was the strangest marriage ceremony that ever took place; the only people present were Edward, me, my father, the clergyman of course, and two servants who acted as witnesses.' Isabella gave a tremulous smile and continued, 'The bride cried silent tears throughout, but they were tears of sadness, not of joy. Apart from my father's impending death, perhaps I also had a premonition of what was to come.

'After the ceremony, Edward returned to his property, Vane Manor. I felt sick with worry, afraid that he would return to consummate the marriage that night. However, he made no demands and I was left in peace to nurse my father. Edward must have known that the end was hours away and was simply biding his time. He offered me no support and I felt angry and let down: I had assumed my new husband would try to ease my sadness a little. Two days later, my father died and I was left alone to deal with my grief. Even though I sent word to him, Edward did not return and I was obliged to make the funeral arrangements myself.

'On the day of the funeral, when the mourners had gone home, Edward informed me brusquely to pack my things. By the time I reached Vane Manor, I felt wretched – not only had I buried my father, but I had left my childhood home and was alone in the world, apart from Harriet who was many miles away and Great Uncle James, a distant relative.

'I hoped that Edward would now be more comforting but I was mistaken. The loving suitor was gone and in his place was a curt stranger. His attitude was terse and cold, and he drank throughout the silent dinner we shared. When I could delay no longer, I went to ready myself for bed.' Isabella shuddered. 'I – I did not know what to expect; I had no mother to guide me and I only knew the fundamentals of what happened between a man and a woman. I hoped that Edward would be patient, b-but when he came to me that night, I was suddenly afraid – his expression was pitiless. W-When I felt the weight of his body and smelt the wine on his breath, I began to struggle. Edward was brutal; there was no tenderness or respect, he was simply doing his duty to consummate the marriage and taking what was rightfully his in law. There was no love for me, there never was.' Isabella covered her face with her hands and began to cry.

Hal, his heart full of hatred towards Isabella's dead husband, held her tightly, murmuring soothing words of comfort. When her breathing began to return to normal, he kissed her, and went to pour her a glass of wine. After she had sipped it, he took her into his arms once more. When he could speak with moderation, he said in a bitter voice, 'I wish I could repay him for what he did to you, my darling. If he were not already dead, I would take pleasure in sending him to hell.'

'Harriet is aware of what happened that night, but I have never had the courage to fully articulate what he did,' whispered Isabella. 'When it was over, he left without a word. I lay there in shock until eventually, I managed to wash myself – I needed to cleanse the feel of his body from mine. When I crawled back into bed, I was afraid to go to sleep in case he returned.'

'You must have felt very frightened, and completely alone.'

She agreed, and said, 'Next morning, I went downstairs with trepidation. There was still a spark of hope that the previous night was an aberration on Edward's part and that he would be remorseful when sober. However, what I had witnessed then was the real man and not the façade that I had been shown during his courtship. He treated me with the same disdain. He said my father's property would be sold and I was to be allowed only a few personal possessions from the contents. I did not dare to argue with him.'

'Did he touch you again?' asked Hal, emotion choking his voice.

Isabella nodded. 'Several times, usually when he had been drinking heavily. I tried to lock the door but he was furious and sheared off the lock. After that, I was too fearful to try again – I thought he might kill me in his rage – so I – I ...'

She fell silent, as did Hal, but he held her close, allowing her time to cope with recounting these memories aloud.

'I dealt with his visits the only way I could – I made no sound and lay completely still until it was over. I hated him, truly hated him,' continued Isabella, another shudder running through her body. 'At first, he remained silent and implacable, but gradually my lack of reaction infuriated him even more. He railed at me that I was frigid, that I had no idea how to please a man and he taunted me with how his mistress, whom I later discovered was a woman in the village, knew how to gratify his desires.'

'God, so he pushed his deficiencies on you as well,' he exclaimed through gritted teeth. 'He was not worthy of being called a man – he was a cruel, vicious monster.'

'I know,' she acknowledged with a sigh. 'My salvation came when, after four months of marriage, I told him I was expecting a child. I wondered if the news might alter Edward, but he made no comment when he heard. However, from that day on he did not venture near me again. Perhaps he thought he had done his duty in producing a child or found more pleasure in the arms of his mistress. Whatever the reason, I was profoundly grateful. My pregnancy was fortunately free of problems and Edward allowed Dr Dalton, who became a good friend, to tend me throughout. Dr Dalton was not fooled by Edward; he had only recently returned to the area but he had previously been the Vane family physician and was aware of Edward's caprices. He had great sympathy for my situation and, when I reached my time of confinement, I was glad Dr Dalton was there.'

'Was he – your husband – there?' Hal could not bring himself to mention the name.

'Edward was away in London, drinking himself into a stupor,' she replied. 'His drinking and gambling were increasing as he spent my dowry and the money released by the sale of my father's estates. When Dominic was born, only Dr Dalton and Mary were with me. There was no loving husband waiting anxiously for news – Edward would not have cared if I had lived or died – and yet, Dominic's birth was my only joyful moment during those years. From that moment on, I had someone who depended on me completely and that knowledge gave me a renewed sense of purpose.'

'What a burden of sadness you have borne, sweetheart,' he said, 'Little wonder that you retreated from the world, yet I sensed the warmth underneath your cool diffidence when we met, and felt protective towards you even then. Did his behaviour improve after Dominic's birth?'

'No, it grew worse. He either ignored me or flew into a drunken, towering rage, calling me a soulless witch, unfeeling and unnatural.' Isabella gave a little shrug. 'Strange to say it, but I grew used to his behaviour. I did not fear physical violence: any signs that he had struck me would be visible and he wanted no talk in the village. Edward had a perverted, magnified sense of pride in the Vane family name and would have been mortified had his treatment of me become public knowledge. So his behaviour was restrained to verbal taunts or to ignoring me. I could tolerate the latter, and learnt to deal with the former by cultivating an air of apparent indifference.'

She paused to take a sip of wine and then slipped her hand into his. 'To be subjected to daily taunts, insults and criticism can be just as effective as physical punishment, and any confidence I possessed fell away under Edward's malicious tongue. However, my pride would not let him see that he was succeeding, so I learned to keep my feelings hidden from everyone … until I met you.'

'Thank God!' muttered Hal. 'I'll be eternally grateful to Freddy for insisting I went to Lady Pargeter's that evening.'

'And Harriet has my gratitude for insisting that I accompany her,' replied Isabella, with a wistful smile. 'As for Dominic, Edward was neither proud of nor pained by his arrival into the world. I suppose Dominic received more affection than Edward gave to any other creature in that he did not like to see him ill, or hurt, but his fondness extended little further. On one occasion, when Edward did not know he was being observed by me, I watched him trying to play with Dominic in the garden. However, his father was effectively a stranger so Dominic was afraid and would not join in. That was the only time I saw any kindness in Edward. Drinking and gambling were now his consuming passions and, although I did not know it then, he was also heavily in debt. Life at Vane Manor became even more intolerable.'

'Did you ever think of leaving?' he asked.

'Many times, but I had nowhere to go – Harriet could not afford to support us – and I could have found myself in even worse circumstances. As long as there was no immediate danger to myself or Dominic, I could bear it. I corresponded with Harriet regularly and told her a little of my circumstances. Eventually, when matters deteriorated still further, I poured out the whole of my situation and Harriet, leaving behind her comfortable life without a qualm, came to live at Vane Manor. I was astonished that Edward agreed, but he said that having Harriet there would keep me and the child out of his way. When Harriet saw exactly what circumstances I was living under, she was appalled.'

'At least you had someone to help you,' he said, raking his fingers through his hair.

'Harriet gave me much needed comfort, and moral support. By then, we were social outcasts to most of local society and I was not sorry for that, being too embarrassed and saddened to care. Harriet and I spoke on many occasions of how I might escape, but there seemed no way out. We had little money between us and, according to the law, I was Edward's wife – even if we had escaped, Dominic and I would have had to live in fear of discovery and I'm ashamed to say I did not have the courage to do it.'

'Don't be critical of your actions, Isabella. It is understandable why you could not escape his tyranny then.'

'I think we would have eventually, but, as often happens, matters reached a crisis one night.'

Feeling a violent shiver run through her, he whispered, 'Do you want to continue? It can wait until another time.'

'I must go on, Hal. It is cathartic and perhaps the circumstances surrounding Edward's death will no longer hold any fear for me if I can describe them.'

He kissed her forehead and waited.

Isabella stared into the fire for a while and then said, 'It was a Friday evening. Harriet and Dominic were staying overnight at the home of one of my few acquaintances. Alicia Knowles was a childhood friend who had married a local landowner. They had a child, a son of Dominic's age, whom Dominic loved to play with. I did not see them often because they made no secret of their dislike of Edward. However, they sometimes invited Harriet, Dominic and me to spend the day at their property. I enjoyed those visits very much, but when on one occasion they asked us to stay overnight, Edward would not allow me to accompany Harriet and Dominic. At that point, I had no inkling that I should be worried and was just pleased that Dominic would enjoy another child's company. I should have wondered if there was a reason behind Edward's decision.

'He had taken to inviting his unsavoury friends to the manor, to join him in all night card games where the wine and the bets flowed freely. Harriet and I stayed well away from these events, but, unknown to me, Edward had arranged for one of these gatherings to take place that Friday night. When I realized this, I was a little afraid because I was alone in the house; Harriet and Dominic were, of course, away and Mary had gone to visit her mother in the village. The other servants knew their place and would not intervene. So I went to my room, determined to remain out of the way until the morning.

'For hours, I listened to drunken laughter and curses emanating from downstairs – I was too nervous to sleep and had decided to sit by the fire and read. Edward came to my room in the early hours. I knew his friends were still downstairs, so I did not imagine that he wanted me in that way – he had not touched me since discovering I was expecting Dominic. He had drunk so much he had difficulty standing and, in a slurred voice, told me that he had lost at cards until he had been forced to lay a wager with his one remaining asset – me.'

'He used you for stakes in a card game?' said Hal incredulously, his voice shaking with fury. 'By God, death alone was too good for him – he should have been horse-whipped first!' His anger suddenly overflowing and needing a physical outlet, he stood up and paced about the room, cursing under his breath, until he looked into her face once more. His expression softened at once and, heaving a deep sigh, he returned to her side and gathered her back into his embrace.

'In a sense, I suppose he was, as you will hear,' she murmured, resting her head against his shoulder once more. 'One of Edward's card-playing friends had admired me and when Edward ran out of anything else to offer, his friend had suggested me.' Bitterly, she added, 'The bet was accepted – one night with me was worth thirty guineas which shows how little I meant to Edward. When he came to inform me that I must make myself available to his friend, I was furious and all my pent-up rage and resentment came pouring out. I denounced his character, his behaviour, his lack of honour, his absence of affection for me and his son, but it was all to no avail – he told me if his friend was foolish enough to want to bed a cold, freakish witch that was his affair. I must comply and if I did not, he would have me certified insane and committed to an asylum – I would never see my son again. Then, he calmly left the room to return downstairs. Frantic with terror, I knew that I needed to escape.'

'No wonder you were so devastated last night when you thought I had courted you only to win a wager,' whispered Hal. 'That must have evoked terrible memories.'

She nodded in agreement and replied in a barely audible

voice, 'She did not realize it, but Lady Portland could not have alighted on a more painful, disturbing subject for me. As I said, I was frantic … I heard the man approaching and rushed to hide. Dominic's room adjoined my own and I waited there, hoping that I would not be discovered. The door opened and I sensed his eyes scanning the room, which was in darkness apart from the glow from embers in the grate. Unfortunately, in my haste I had not hidden my dress and he must have seen the pale muslin cloth protruding from behind the chair. He grunted and came in and I sensed at once that he had guessed my hiding place. Terrified, I took hold of the only weapon to hand – a poker which had been sitting in the embers and was searing hot.'

'My God,' he breathed, proud of Isabella's courage yet afraid as to what he might hear had happened next.

'Taking hold of it, I lunged towards him. I knew I had only a moment before he overwhelmed me but I managed to strike home. The hot metal scorched his cheek, adhering to his skin.' She drew in a sob, and stammered, 'I – It was hideous; the smell of burning flesh rent the air as he screamed in agony. In my haste, I burnt my hand – there is a scar here' – Isabella pointed out a small mark on her trembling right hand, near her thumb – 'which has acted as a reminder of that terrible night ever since.'

'I can well imagine,' he said, touching his lips to the scar as if to try and erase it. Then, with a catch in his voice, 'Did you escape?'

'Yes,' she replied, aware of him exhaling in relief. 'I left him writhing in agony and found my way out of the house. There was uproar inside; I could hear the man cursing and Edward's angry shouts. My best chance was to hide until morning – if I tried to run away, I would not get far and then who knows what my fate would have been? It would not have been pleasant – they were all drunk and beyond reasonable behaviour. Eventually, I found a small loft above one of the stable buildings. It was a curious coincidence that Sarah chose to hide Dominic in a loft, because I found a similar hiding place. The wooden door was directly above one of the stalls and I had to stand on the dividing partition to reach it. The horses were nervous, but they were used to me and made no great noise. Shortly after I had climbed in and replaced the door, they came into the stable looking for me.

'I hid under the hay, trembling and listening to the murmur of their voices below as they searched. After a while, when they could not find me, they went out and all fell quiet again. I could not move – even though rats ran over my feet and I was numb with cold, fear kept me motionless. Stiff and sore, I did not stir until I was certain that it was dawn and Edward's friends had given up and gone home. I decided that I must leave the manor that day because it was no longer safe to remain there.'

'Had they indeed gone when you left your hiding place?' he asked. Rage constricted his voice and he had clenched his fists as Isabella had recounted Edward's monstrous behaviour.

'They had, but I did not know it then,' said Isabella. 'When the first streaks of dawn were visible through a hole in the roof above me, I hoped that the thirst to hunt down their quarry had abated. I lowered myself down into the stall below, trying not to frighten the horse stabled there. It was Conqueror, one of Edward's mounts, a huge black stallion of uncertain temperament that Edward controlled with cruel methods. I spoke soothingly so he would be calm enough for me to slip by. However, Edward appeared at that moment.'

Isabella, feeling Hal's body stiffen again with anger, hurried on, 'He was still drunk, but when he saw me, his expression was one of pure hatred – you see, I had embarrassed him in front of his friends, as well as injuring one of them badly. I truly believe he wanted me dead at that moment. He had a scythe which he had taken from the wall and he swung it down towards me, intending to kill. However, I stepped back and the blow struck the horse, gouging a deep cut in his flank. Conqueror reared up instantly. I glimpsed fear in Edward's eyes before the stallion's flying hoofs knocked him sideways. The horse then lunged to the right, crushing him against the side of the stall. He cried out and then sank to the ground, where he lay silent. I – I could not touch him – I could see that he was unconscious and not dead, but I think I sensed that he was mortally wounded. When Harriet returned, she found me in the stable, still staring at Edward's body, and sent for Dr Dalton.

'Harriet and Dr Dalton know what happened, but not Dominic, and I shall not tell him until he is older and can deal with what he must hear,' said Isabella, looking up into Hal's face. 'Harriet rejoiced at Edward's death, notwithstanding her gentle nature, and Dr Dalton also felt that Edward had received just reward. The doctor knew that there was little hope and when Edward died some hours later, Dr Dalton promised that for my sake and Dominic's, the truth of what had happened would not emerge. Edward's death would be explained by saying that he was killed while in the stable alone; there was a terrific storm during the hours leading up to Edward's death and it would be perfectly feasible for the horse to have been disturbed by this while Edward was in there. Afterwards, I wanted to get away from a place that held so many awful memories. I decided to sell the manor, but I was to receive a final, sickening blow; the attorney told me then of Edward's debts and said that by the time the manor and its contents had been sold to pay off his creditors – it was not entailed – there would be no more than a few hundreds pounds a year to support Harriet, Dominic and myself. I had not expected much, but to hear it was so little was a shock and I fretted for months about our future.

'When the sale of the manor was almost complete, news came to me that Great Uncle James had left me this house and Dr Dalton's sister, Lady Bingham, had offered me use of her London townhouse for the season at a minimal rent. Perhaps you understand now why I was so reserved in my manner when I arrived in London, Hal – experience had left me unwilling to trust a man ever again.'

There was silence for a time; Isabella felt emotionally drained while Hal was still struggling to take in everything he had heard.

Eventually, he murmured, 'Now I can conceive why you were so fragile and withdrawn ... you had suffered so much and if

Edward were not already dead ...' Jaw clenched, Hal said after a pause, 'He took a young girl whose father had just died and who had little knowledge of the world, and violated you – for which crime alone I wish I could tear him limb from limb – and then continued to treat you and his son with cruelty and contempt for years ... I hope he is rotting in Hell for his wickedness.'

He ground his teeth in fury until Isabella laid a hand on his arm. 'Edward is dead, Hal; he cannot hurt me any more. Dominic will have to know the truth about his father one day, but he will understand and perhaps remember enough of Edward's behaviour to know I speak the truth. At least now I have you to love me and that is all I ever want.'

He looked into her face and his heart quickened with love. Both his eyes and Isabella's were wet; they were not only tears for the past, but also tears of joy for the future. 'Isabella ... I swear ... I swear that I would never force you into anything,' he said, the timbre of his voice roughened with emotion.

'I know you would not.'

'And I will love, cherish and protect you always, putting your welfare and happiness above my own.'

'I know that too,' she whispered.

Folding her into his embrace, Hal kissed her fiercely, eager to ensure all she would know from this moment would be the pleasure and security that his love would bring.

Chapter Nineteen

DURING the days that followed, Isabella talked, laughed, made plans and shared passionate kisses with Hal, and could hardly believe that her life was so altered. She was relaxed and content for the first time in her adult life. Hal cursed good-naturedly that they had to wait even a day to be married and Isabella agreed; despite those exquisite kisses, she longed for something more.

On their return to London, Lady Bramwell welcomed her with open arms. 'My dear Isabella, if you had refused to marry my son, I would have feared for his reason,' she declared. 'I'm so happy for you both – having enjoyed a loving marriage myself, nothing will give me greater pleasure than to see you and Hal rejoice in the same.'

Sir Seymour and Harriet were married at St George's in Hanover Square, Dinny looking every inch the proud and sartorially extravagant bridegroom in his claret coat, puce and gold waistcoat, and his cravat tied in a style created and named for the occasion: the Dinniscombe Dash. Afterwards, they departed to spend a few days on Sir Seymour's estate in Gloucestershire. Marguerite, Isabella and Julia, meanwhile, left London with Hal and Dominic for the journey to Chenning, where everyone was to join them for Hal and Isabella's wedding. Lady Bingham, Dr Dalton and Alicia Knowles and her husband had also been invited to the ceremony.

When it arrived, Isabella's wedding day was filled with many happy moments, in sharp contrast to her first marriage ceremony in Yorkshire. It was late evening when she and Hal were finally alone – Julia and Freddy had gone to visit Freddy's parents before returning for their own wedding; Harriet and Sir Seymour had invited Dominic to Gloucestershire and he had been eager to go when he discovered one of Sir Seymour's tenants possessed a tame barn owl; Theo, having finished his essay, had returned to London while Lady Bramwell had decided to visit Bath with Lady Bingham, Lukas and Hugo.

Dr Dalton was the last guest to depart and, while Hal was saying goodbye to him, Isabella went upstairs to soak in the luxuriously scented bath that Mary had prepared in her dressing-room. After drying herself, she applied a few drops of the perfume that Hal loved and slipped into her nightgown, a diaphanous garment with ribbon fastenings given to her as a wedding gift by Julia.

The bedroom was bathed in the rosy glow of candlelight, and Isabella sat at the dressing-table to take the pins from her hair. The door opened and Hal came in, moving to stand behind her and place his hands on her shoulders. He was dressed only in a loose robe which revealed the hard musculature of his chest dusted with dark hair. Desire began to curl slowly outwards from Isabella's core; every look, glance and touch they had exchanged since their first meeting had affected her, but to see him like this took her breath away and made her quiver with anticipation.

Reaching up to cover his hand with her own, she said, 'It has been a wonderful day.'

He smiled lovingly at her reflection in the mirror. 'Have I told you today how lovely you are?'

'At least twenty times,' she replied, smiling back.

'That is not nearly enough.' His mouth coursed slowly over her skin, smoothing away the locks of hair from her throat and whispering a new endearment each time he pressed his lips to her flesh. She gasped, arching her neck and leaning back to let him continue his trail of kisses. When he had completed the task to his satisfaction, he murmured into her ear, 'I have a gift for you, my love.'

Hal took a slim black box from the pocket of his robe and gave it to her. She smiled again at his reflection in the mirror and opened it to reveal an exquisite necklace: a string of pearls interspersed with diamonds, with a single tear-shaped diamond at its centre. Isabella drew in a breath. 'Oh, it is enchanting! Surely it was very expensive?'

He did not answer this, but grinned at her obvious pleasure. 'Let me put it on for you.'

He placed the necklace around her throat, tiny shivers running through her where his fingers brushed against her skin. Isabella looked in the mirror; the pearls shimmered and diamonds sparkled with inner fire as they caught the light. She touched her fingertips to the necklace and said in an emotional voice, 'Are you sure, Hal? It is the most beautiful thing I have ever seen.'

'*You* are the most beautiful thing I have ever seen. It is my wedding gift to you so wear it for me tonight.' When she stood up and turned to face him, Hal saw her nightgown clearly for the first time; one glimpse at her body, tantalizingly revealed through that gossamer fabric, sent his pulse soaring. He looked into her eyes and saw the flicker of apprehension there. 'Don't be afraid, my love,' he said, gently. 'Tonight will be like nothing you have experienced before.'

'I'm not afraid in that way – not with you. I'm only ...' she hesitated, before whispering, 'I'm only afraid of disappointing you.'

He took her hands tightly in his. 'Then don't be because you could never disappoint me,' he said, his gaze brimming with passion. 'I love you so much – you mean everything to me. I want to show you such pleasure that it will wipe away painful memories, to love every inch of you until our heart and souls meld. I want to love you like never before, Isabella. Let me worship you with my body, and my spirit.'

Visibly trembling, Isabella forced her lips into a smile. 'I love you, Hal, and I want you to love me ... love me until I forget the past.'

'I will,' was his murmured promise. Then, 'God, you're so beautiful.' Taking her face gently between his hands, he pressed a slow, smouldering kiss against her lips.

His nearness, the scent of his skin and the whisper of his breath, filled Isabella's senses. Unable to think or speak any longer, she melted into his embrace, running her hands over his chest and finding the sensation of his bare skin beneath her fingertips intensely thrilling. His lips never leaving hers, he reached up to remove the remaining pins from her hair, threading his fingers through its silky weight.

Soft kisses blazed a trail along her jaw, down her throat and across her shoulders, the slight roughness of his stubble rubbing provocatively against her skin. Isabella gasped with pleasure as the heat inside her was teased into an inferno by his lips and his fingertips. She felt almost light-headed, every inch of her tingling with awareness. His caresses were in turn gentle and insistent and no part of her was excluded from his slow seduction until, when she thought she must faint from the pleasure he was building within her, he lifted her up and carried her to the bed.

They lay close, facing each other and sharing an ardent gaze, before his hands and lips continued to weave their magic. Sighing with delight, Isabella curled her fingers around the back of his neck. Craving his touch yet compelled to explore him in return, she ran her hands tentatively over his body; he groaned softly and she felt him shudder in response.

Discarding his robe, he began to untie the ribbons on her nightgown until her body was exposed to his gaze. Another shiver of pleasure ran though her. The rosy tips of her breasts, already aroused by his touch, ached for more and she moaned with relief when the caressing strokes of his fingers were followed by the subtle, teasing ministrations of his mouth.

Isabella was lost in a dream of new sensations. She felt no fear, no embarrassment and under Hal's loving, patient touch, her body felt supine and boneless. Terrible memories were banished forever as she surrendered to the rapture which threatened to overwhelm her.

Still kissing her sensitive, aroused peaks, he pushed aside the silky material until there were no barriers between them. He trailed lingering kisses over her body, murmuring words of love against her skin and drawing gasps and whimpers of delight from her. Long, delicious, pleasure-filled moments passed until it seemed her body was no longer her own. *Hal* ... she could not say his name, but he seemed to sense her need, abandoning his slow exploration to move his body over hers. Hands skimming the firm surface of his chest, she felt a tremor run though him and opened her eyes, her gaze slowly focusing to see his eyes glittering with passion.

'Kiss me, love,' he said, in a husky whisper.

She slid her arms around him and touched her mouth to his in a deeply sensual kiss. She had never experienced such a sense of fulfilment – it was wondrous, visceral and she loved and needed Hal more than she could express. Wrapped in his embrace, the delicious feeling at her core increased until the torment of pleasure he had taken her to splintered in shuddering ecstasy.

Isabella drifted on a slow tide of elation. Utterly replete yet vibrant, she was conscious of even greater love for this man whose body was still entwined with her own. A sudden deluge of emotion – gratitude, respect, desire, love – welled up in her soul and, from under closed eyelids, large tears formed.

Hal, who had been running his fingers through her hair as she lay cradled against his chest, looked down to see her tears. 'Sweetheart, what's wrong?'

'Nothing,' she whispered. 'It's just that ... you see, I never knew ... I never understood it could be that beautiful.'

'It was beautiful because we shared our hearts, minds and bodies out of love,' he said, before brushing his lips over hers once more.

Isabella responded, luxuriating in being thoroughly kissed and in what they had shared. In her blissful, drowsy state she asked some minutes later, 'When did you realize you loved me?'

'Shortly after we met.' Hal smiled, remembering. 'I saw the vulnerability in your eyes and, in spite of your disdain, I think I fell in love with you then.'

'I could not acknowledge I loved you, even to myself, because I was afraid,' admitted Isabella. 'By stifling my emotions, I thought I could protect myself from getting hurt again. Thank God you saw what was really in my heart, Hal – your love has proved that I am not the frigid creature I was branded.'

'You never were, my darling. It was cruel treatment that made you outwardly cold. You are warm, passionate and loving, and all you ever needed was our love to guide you.'

She reached up to place her palm against his cheek and, after another lingering kiss, they lay in silence, embracing the languid aftermath of passion. Hal stroked his fingers rhythmically over her back and, after a time, the slow movements sparked new desire and she began to stir against him. This time Isabella's incipient confidence in her sensuality allowed her to explore every contour of Hal's body before she succumbed to the glorious, unhurried way he brought her to those rapturous heights once more.

When sleep claimed them, Isabella remained within Hal's arms until dawn. She was awakened by his tender kisses, love and desire combining to take her to another ecstasy of fulfilment. Afterwards, they shared caresses, endearments and soft laughter as they planned their future.

Epilogue

Late June, one year later

LATENT, oppressive heat hung in the air as the first rain-drops of the gathering storm began to fall. Thunder rumbled in the distance and the dark clouds overhead had already covered the sun, leaving the evening light outside Chenning gloomy and threatening.

But the elegant, dark-haired woman who waited anxiously outside the bedroom scarcely noticed the rain on the window. She paced to and fro, glancing occasionally at the closed door. Murmured voices rose from downstairs on the humid air, but she listened only for sounds from within the room.

Suddenly, the door opened and, after quietly closing it behind him, Hal looked at his mother. 'It is over,' he said with a deep sigh, raking his fingers though his hair.

Lady Bramwell started forward in concern; she could see that his eyes were wet with tears. 'Isabella, is she—?'

Pushing a hand across his eyes, he said in a wavering voice, 'Isabella is well, as is the baby – we have a beautiful daughter.'

'Oh, how wonderful!' Marguerite embraced him, smiling now she appreciated his tears were of joy and relief. 'Congratulations! May I see Isabella soon? And my new granddaughter, of course.'

'She is tired, but she would like to see you; Dr Dalton has finished attending to her and the baby.'

'I shall go in, just as soon as I have told everyone – they have been waiting anxiously.'

'Tell them the good news and ask Dominic to come up,' replied Hal. 'We want him to see his sister.'

Ice Angel

Elizabeth Hanbury

ROBERT HALE · LONDON

© Elizabeth Hanbury 2009
First published in Great Britain 2009

ISBN 978-0-7090-8784-7

Robert Hale Limited
Clerkenwell House
Clerkenwell Green
London EC1R 0HT

www.halebooks.com

The right of Elizabeth Hanbury
to be identified as author of this work has been
asserted by her in accordance with the
Copyright, Designs and Patents Act 1988

2 4 6 8 10 9 7 5 3 1

Typeset in 10.5/14pt New Century Schoolbook
Printed in Great Britain by the MPG Books Group, Bodmin and King's Lynn

Acknowledgements

My love and gratitude go to Tim, Adam and Andrew for their patience, forbearance and support while I disappeared into my Regency world; to the rest of my family for their encouragement and for being a source of inspiration; to Julia and Gill for their help and feedback at every stage; to my friends at the C19 message board, especially Glenda, Wendy, Jo, Eve, Christine, Sally, Rachel, Diane, Steph, Debbie, Viola Jane, Nora, Neelma, Phillipa, Rosy, Maggie, Yvonne, Janet, Bernie, Ruth and Annalise; to Mags and Gilly for their assistance with historical research.

Finally, to Karen, Nicola, Lisa, Jo, Jane, Helen, Lorraine, Jill and Jackie – thank you for sharing your stories.

Prologue

Yorkshire, England – January 1814

A STORM raged outside and torrential rain fell against the window pane, but the young woman waiting anxiously took little notice of these turbulent conditions, which were in stark contrast to the quiet bedchamber.

Having drawn up the sheet over the corpse, the doctor turned away from the bed and lifted his candle. The flame threw eerie shadows on the walls, and revealed both her startling beauty and the large expressive eyes regarding him gravely.

Giving a brief shake of his head in response to her unspoken question, he said, 'It is over, Isabella. He is gone from this life and you may rest easy; the end was peaceful when it came.' Observing that she pressed trembling fingertips against her lips and her eyes, full of indiscernible emotion, were now wet with unshed tears, the doctor touched her hand in a reassuring gesture. 'You must tell the boy in the morning. The sooner he is told, the better, and you must make plans for the future.'

Quiet as a sigh, her voice stirred the candle flame. 'I know, Dr Dalton, but it will be difficult. Sometimes I fear I shall never enjoy life again—'

'Isabella,' he interjected, 'you must not allow tonight's events and those of recent years to affect your judgement. There are many things to enjoy in this world. Take heart – you will come about.'

'I am too numb to think or feel anything after what I have endured,' she said, tears now falling down her pale cheeks, 'but

I shall do my best for Dominic. He deserves to find some pleasure.'

'Do not channel all your energies into your child and neglect your own feelings, my dear; perhaps one day they can be awakened by the right person.'

'No!' she whispered fiercely. 'My very soul is frozen from the anguish I have suffered and I will never be beholden to a man again.'

As Lady Bramwell hurried away downstairs, Hal went back into the room. A tired but content Isabella sat in bed holding their daughter, who was wrapped in a shawl and sleeping soundly. He kissed his wife before reaching out for her hand and gazing in wonderment at the life they had created.

Tears still stood in his eyes and observing them, Isabella said softly, 'My love, I am quite well, I assure you. Tiredness is to be expected, you know, and at least my confinement was quicker this time.'

Dr Dalton, who was packing away his medical bag on the other side of the room, shook his head and chuckled. 'I have never seen a husband so anxious during his wife's confinement; for the first time in all my years of experience, he refused to leave the room during the baby's arrival. If I did not know you well, Hal, I would be offended and think you did not trust me to look after your Isabella.'

'It is not that I did not trust you,' explained Hal, 'but Isabella is everything to me and I needed to assure myself that—'

Dr Dalton waved a hand and interjected, 'I quite understand. Perhaps you will start a new fashion for fathers to be present at the arrival of their offspring. What did you think of the experience?'

'It was incredibly emotional – in spite of feeling like my heart was being ripped out to see Isabella in pain.'

'But it was worthwhile because we have a beautiful baby,' she replied, looking down at the sleeping child. 'The names we have chosen suit her well, Hal, don't you think?'

'Elise after your mother and Helena, meaning bright and shining. Elise Helena – it sounds as perfect as she is.'

'I shall return in the morning, Isabella,' said the doctor. 'Make sure you have as much rest as that lovely scrap of humanity will allow.'

Dr Dalton received no reply to this and, observing that they were now oblivious to his presence, slipped out of the room.

'You never looked more beautiful than you do at this moment, my love,' said Hal, running his gaze over her face.

'I look completely exhausted,' replied Isabella, laughing.

'Not to my eyes.'

Teasingly, she murmured, 'But then you are very biased.'

'I don't deny it,' said Hal, with a grin.

The safe arrival of their daughter was the culmination of a wonderful year, thought Isabella. They had spent the summer after their marriage at Chenning. She and Hal had not wanted to leave Dominic immediately after the wedding, so they had delayed their time alone until they were certain he was settled in his new surroundings. Dominic, however, had adapted quickly, discovering two more heroes in Lukas and Hugo who spent the summer initiating him into the delights of their latest inventions. Harriet and Sir Seymour had visited often and Hal, Isabella and Dominic had journeyed to Gloucestershire to spend a fortnight at Sir Seymour's estate.

Lady Bramwell had moved to the Dower House half a mile away, in spite of Isabella's protests that it was not necessary – the house was big enough to accommodate an army, she had argued. Her mother-in-law had merely laughed and declared, 'I was newly wed myself once and very much in love, as you are; you need time to enjoy each other's company without fear of being disturbed. Lukas and Hugo can stay with me at the Dower House until they return to school.' Marguerite's eyes had twinkled as she added, 'And you may send Dominic to me any time you wish to be alone.'

Julia and Freddy had also visited often. Julia's vivacious nature complimented Freddy's intensity and ensured their marriage was as loving as their reconciliation in Sussex had promised. Now, they too had additional joy since Julia had discovered she was expecting a baby at the end of the year.

Theo had left Oxford and, as well as cutting a dash around London, occasionally descended on Chenning to talk animatedly about his new wine importing venture. The wine he had discovered in the cellar at Haystacks had proved the starting point for his interest and, with his usual vigour, he was persuading his friends to purchase far more wine than they needed by convincing them it would be an excellent investment.

Haystacks itself had been fully renovated. The house was connected with so many delightful memories from that night the previous June that neither Isabella nor Hal could part with it and had decided to use it as a summer home near the coast. They had spent two blissful weeks alone there in October, their happiness finding expression in tender moments by day and passionate nights. Isabella's lips curved into a smile at the memory; their baby had been conceived during that autumn idyll at Haystacks.

Hal watched her smile and, finding her as irresistible as ever, leaned over to touch his mouth to hers again just as Dominic entered, excitement visible on his face.

He climbed on to the bed. 'I want to see my new sister. What's her name?'

'Elise Helena,' replied his mother. 'Do you like it, Dominic?'

'E-lise Hel-e-na,' he replied, sounding out the syllables approvingly. 'I like it very much, Mama.'

Isabella moved the shawl so that Dominic could see the baby's face. The movement disturbed her, making her wriggle and screw up her features before yawning.

'She's very tiny,' murmured Dominic, eyes wide with amazement. 'Will she be able to play with me soon?'

'Not for a little while yet, love, but she will soon be chasing after you and Aesop.'

'Good,' observed Dominic. Then, with a satisfied grin, he added, 'I love Theo, Freddy, Julia, Hugo and Lukas, but they are all bigger than me – now I have a sister, I'm not the littlest any more!'

Hal and Isabella laughed at this, and then Hal said, 'You're a very special boy, Dominic, and your new baby sister is an angel.' He looked up at his wife and added with a loving smile, 'Just like her mother.'